Everyday Ghosts

by Chris Gregory

Dedication:
For the ghosts.

EVERYDAY GHOSTS

First edition. May 21, 2022.

Copyright © 2022 Chris Gregory.

ISBN: 979-8224905683

Written by Chris Gregory.

Other books by Chris Gregory

Science Fiction by **Chris D Gregory**
Seconders
Second Generation
Distant Son

Rescue

Urban Fantasy by **Chris Gregory**
Everyday Ghosts
Everyday Spirits
Everyday Legends

Historical Fiction by **CD Gregory**
Crystal
Resister

Pendragons
Uthyr Pendragon

The Patient

Women's Ward B, Queens Medical Centre, Nottingham, December 2019

"I buried Robin Hood," she said, white knuckles gripping her sheet. I hadn't given the young woman my attention until she spoke. Now I saw livid grazes on her palms and knees as if she'd fallen, hard. She pulled a gown around her slight shoulders with a shiver and a mess of brown hair fell across her frown. She held my stare.

"It didn't happen as it should have," she asserted. "He didn't shoot an arrow and tell me where to bury him." I noticed her eyes were bloodshot, and I wondered if she were tired, in pain, or had been crying. Perhaps all three. Despite their rawness, I sensed those eyes had seen more than someone so young should have. They seemed weary yet penetrating. Searching for trust. Whatever she had to say seemed to weigh heavily.

I'm not alone in hating hospitals: they're full of sick people. I would rather have been anywhere other than this women's ward on a wet December morning close to Christmas. The attempts at festive decoration were not filling me, or anyone one else I could see, with fun. I was stuck, waiting for my operation, and trying hard not to dwell on it. Part of me wanted to be alone with my thoughts and I could have rolled over to ignore her. But her eyes compelled me to look and listen.

"I'm the only one who knows where he is," she continued. Perhaps she'd decided I was worthy of her trust. "I'm the only one who knows who he is. I should go back to him…"

"No, you don't, sweetheart," soothed the nurse. Nurse Christine Lamwaka is a star, everyone in the ward agrees. "You lie back and rest. You're dehydrated, malnourished and weak as a kitten. Just like the last time you arrived in my ward. What are you doing to yourself, dear?" Christine lowered her voice but I could still hear. "At least you're clean. Lord knows the temptation is there when you're going from shelter to streets and back again." Christine took the young woman gently by the shoulders and eased her back, plumping up the pillows behind her. She didn't resist, though I sensed she could have. The eyes held a spark of rebellion. Instead, she waited until Nurse Christine had poured a plastic cup full of water, checked the notes and moved on to another of her waifs. After studying the cup of water, the young woman turned back to me, leaning awkwardly on a grazed elbow. She continued, voice a little quieter and controlled. Conspiratorial.

"I can see people who lived a long time ago," she said, holding my dubious stare. "Yes, I know, you don't believe me, but please hear me out. I sense when they're near me. Some places make it easier: where it's quiet and old. I don't think of them as ghosts, they feel more like… echoes, to start with, but they become much more. Real people, full of life. I know it sounds crazy, but I really need to tell someone." She looked at me, begging me to listen and treat her as if she were not as crazy as she sounded.

She seemed earnest and dishevelled. She also sounded articulate and educated, which I admit surprised me in view of what Nurse Christine had let slip about her being on the streets, though in retrospect it shouldn't have. I don't normally prejudge like that. As someone trained in archaeology, I look at all the evidence before suggesting an opinion, even in my new job. Whatever trauma she had been through, she obviously believed it to be true, and if she were dangerous, I'd like to think she wouldn't have been put in a general ward beside me. Despite her wild claims she seemed lucid and engaging, if agitated.

In any case, it was drizzling outside, and I was stuck in a hospital bed waiting for an operation I didn't want. I felt sorry for myself. I decided I needed to be diverted by a good story. Indeed, I have a professional interest in stories of the past, and like many I have a weakness for the folktales of Robin Hood.

After pause for thought, I smiled and nodded for her to go on. Let me tell you the story she told me.

Hope

Market Square, Nottingham, October 2019

She hadn't slept. It's almost impossible to sleep on frozen stone slabs under electric lights while wondering who's watching you. Who's looking for a chance to steal from you when you finally close your eyes. Or worse. She felt a rude shove in her ribs. She swallowed back the curse on her tongue and focussed on the uniform outlined by the harsh glare of early daylight. She felt bleary. The smell of other people's piss made her cover her nose with an unravelling scarf.

"Get up," the policeman said and pulled his jacket tight against the wind. "You can't sleep here."

"I was trying to sleep when you shoved me with your boot. Have you any idea how dangerous it is to sleep rough after dark?" the young woman gave the copper a stare that could split walnuts. She peered at the ID half hidden by his jacket. "What's your number?"

The policeman took a step back looking uncomfortable. "You can't stay here, miss. Move on."

"Boot first, 'miss' after. Is that how they train you?"

"Look, you just can't stay here," and after a pause, "You don't want me to arrest you, do you?" It sounded like a question he asked to make people stop and think before causing him more paperwork. Maybe sometimes it worked.

"Don't know. Will it get me a cup of tea somewhere warm?" she asked.

The policeman looked up at the sky, then back at the huddle of shabby clothes and straggly brown hair hunched beside the Council House archway. It seemed his question wouldn't work with her. "'Clear the Market Square' my sarge said. 'We don't want undesirables making the place look bad when the mayor's guests come this evening', he said." The copper looked at the young woman and shook his head. "Look, you don't want a record, miss," though perhaps he wondered if she already had. "Try Hope House, bottom of Goose Gate."

She glared at the policeman and pulled herself up, then stooped to collect her bag. She stuffed her makeshift ground sheet into the back of it and a couple of empty Mars bar wrappers fell out. The policeman was already walking down the loggia looking for more undesirables. Not for the first time she felt discarded – someone else's problem. Invisible.

She wondered if she could head around the back of the Council House and straight back to her pitch without being seen. The open sided colonnade was raked by the wind, but she felt slightly safer there than in a secluded porch or alley, where she could be cornered. She didn't like dark corners.

The policeman had made her even more depressed and angry. She found herself getting angry with of a lot of people in authority, especially after the woman on the desk at the Welfare Rights office declared she had made herself 'voluntarily homeless'. Until yesterday she hadn't even heard that insulting phrase. She couldn't imagine someone volunteering to freeze, beg, starve, be spat on, be ignored (she wasn't sure which was worse), or have a copper's boot wake you up. She had a sneaking suspicion that 'voluntarily homeless' was a phrase used by some people to ease their conscience. She wasn't sleeping in a fetid archway out of choice.

She had found herself arguing back at people like the welfare officer more and more. She was repeatedly told what she couldn't do, or what they weren't allowed to do for her, as if it were her fault. At least the policeman had tried to make a useful suggestion, after inserting his size ten, but she was wary of taking it up.

A gust unbalanced her. She grabbed a stone column to keep her upright, pulled the mustard wool hat down over her ears and set off around the side of the tall Portland stone edifice. It called itself the Council House, but it wasn't somewhere the council would let you sleep. Peering into the Exchange Arcade that ran through it she could see a Patisserie Valerie and a line of posh clothes shops all selling beautiful expensive things to beautiful expensive people. It felt welcoming and hostile all at once. She could remember browsing nice shops in Blackheath at weekends with her mum, before they had to move. She could even remember being taken into Selfridges for a posh ice-cream by her father, when he was on one of his rare guilt trips to see her. Now she felt ashamed to go in, because she knew she couldn't afford anything in there and people would stare if she did. That seemed to be the only way she got seen now: go somewhere where she wasn't welcome. That kind of notice only lasted for as long as it took her cheeks to start burning and force her back out. After that she was invisible again.

She steered between the commuters, pouring into the Market Square to get their tram home. No one paid her attention unless she got in their way. The wind caught a sandwich board outside The Loxley pub on Pelham Street and knocked it flat with a bang, making her jump. None of the shoppers seemed to notice. A bus swung across her as she tried to cross into Carlton Street, and she staggered back to avoid being hit. She steadied herself against a curved glass shop window, waving her fist at the driver. She may as well have blown him a mocking kiss; he couldn't see her.

It was a mercy she had some knowledge of central Nottingham from her childhood visits to her aunt, Jane. As if following some half-remembered journey, she found herself wandering into Goose Gate, though it wasn't her original plan. Not a conscious one. A casual visitor might have looked for an actual gate there rather than a scruffy street that led east from the city centre. On the far corner, past the Sue Ryder and the boarded-up shops, she saw a faded art-deco office block set back from the street with a white banner that read 'Support Centre'. Underneath an afterthought: 'Hope House.'

She could do with a little hope, but she had learned not to expect it. Despite herself she had arrived at the shelter suggested by the boot brandishing policeman. She wavered. She didn't like asking strangers for help. She didn't like the questions they asked, but the wind blew through her man-size coat and hoodie making her shiver. She breathed in, pushed the door open and walked up to the woman on the desk. The laminate was peeling a little at the edges to reveal bare chipboard underneath, but the woman gave her a friendly smile.

"How can I help, duck?" said the woman.

"I haven't got anywhere to stay." It felt shameful to admit, but the woman made her feel it was okay. More than that, she looked at her with some measure of compassion and respect, more than she had experienced since she climbed aboard the coach at Victoria Station and paid her last few quid to get a ticket to Nottingham.

"What's your name?"

She hesitated. She guessed the woman wanted her full name, "Mary Ann Partington... but I prefer Anna."

"I'm Maureen. Come, sit y'usen over there, Anna. I'll see what we can sort out."

Anna suppressed a small cry of relief. Instead, she smiled and sat down, gathering her bag and dignity like a rusty shield and sword. As she waited, she cast her eyes around the entrance hall. The floor was terrazzo tiles with brass inlay strips, probably 1930s. Someone had laid a few carpet tiles over the corner she was sitting in, to take the hard echoes off, but they were swamped by the double height space and the grand staircase. A pair of dark oak doors with tiny Georgian wired windows hinted at a cavernous room beyond, but Anna suspected it was more likely a warren of little office cubicles, with charity workers battling bureaucracy. A slight whiff of floor cleaner reinforced the institutional feel, but an older smell of polished oak and dust lay beneath. She felt a familiar tingle, somewhere at the border between her conscious and sub-conscious mind. She knew this was significant. A good place to look. So, Anna closed her eyes.

She focussed on that part of her mind that was tingling, reacting to something that lingered in the old reception hall. A weird yet familiar detachment occurred in her mind, as if floating away from her body. For a moment it felt as if the floor was falling and she were looking down from a great height. It made her giddy. Then she sensed a flickering, as if sunrise and sunset had accelerated and the world was shifting in a stop-frame video. Or pages of a picture book flipped rapidly before her. Her mind's eye filled with phantoms gliding across each page. The faded outlines of people moving in and out of view. Some pushed ghostly doors wide and other followed, wheeling silent trollies or carrying stacks of papers that teetered and slid. It was as if an artist had sketched the outline of an animation and had yet to paint between the lines with colour.

Slowly her mind steadied. Some of the sketched figures started to fill with hues and tones while others faded out of sight, becoming ghosts again. Her view steadied and sharpened, became solid. She looked about her. It was the same hall, but it had changed. She had taken this peculiar viewpoint, felt the vertiginous lurch, almost every day for most of her life. Yet it always filled her with excitement. If she visited somewhere for the first time, like this, she had no idea who she was about to see. Or when.

A large clock ticked off the minutes over the tall oak doors. Carefully groomed clerks in suits walked slowly and purposefully up the stairs. A huge portrait of a man with a walrus moustache filled the opposite wall and below it an elegant receptionist in twin set and pearls sat to attention behind a large leather topped desk with stylish stepped mouldings in mahogany legs. The receptionist did not look up at the young woman sitting in the corner in an oversized overcoat. The clerks didn't stop or glance at her before climbing the next flight. Anna was invisible to them all, just as she always had been. But she never stopped looking for them, whenever she went. She had been doing this since she was small, and it comforted her. They were her secret, in her world. They kept her company when no one else would.

"Anna?" She was jolted out of her visit to the past by Maureen, who had returned to the laminate desk and snapped her back into the twenty-first century with a physical jolt.

"Oh, sorry, I was just imagining what this place must have been like when it was new." Anna had been doing more than imagine, but she had learned not to go into that. How could she begin to explain? And Anna got sick of explaining things very quickly.

"Dev here will take you for a chat," Maureen said and beckoned Anna to follow the middle-aged man in the baggy red pullover. Dev's smile looked as tired as his jumper. Dark shadows lined his eyes. He sat Anna down in a glass booth, one of many, much as she had imagined. He took notes, nodding while she told her story, explaining her journey to Nottingham to search for her aunt. Anna guessed that Dev had heard many stories, judging by the weary gestures and well-worn smiles.

"You said your aunt has moved, but you don't know where," said Dev.

"Yes, last time I visited was almost three years ago."

"Have you any other family you can go to? Any brothers or sisters?"

"No," said Anna, looking at the forms scattered across his desk. "Not really." She had only ever known her close family of two: Anna and her mother. She had never felt the need for more, not until now.

"What's your aunt's full name?" asked Dev.

"Jane Trudy Fitzwalter, I think. She was married and divorced. I don't know if she took her ex-husband's name or kept her maiden name."

"Fitzwalter was her married or maiden name?"

"Maiden, she was my father's sister."

"Are you married?" Anna looked at Dev blankly, so he went on. "Because you give your surname as Partington."

Anna closed her eyes, preparing herself for another difficult explanation, then opened them again to fix Dev with a steady glare. "My father christened me Mary Ann Fitzwalter, but after making his mark he took no interest, so I have no interest in his name. Instead, I use my mother's maiden name, Partington."

"I see," said Dev, scribbling notes. Anna doubted if he did. "So why are you searching for his sister, your aunt?"

"I like her," shrugged Anna, as if it should be obvious. "I spent holiday breaks and long weekends with her here in Nottingham as I was growing up. Now my mother's dead, she's the only close living family I have," who can give a toss, she wanted to add.

"And you don't know if she's still in the Nottingham area."

"No." Anna could already see where this was going.

"You've tried searching social media, haven't you?"

"She hated it. She's a media ghost."

"Oh dear," Dev shook his head. "You say the current owners have no forwarding address for her."

"No. They didn't want me back either." Anna remembered what the guy had said when she turned up on his doorstep in The Park and decided not to repeat it. She folded her arms and slumped back into the chair, bracing herself for what Dev would say next.

"So, we've no address, no media presence and we're not even sure of her current surname," summarised Dev in a dispassionate tone.

Anna wished again she had kept in touch. The last couple of years had been so difficult: all the moves and her mum's illness. "It's not my fault," she threw her hands up and raised her voice, angry. "If I knew where to find her, I wouldn't be here," she gestured at the shabby office booth.

"Okay look," Dev made a calming gesture with his palms down. Anna's strop hadn't phased him. "We'll have a go at tracing her for you, but don't expect miracles." She didn't, and was starting to feel bad about taking it out on Dev. "We can arrange a bed for tonight, help you sort yourself out, but we can't do more than that for now." He stood to show her the way.

Anna gathered her scruffy bag and stood too, looking at the other booths down the corridor. Either they had people like her talking to people like Dev, or the Devs were busy making phone calls, searching for phantom relatives or beds. She was just one of many.

Goose Gate, Nottingham, October 2019

The centre gave Anna a chance to fill her empty belly, shower the grime off and wash the clothes she had been standing in for the past week. Especially the luxury of falling asleep without the fear of not waking again. Or worse. She zig-zagged between pathetic thankfulness and dignified acceptance of the basics that a civilised society ought to provide. She still felt resentful: it was as if she had been forced to admit her own helplessness for people to stop passing her off and help her. She hated feeling helpless.

The best and worst parts were finding she was not the only one. Not by a long way. After the first night of uninterrupted safe sleep for a week, in a spare white dormitory that smelled of disinfectant, she pulled a borrowed hoodie on and went downstairs to a crowded canteen serving breakfast. There she saw a wiry young man with wild dark hair. After some hesitation she decided to do what she would normally have avoided. She went to say hello.

"Hi, I'm Anna."

His shadowed eyes flicked in her direction, skewering her momentarily with a mix of accusation and distrust, then returned to the plate of scrambled eggs in front of him.

"What's your name?" she persisted. Having decided to make conversation she wasn't going to be fobbed off. He was probably as lost and scared as she was, she reasoned.

"...Rob," without looking up again.

Anna faltered. In other circumstances she'd have left him alone, he was making it clear enough, but it was a long while since she had spoken to anyone other than to fill out a form. "Where're you from, Rob?" she tried again stubbornly.

"Loxley House," was his toneless reply, still concentrating on his plate. The old woman at the table behind him snorted, as if sharing some black humour.

"Where's... oh, right, ha-ha," she finally connected the name with the Welfare Office she'd been to on Station Road. Was he making fun of her? "I guess we all come from there now," she tried, "but before?"

Rob chased the last scraps of scrambled egg around the plate with his fork. His focus on the task was extraordinary.

"I'm from Blackheath, in London," volunteered Anna, hoping to encourage him, "and I've come here to look for my aunt." That got another flick of the eyes, a little longer this time: looking, judging. Was that scorn or caution, she wondered? "But she's moved, and I don't know where to start looking," she added. "I've nothing to go back to."

"Well, I don't know where she is," he said, not harshly, just matter of fact.

"Didn't expect you to," Anna was starting to get annoyed. "I just wondered where you were from, that's *all*." She put more bite in the last word than she meant.

"Sherwood for a bit. Then St Ann's." He eyed her warily over his empty plate. Was she bullying him into an answer?

She calmed herself again. "Okay, nearby. How did you end up in this place?"

Rob emptied his coffee mug, picked up his plate and walked off.

Anna watched his back disappear through the door, struggling to hide her anger and frustration. "What did I say?" demanded Anna, clattering her breakfast plate down on the empty table. The egg scrambled across it.

The old woman on the next table leaned back to look at her. "We all have a story, duck. Bet you have yorn. But some don't like telling theirn, not to someone they don't know."

"Okay," she said, scooping up bits of egg. "Guess I was a bit pushy." She sat down and hung her head. "Just wanted to talk to someone."

"We're all alone together, duck. It's hard but there y' are. Get y'usen more egg an' fill up."

Anna closed her eyes for a few moments. She felt for that tingling at the borders of her mind. Sensed her disembodiment, her lurch out of the present and the flickering of past days. At least she could look for the people others couldn't see; at least they didn't turn their back on her. She felt her mind detaching, then her downward view as she looked through the pages of time, searching for the memories of people who had been in this room many years ago. Echoes from the terrazzo floor of the canteen. She discovered a particularly vivid scene as a round faced woman in a white pinny and serving hat approached her from the far end of a kitchen corridor. She was pushing a trolley piled high with cream buns, cucumber sandwiches and scones. A queue of office clerks were following and were trying hard to look proper while surreptitiously eyeing the mountain of freshly baked food. One clerk with a drooping moustache and cheeks like a hamster was wiping the dribble from his chin. As usual the scene dissipated when she opened her eyes, but the secret spectacle had made her grin.

Heeding the old woman's advice, Anna walked back to the self-service table to fill her plate again. Then, with a mischievous twinkle, she stuffed the fold of her hoodie full of fruit and Mars bars, silently resolving to come back down, wearing her oversized overcoat with its oversized pockets.

Alleys

Upper Parliament Street, Nottingham, October 2019

A paramedic pressed a phone to his ear and slumped against the ambulance. His teammate crouched over a bundle of rags in the mouth of a tiny brick archway, squeezed between a pub and a curry house. Anna wondered what they were doing, why poke around old clothes in a foul-smelling alley? The truth dawned slow and cold: the squalor of the alley, the drained faces, the lack of any flashing lights or hurry. It was a dead body, likely homeless. Likely there some time before being reported.

Anna's mind surged with questions: who were they, what was their name? How did they die: exposure, starvation, TB, overdose, assault? Would there be anyone to identify the body; would anyone care? Just like the commuters and shoppers, she put her head down and walked on. But unlike them, she had noticed that small quiet death. She was shaken.

She looked along the rain-slicked road lined with buses and lorries and walked towards a copper-turreted office block. There she turned north and wove through the side alleys. Dev had apologised that Hope House could only offer temporary help. He suggested the Women's Centre may give Anna counselling on job searches and long-term support.

She arrived, late, in front of a huge fortress of Victoriana on Chaucer Street, capped with gables and turrets. A pale blue door looked incongruous against the rusticated stone base and, if it hadn't been for the tiny 'Women's Centre' sign on it, she wouldn't have dared knock.

While she waited a couple of young guys walked past on the other side of the street. The shorter one with blonde hair called out to her: "Oi! Scrounger, do some work."

Anna pulled the hoodie down over her face and balled her fists into her pockets while she waited for someone to answer the door. The taller one with a black leather jacket muttered something behind her and they snorted with laughter. She wanted to shout at them, tell them how hard she'd tried. Ask them how they'd get a job if they had no address to give and turned up to interviews in the clothes they'd been sleeping in for the last month. Of course, she wanted to work. Of course, she was ashamed she needed help, but they wouldn't understand. She could sense the guys were still there, waiting for their prey, so she willed someone to hurry up and open the door.

At last, a kind faced woman wearing a bright green sari appeared and beckoned her in off the narrow pavement. "I'm Preet. Come and take a seat. You're a little late but I'm sure I can fit you in. I'll be back for you in a moment."

Anna swept the hood off her face and leaned against a plump cushion, savouring the comfort like a wine buff with a fine Malbec. Normally a moment to herself like that would encourage her to close her eyes and search for the ghosts who might dwell in the old building, but she kept her eyes wide open and her mind firmly closed. The lads outside had scared her and there was a harsh feel to the place that suggested it may once have been a workhouse or a sweatshop. She didn't want to look.

Her ability to sense memories from the past was starting to seem more of a curse than a gift. It used to provide her with an entertaining diversion or educational insight, an escape from her present. More often now it would disturb.

Until she was five, she thought everyone could do it, so it confused her to find that none of her playmates in the school could see the other children playing outside in their long shorts and pleated skirts. The adults remarked on her wonderful imagination and told her not to use it. Then she noticed how her mum would smile, tousle her hair, and change the subject every time Anna said she saw the other family in their house. It made her sad because the tall girl was so pretty, and the mother and father had such kind smiles. No one could share them with her.

Over time Anna realised she was slow to make friends. There was a part of her life that she could not share, so more and more that part took the place of friends. She knew the faces of so many people in her neighbourhood, all of them dead, yet very much alive to Anna. When she was small, the memory of a young woman would come to sit on the steps near Anna's window and talk to herself. Anna would stand on the cill in her room, pull the top sash down and cling to it while she listened. The young woman often seemed to be there when Anna was tired of playing or at a loose end. Though too small to remember what she said, Anna enjoyed her company. Sometimes she wondered if the woman knew Anna was listening. Anna thought of herself as a self-contained person, happy with her own company, but she felt she needed someone to listen to her now. Someone alive who could help her.

In the last few years, her unique insight had only made her problems worse. She had missed too many lessons taking her mum to chemo sessions and when she did turn up her eyelids would droop and she would drift, sifting through the students from past decades. When cancer overcame what little resistance her mum had left, the places they had enjoyed together felt closed to Anna. She was not ready to see the ghost of her own mother. Not yet.

Preet took Anna into a tall ceilinged room with flowers on the table. The gesture felt lost in that building. She listened carefully to Anna's story, with an encouraging tilt of her head. Preet had no easy answers but she agreed that finding Anna's aunt would be helpful. Anna may be able to use her address when job searching if nothing else. While it was no guarantee of an offer it increased her chances significantly.

"Have you sought help from your father?" Preet asked.

Ann rolled her eyes and blew her cheeks out. "He hasn't shown any interest since he found out mum was dying," said Anna, "and I'm no longer young enough to be fobbed off with ice-cream."

Preet frowned. "You're only seventeen. Legally you are still his dependent, and he also has a moral duty towards you."

"Really? A moral duty?" she almost spat the word. "He hasn't shown any sense of duty, let alone compassion. It was me who held mum while she threw up after each chemo session. It was me who sat at her bedside while she died. Do you want to know how he fulfilled his duty at her funeral?"

Preet was leaning away from Anna and shook her head, wide eyed. Anna realised her voice had got much louder, so she took a breath and lowered it. "He sent flowers."

Preet looked sad. She was probably wondering what kind of monster Mr Fitzwalter was, but Anna didn't know him well enough to hate him. She certainly didn't look on him as family, despite being given his surname. The only family she could think might have an interest was his sister, Jane.

"I want to find my aunt," finished Anna, almost whispering now. Because, she thought silently, I don't want to die alone in an alleyway.

It was dark when Anna left, clutching a folder full of leaflets, phone numbers and websites. She took a moment to stuff pamphlets into pockets so she could get rid of the folder, she wasn't keen to advertise where she'd been, though she was oblivious to the way her overcoat bulged. Appearances had never bothered Anna much, which was just as well these days.

She looked up and down the street for blonde guy and leather guy, but there was no one except a middle-aged man in a smart dark blue jacket and tie who was thumbing his phone. She started downhill towards the Trent University blocks and the main road running towards the centre. As she walked, she heard the man's steps behind her. She glanced behind but he still seemed distracted by his phone, so she carried on towards the tramlines and the pale grey tower of the Newton Building.

Hunger gnawed and she remembered that Dev had mentioned a place called Tina's Pantry, only a few minutes away in Trinity Square. Anna had imagined one woman with an urn of soup and a stack of plastic cups. Tina had a bustle of helpers in fluorescent yellow jackets lined up behind trestle tables that bowed beneath a feast of pasties, sandwiches, buns, crisp packets, apples, and pots full of steaming curry. The reassuring smell of warm naan bread wafted over her. The homeless and hungry peered over each other's shoulders or chatted quietly to their neighbour in the queue. Anna joined the end. Even if she didn't know any of them, she felt the protection of numbers. People in the same mess as her.

"Thank you," said Anna as one of the helpers offered her a cob and a hot cup of tea. "Which one of you is Tina?"

"Over there in the pink high-vis and the ponytail, chatting to her regulars," said the helper. "She was on the streets herself."

Anna didn't know how to react to that. Having been through it herself didn't mean Tina could solve Anna's problems, neither did it mean that Anna would make it through like Tina had. However, it was telling that she cared enough to help those going through it now. "Tell her thanks."

"I will, love. Look after yourself."

The commuters had gone home. She struggled to remember which day of the week it was without any structure to her life, but as there weren't many students out, she guessed it could be Monday. The road wasn't empty, but it was quieter than normal so she could hear footsteps behind her. Over her shoulder, a few yards back, she saw a man in a smart jacket and tie. It looked like the man she had seen in Chaucer Street. Anna walked faster, aiming for the light that pooled under the next lamp. The footsteps behind her kept pace, no indication of hurry. She was probably overreacting.

Anna reached the lamp only to realise that she would need to keep going to the next one and the one after that. Not far from Hope House, she thought, only a couple of minutes away. She calmed herself and kept walking. Each footstep had its echo. Her shadow reached around in front of her as she passed the lamp. In a few steps she saw a second shadow, just behind hers. There was a couple at the far end of the street, perhaps if she could reach them and...

A hand clapped over her mouth and another shoved her sideways into a doorway. "Shh! Good girl," he whispered. Hot boozy breath against her face.

Anna didn't think, she reacted. Her knee found his groin and he doubled over. She took his momentum and shoved his head against the metal bars across the door then ran and screamed. The couple she had seen looked more like a couple of guys as she approached, and the nearer she got the more they reminded her of the two who had shouted at her in Chaucer Street. She veered sideways down another alley and saw a small girl in a dirty grey slip waving at her. Anna had no idea who she was, but she didn't look threatening and she was beckoning her to follow.

Anna stole another glance over her shoulder. The man in the jacket was staggering after her, looking to beat a bloody revenge. He pushed himself to lunge at her then tripped over a dark shape in the road and fell. Anna ran. The girl waved again and slid through a loosely tied construction site gate. Anna could hear loud cursing from behind so she followed, squeezing through the gap and snagged her coat on a steel bar. She gave it a sharp yank that tore the coat and lost her balance. She couldn't see the striped warning tape behind her or the blackness beyond, so all she was aware of was a sudden lack of anything beneath her feet and a moment of weightlessness.

Beatrice

Holland Street, Nottingham, October 1831

"Have ye hurt y'usen?" A little girl's voice. The one Anna had followed into the building site? She felt a small hand shaking her gently – more gently than a copper's boot. Where were the police when she was being chased down a dark alley? And where was she now? Anna was sure her eyes were open, but the darkness drowned her sight. Concentrating, she caught a hint of light creeping down a rough wall from above, assuming she was looking upwards. She felt around the floor she lay on. It was gritty and cool. There was pain at the back of her head, so she reached behind to feel for blood. Nothing wet, but she could feel a whopper of a bruise.

"I'll live. Who are you?"

"Beatrice."

"I'm... Anna. Isn't it late for you to be out, Beatrice?"

"Nay. I work any hour."

"Work?"

"Fetching water. I get mesen tuppence a day." Her language seemed odd, but it was obvious she was proud of her earning potential.

"How old are you?"

"Mam says I'm eight." And even more proud of her age.

"You're only eight and your mum sends you out all hours of the day and night to fetch water?"

"Samuel's seven an' he does cesspit. I got mesen a right belt job!"

"What's a belt job?"

"Easy! Sammy shovel's poo, an' I fetch water."

"I guess you have got it easy compared to poor little Sammy. Doesn't sound right making either of you work, though."

"Why's that?"

"You shouldn't have to work until you finish school."

"School's for rich kids, says mam."

"School should be for everyone, that's the law."

"Is it? S'pose we're law breakers then. Don't seem fair though, we can't afford schooling."

"State schools are free."

"What are stately schools? Sounds like they're only for toffs."

Anna paused before the conversation ran away from her. It was dawning that Beatrice lived a very different reality from her. "This is Nottingham, isn't it, Beatrice?"

"Ay. We're in well, off Holland Street."

Anna realised she was asking the wrong question. "What year is this?"

"Knocked yourn head right 'n proper, haven't ye!"

She didn't think that was the problem, though it was easier to go along with it. "Yeah, I have, can you remind me?"

"Eighteen thirty-one."

"…"

"Y' alright, miss?"

This was all wrong. Anna knew her limits: she would close her eyes and focus carefully, feeling for the memories, like peeling back pages in a book full of other people's stories. Some pages would be empty. Some would be very faint; others would spring to technicoloured life like a children's pop-up book. But all she could do was look at the pages and admire them. She had never ever talked to one of the characters on the page, let alone touch them. The pain at the back of her head had been taking much of her attention, but now she stopped to think about it she sensed a familiar tingle on the edge of her conscious thoughts. "Do you mind if I hold your hand for a moment, Beatrice?"

Beatrice trustingly found Anna's hand and gave her a firm hello grip. This was definitely not normal, even for Anna. "Ye feeling woozy?" asked Beatrice.

"Yes. Would you help me? I think I'd like to get up, out of this well." Anna felt tense in dark confined spaces and her breaths were coming short.

Beatrice gave a surprisingly strong tug which was exactly what Anna needed to get on her feet. "Are y' a toff, miss?" The question almost made Anna fall again. "Only ye talk funny." It wasn't said harshly, just matter of fact. Anna had to admit she must sound like a toff to Beatrice. After all, she was a southerner and a lot of southerners sounded like toffs to people from the midlands and the north.

"No. I don't have much." That was an understatement. "I suppose I sound like one because I'm from Blackheath."

"Where's that?"

"London."

"Are ye a runaway?"

Anna hadn't stopped to think about it like that. She had run away from the druggies and the alcos in the B&B. She had run away from the strain and embarrassment of sofa-surfing with her two friends in Hither Green. And she had just run away from someone who had tried to rape her. That was what he was going to do: rape her. The memory hit her hard in the gut. She bent double and threw up.

"Better out than in, miss. That's what me mam always says."

Anna wiped her mouth with the cuff of her overcoat. One more stain wasn't going to make a difference. "Your mum sounds a wise woman," she croaked.

Beatrice took Anna to the side of the well shaft and guided her hands and feet into little holes in the stone that served as a ladder. It was only when they reached the top that she could see enough to realise Beatrice had a leather bucket full of water in one hand and had been guiding Anna while climbing with the other. Beatrice seemed determined to earn her tuppence.

It was night-time and far darker than Anna had ever experienced in a city. Beatrice led Anna onto the main street where a few fluttering gas lamps shed a pale light. Anna's mind did summersaults as it told her she was on Goose Gate and yet it all felt so strange. Not a single illuminated signboard. No plate glass windows stretching from ground to ceiling. No Oxfam, no Pizza Express, no Sainsbury's Local. But if she looked up, there was a strong familiarity: most of the buildings above shop-front level were the ones she knew. Anna started to realise that this part of Nottingham had existed (would exist?) for at least two hundred years. The sole contribution of the twentieth and twenty-first centuries had been to blitz it with light and trash it with ads.

At least the side alleys still smelled of pee. Beatrice led her down a particularly ripe and narrow one that wiggled south. There were no gas lamps in the alleyways. Anna gripped Beatrice's hand to guide her as all she could see was the stars in the narrow gap of sky between the dark hulks rising either side of her.

Beatrice stopped at a door and pushed it open. The candle lit room beyond smelled of wood smoke and at least half a dozen people huddled around a small stove in the corner. The children ranged from a little above Beatrice's age to a baby held by the mother, wrapped in a dirty cloth. The mother thanked Beatrice as she poured some water from her bucket into an earthenware jug on the bare wooden floor.

Anna was taken down some rough-cut stone stairs into a basement where another family sat under blankets. They too had a jug which Beatrice filled. No windows. Anna couldn't imagine living in a basement without any fresh air or view of the sky. The place was rank. It was so damp she could see mushrooms sprouting from rotted timber boxes that served as a table and chairs. One of the boys looked pale and unwell. Anna was surprised only one of them did and was relieved when Beatrice led her back up the stairs, all the way up to the top floor.

"Hello mam!" said Beatrice to the fair-haired woman, stirring a black pot over an even blacker stove.

"Hello dear. Who's this, a friend of yourn?" The mother inspected Anna with her blue-grey eyes.

"This is Anna. She's runaway from London. She sounds like toff but she en't an' she had nasty bump on head. Found her down well."

Anna found it difficult to add anything to such a concise summary, so she just smiled and said hello. Beatrice's mum ladled some soup into a bowl and handed it to Anna with a warm smile and a shrewd look. For a moment Anna thought she saw something familiar in the woman's face: a familiarity that hovered at the edge of her mind, just beyond grasp. The woman poured another bowl for Beatrice while she filled their own jug with the last of the bucket. Anna looked around for a spoon, then saw Beatrice put her bowl to her lips and tip it back. She followed Beatrice's lead. Parsnip soup – it was good.

Anna felt the comforting sense of a home, despite the damp and sparse conditions. Not her home, but Beatrice and her mum's home. A sense of refuge and reassurance. Of unquestioning support. Like the soup, it warmed her. It also reminded her how much she missed her own mum and the home they had carried from one place to another. Anna was trying to work out why she might recognise Beatrice's mother when a glow at the window caught her eye and she pointed over the dark rooftops to the west.

"What's that?"

"Ooh! Let's go see." chirped Beatrice.

"Go careful m' duck," called her mum.

Beatrice led Anna back up to Goose Gate then down the hill to where the Council House should be. It wasn't. A Georgian building sat in its place: just as tall and grand, but not nearly as deep, no dome and no shopping arcade full of beautiful people. She could hear plenty of people at the far end of the Market Square, but they didn't sound as if they were in the mood for shopping. In fact, they sounded pretty pissed off about something.

"What's going on?" asked Anna, getting nervous.

"I'll ask," said Beatrice brightly.

"Hey, wait, you could get hurt." But Beatrice had already sprinted ahead, leaving Anna with a head full of questions. She crept to the corner of the Market Square and looked out on a sea of closed-up wooden stalls with shadows milling among and beyond them. Above the rooftops she could see the red glow of fire, unmistakable in its intensity, yet it seemed to be coming from somewhere above and beyond the square.

A familiar grey slip re-emerged from between the stalls. "Follow me!" grinned Beatrice, "they're burning duck 'enry." At least that's what Anna thought she said. Beatrice explained with the patience of a junior-school teacher that it was Henry, Duke of Newcastle, who of course had a mansion in Nottingham (not just Newcastle, silly). After more silly questions she learned he had been one of the toffs who had opposed 'the Bill' for the umpteenth time. Not for the first time, Anna was grateful for her mum having been a history researcher. She guessed that if this was 1831 then Beatrice must be talking about the Reform Bill, which her own mum had described as one of the biggest attempts to force some kind of democracy on Britain since the beheading of Charles the First. The Commons had passed it only for the Lords to throw it out again, despite extraordinary support from the privileged voting elite and ordinary people alike. It seemed that Duke Henry (she liked the sound of duck 'enry better) was one of the toffs who had a poor grip on the popular mood. A dangerous misjudgement so soon after the French Revolution.

They hurried down a street where the shouts of the mob grew louder, just as the fiery glow rose above. She guessed it must be Friar Lane because they were running uphill from the far left-hand corner of the Market Square, though all other clues were gone. The flat-faced glass and concrete blocks had vanished and in their place was a crowd of half-timbered medieval buildings, punctuated by the odd Victorian turret or genteel Georgian facade. Above them she could see flames leaping from a mansion building at the very top of the Castle Rock. It seemed duck 'enry was being roasted.

"Is anyone one in there?" asked Anna.

"Nay, it's been empty last two years," said Beatrice. "Duck 'enry never comes here anymore. Nott'n'm's too grimy for likes of him. 'sides, he said he only had to show his face here to start a riot. We had cheese riot, bread riot and meat riot." Beatrice seemed proud of the locals' revolutionary achievements.

"He's not liked then?"

"Mam said even duck Wellington thinks him a fool." And who would argue with her mum? The knowing look she had given Anna had suggested a sharp intellect despite any possible lack of schooling. "Half of us be on poor relief here," continued Beatrice, "and duck 'enry don't give a fart."

Anna supressed a laugh. Beatrice was a tiny tornado of rebellion, but her circumstances seemed just as chronic as her own. It made her wonder how many gave a fart in the twenty-first century; she'd struggled to find many away from Tina and Hope House. Anna watched the rioters carry furniture and rugs from the burning building. A couple of lads were trying to sell stolen wall hangings for a couple of shillings a yard. She could hardly blame them.

Hooves clattered on cobbles, echoing off the street walls. The lads looked up, dropped the hangings, and ran. Beatrice tugged at her sleeve. "Run! 'oozars are coming, RUN!"

Anna didn't stop to ask what an 'oozar was, she could guess they came on horse-back and took a dim view of looters, arsonists and anyone stupid enough to be caught standing next to them. She ran.

Beatrice pelted down Friars Lane like duck 'enry's hunting hounds were after her. In a sense they were. Anna stole a glance over her shoulder and saw three horsemen wearing tall bearskin hats, taking wide swipes at hapless bystanders with wicked curved swords. Anna decided that at least one thing had improved in the last two centuries: you were less likely to be gutted by a cavalry sabre.

Beatrice was ahead of her, beckoning for Anna to follow her, weaving between the stalls in the marketplace. The 'oozars thundered after them, scattering rioters and upending carts. Anna chased after Beatrice, pelting up Pelham Street and into Goose Gate. Hooves still clattered off the cobbles behind. Beatrice veered off a side alley to the left. Anna leaned into her run, panic rising. The raw memory of being hunted clawed her. The clatter behind grew louder and she could hear a horse snorting. Almost level with the alley she had her hand out to grab a timber post and swing herself in. There was a swoosh of sliced air behind and a blinding whack on the back of her head. Then nothing.

Ghost from the Past

Queens Medical Centre, Nottingham, October 2019

Blinding white light. Anna screwed her eyes shut again, wincing at the pain from the back of her head. She risked prising one eyelid open to squint at her surroundings. A grid of soulless white ceiling tiles interrupted at random by shiny metal light diffusers. Bright blue plastic curtains hung from stainless steel rails and the sound of a phone being ignored. It was horrible. Thank god she thought, I'm back in the twenty-first century. And I'm alive.

"Hi there, sweetheart. Good to see you're awake," A kindly nurse leaned over her and smiled. She wore a badge that told Anna her name was Christine Lamwaka. "You lie still, dear. You've had a bad night. Some archaeologists found you in an old cave cistern they were excavating under a building site on Brightmoor Street. Gave them a right old fright, you did. Thought you were a ghost from the past!"

Anna was confused. She was sure the girl had said Holland Street. And a cave cistern? "A cistern is a water well, isn't it?"

"That's right. They said it was dug out of the sandstone to get to the water table below. They reckon it's at least two-hundred years old."

"At least," nodded Anna, sagely, then stopped. Her head still hurt.

"What were you doing down there, dear?"

It was a simple question, but Anna felt overwhelmed by the complications of answering it. "I fell," she started.

"I can tell that by the bruising on the back of your head and shoulders. But why were you in the building site?"

"I... I was attacked..." she hated herself for being so weak, but her eyes welled up. A dark cocktail of memories swirled: a man in a jacket pressing her into a dark doorway, boozy breath, eyes undressing her; a burning skyline; a sabre swung by a soldier on a black horse.

"Attacked? You mean you think someone was trying to rape you?"

Anna nodded and screwed her eyes shut.

"You poor thing. You're safe here. We'll look after you and when you're feeling stronger, I'll see if you want us to call the police."

The police. Anna's recent memory wasn't a shiny one. To be fair the officer had suggested Hope House, but that was after he had woken her with his boot. Her head throbbed and she tried to roll over but found it too painful, so settled for lying stoically on her back with her eyes shut to keep the world out. She felt a sympathetic pat on her arm from the nurse who left her to rest.

Anna was released from Queen's Medical Centre two days later. By the time the harassed looking consultant got around to her it was six in the evening and getting dark. Not the best time to be wandering around Nottingham after an assault but she had no choice. At least nurse Christine had been kind enough to lend her a phone to call Hope House, so they were expecting her when she arrived back after seven.

It was the same woman on the door, Maureen, who greeted her, "Hello m' duck, take a seat over there." While Anna waited for a bed to be organised, she mused on the Nottinghamshire greeting. Anna used to think it was just a daft and friendly thing to say. Maureen may not have realised, but if Anna's encounter with Beatrice held any truth, then she was actually saying 'hello my Duke'. She found it respectful in a gently mocking sort of way. Anna liked it even more now.

She thought she ought to feel relieved to be back at Hope House, but instead she felt sad because she was still homeless, just not on the streets. She also felt scared. The walk to Hope House in the dark had shaken her. Fortunately, it had been busy with commuters for most of the way, but there were some stretches where she found herself searching for a group of people or better streetlights to get close to. She was back in an institutional bed in another institutional room, but at least she felt safe.

Anna started thinking about what she had experienced in the cave. The rational explanation was that she had fallen in, knocked her head and imagined going back in time. That would seem logical to anyone other than Anna, who knew she could see people from the past but had never talked to them before. Why had she seen the same girl prior to falling down the well? She could tell herself that talking to Beatrice and touching her was just a dream if it hadn't felt so shockingly real. She knew her unfathomable skill for rifling through the memories of the past was a genuine ability, so it was unlikely Beatrice had been conjured in a dream.

As a child, Anna's mum had taken her to Eltham Palace, not far from Blackheath. Anna felt a familiar sensation at the edge of her mind, closed her eyes, and watched a woman kneeling to pet a lemur. Anna had wondered whether she imagined it or confused the thought with some local menagerie. The guide then started telling the story of how the Courtauld family kept a pet lemur called Mah-Jongg in the nineteen-thirties. From then on, she had looked up the historic facts behind anything she saw. Whenever there were any records, she found she had witnessed a startling truth. It was real, but it had happened long ago.

She looked at her phone. Her last pay-as-you-go had been used up weeks ago and she wondered why she still carried it other than comfort or a misguided hope that things would get better. Anna decided to find the library next morning and look up whatever she could about Nottingham in October 1831.

Nottingham Central Library was a grand four-storey Victorian pile near the top of Angel Row. Anna wondered if it had been there in October 1831. She was damned sure the automatic glass entrance doors, and the sickly green signage hadn't. She cuffed some dirt off her coat and walked in, hoping no one would tell her that her kind weren't welcome. No one took any notice. She found one of the public computers on an upper floor and settled herself into a chair. Ignoring the lurid signage, she instantly felt happier. She was warm, dry, comfortable, and about to do some research. She could kid herself that she was a normal functioning member of society for a while.

Anna found Henry Pelham-Clinton, 4th Duke of Newcastle, easily enough on the web. She wasn't in the least surprised to find him described as a cold and pompous opponent of reform. Her eye was drawn by an image of the burning mansion house and was startled by the notes below it. Despite being no liberal himself, the Duke of Wellington was quoted as saying 'there was never such a fool' as Pelham-Clinton. She could imagine Beatrice's mum nodding wisely. The article listed all the food riots Beatrice had been so proud of and it even quoted the Duke of Newcastle saying he 'only had to show his face to cause a riot'. Depressingly, it also declared Nottingham the worst slum in all the Empire, apart from Bombay, and confirmed that half the population of the city had been on poor relief.

It had been real.

EVERYDAY GHOSTS

In some inexplicable way Anna had been at the riot which ended with the Duke's mansion being torched. The article even confirmed that a few of the 14th King's Hussars ('oozars) had tried to stop the rioters. What it failed to mention was one of them trying to take her head off with a sabre.

Anna sat back in the chair feeling tired and overwhelmed, an unwelcomely familiar feeling. It was all but impossible that she would have read so much and recalled every detail in a dream. Even the lads selling off the tapestries were there in print. And the date of the riot was the eighth of October. She looked at the bottom right-hand corner of the computer screen confirming that it was the tenth of the tenth: two days and almost two centuries after. She wondered if all the ghosts she saw were locked in some eternal loop that played out over time to the present, or whether this was just a coincidence. Perhaps a memory got stronger and so easier to find on its anniversary?

She remembered that nurse Christine had called the street with the well Brightmoor Street. After searching through a few historic maps, she found that Brightmoor Street used to be called Holland Street, exactly as Beatrice had said.

Anna felt miserable for Beatrice. She was beginning to accept that Beatrice was real, and she ached for the loss of her childhood. Beatrice had been put to work when she should have been playing. She was prematurely wise of the world when she should have been discovering its mysteries. Anna may be homeless but at least she had enjoyed a childhood and an education. Poverty and destitution may persist, but a few victories had been won by the reformers. She wondered if that was cause for hope.

Anna was reluctant to leave the comfort and safety of the library, but she was hungry, and she couldn't afford anything from the library café. She remembered Tina's Pantry and decided to brave the grey skies and wind. Reluctantly she descended the stairs. Brash yellow posters told her Goose Fair had been extended and she could catch the last day today. She remembered her aunt taking her once when she was younger. She had never seen so many rides, stalls, and coloured lights all in one place before, nor since. She thought about going but was afraid to be out alone after dark.

Just past the steak houses and burger joints in Trinity Square, she found the queue and Tina's trestle tables. She also found Rob. He was eating a sticky bun and licking his fingers, immersed in the joy of comfort food. After their last encounter she felt inclined to leave him to his bun, but his dark brown eyes flicked up and met hers. He nodded. Not an effusive greeting but he was acknowledging her existence.

"Hi Rob," Anna tried, "That looks good."

"Mm. Favourite."

Breakthrough! He had volunteered a nugget of personal information. "Sorry I hassled you at the refuge," she said.

"'s alright. Still looking for y' aunt?"

"Yeah. No luck yet."

"Not much luck 'round here," Rob gestured to the line of faces queuing for the trestle tables.

"Guess not." On an impulse she asked, "Have you been to Goose Fair?"

Rob looked surprised, "Course!"

"Yeah, of course you have. Sorry, stupid question."

"Well, s'pose some people live in Nott'n'm their whole life an never go." Longest sentence yet, thought Anna. Must be getting somewhere. Then he surprised her. "D' y' want to go?"

For a moment Anna thought it was a taunt. She'd say yes and then he'd tell her to go by herself. But he was looking at her, giving her his full attention. She felt unsettled yet a little beguiled. His expression hinted at mischief and adventure which many months on the streets had failed to drain away. "Yeah. Okay."

Rob licked the last of the bun off his fingers and tilted his head to say come on then. Anna grabbed a bun for herself and followed.

Fair

Forest Fields, Nottingham, October 2019

They heard it long before they saw it. Between the trees that lined the cemetery on Mansfield Road, they glimpsed the lights of the fairground rides. When they passed the ornate stone pillars at the corner of Forest Fields it seemed as if the whole of Nottingham and half the Midlands had descended for a party. They had.

Anna remembered Jane telling her it had been going almost every year since Saxon times. She said they used to bring geese to the market square, many of which waddled up Goose Gate having come as far as Lincolnshire. Their webbed feet were covered in tar and sand like little boots, to help them make the journey. The fair grew and grew until it was too big for Market Square and was moved out to the huge recreation ground called Forest Fields, a mile north of the city centre.

Rob stood for a moment, searching the tops of tents, rides, and stalls, as if looking for a place to start. With a gesture of his head, he beckoned Anna to follow him as he dived into the crowd, sliding between punters like a spirit. She found it hard to keep him in sight, he seemed practised at slipping through crowds. She saw him enter a large gaming marquee where the noise at the entrance was overwhelming. Hundreds of arcade games competed for attention. She glimpsed Rob's dark green hoodie disappearing towards the back of the marquee and followed. When she caught up, he was standing in the middle of a long row of fruit machines, what her aunt used to call one-arm-bandits, 'because they only have one arm, but they still rob you blind'. He looked carefully at each machine in turn before choosing a comparatively small and out of date one decorated with Pokémon monsters. He pulled a coin from his pocket and put it in the slot. Anna was going to say something lame about not wasting what little money he had, when he placed his hand carefully at the side of the machine and pulled the lever. Half-way through the whirl of characters he gave the machine a sharp slap that made her jump. Each drum came to a halt, one after the other: Pikachu, Pikachu, Pikachu... Pikachu. An unbelievably lucky line of little smiley yellow monsters which heralded a cascade of coins overflowing the metal bucket at the bottom. Rob pulled the bottom edge of his hoodie out to catch the coins.

"Give us a hand," he called over his shoulder. Anna rushed over, her own hoodie outstretched, and helped scoop the coins up. "Half each, that's fair," he said.

"What about the coins on the floor?" asked Anna, still unsure what had just happened.

Rob nodded at a pair of small boys who had heard the windfall and come to gawk. "Looks like y' lucky day," he said to them with a grin. Their jaws dropped. Then they dropped to their knees and started scooping handfuls into their pockets. "That's fair too," Rob said with a sly grin.

It was the first time Anna had seen him smile and it had an unexpected effect on her. This taciturn down-and-out had transformed into a mischievous charmer. She was charmed.

Stuffing their bounty into all available pockets, they went out to buy hot dogs, candyfloss, and the wildest ride they could find. Anna pointed to a towering carousel just as the last turn's punters were hopping out of their seats. Rob and Anna each grabbed a seat and pulled the bar across. Anna was trying to pick candyfloss out of her hair when she noticed they were moving, slowly at first before picking up speed. The spin sent them further and further out over the crowds while the top of the carousel rose and rocked. Anna wondered whether she should have had that hot dog so soon before the ride and started giggling. Rob grinned back at her, keeping her steadily in his sight as their seats danced around on the ends of their chains. Unconsciously she rubbed the last of the candyfloss off and tugged at her straggling hair.

Anna wanted to hook ducks off water slides next, but Rob led her to the archery stall. He spent a few moments examining the bow as if he might know what he was looking for. Then he inspected each arrow in turn, looking along them to see how straight or otherwise. Otherwise, judging by his grimace. He asked for a different batch but didn't seem much happier. Just when Anna thought he was going to lose interest and find another stall, he pulled way back on the bow until she was sure it would snap then loosed his first arrow. It grazed the outer edge of the bullseye and Anna jumped up and down with childish excitement. The next one straddled the line, the third one followed swiftly and smacked dead centre. Anna's mouth hung open.

The stall keeper squinted at Rob through a pair of thick rimmed glasses, as if suspecting him of pulling a stunt.

"Prize please," said Rob, calmly.

The stall keeper grunted then nodded to the top shelf of soft toys and trinkets. "Take a couple an' bugger off!" It seemed that winners were not welcome.

Rob grinned, took two of the largest yellow teddies, one under each arm, then passed one to Anna. Neither of them could think what to do with the trophies so they found a youngsters' merry-go-round and left them for the first ones to get off.

Somehow Anna lost all sense of time or place. They ran from stalls to rides like kids let out to play. She laughed at the very thought she was alive. Only the rain knew when it was time to stop and gradually it drove the punters away, closing the rides and shutting the stalls. Rob and Anna pulled their hoodies over their heads and ran for shelter.

"This way," called Rob. She thought he was heading for the gate they had come in, but part way there he veered off towards a high brick wall. He jumped nimbly up a tree that grew close to the wall and wedged himself between them before reaching down to take Anna's hand. He pulled her onto the top of the wall. Then he leaped up onto it himself, bouncing off the coping and down the other side, using a standing stone as a step. Anna followed him across the stone before she looked back and saw it was a gravestone. She felt guilty.

Rob was already running up a gentle slope, weaving between the crosses and tombs, so she followed. Ragged outcrops appeared either side of them. It felt like she was running into a creepy film set where vampires lurked between the rocks and the graves. Where the hell was he taking her? The fading light barely reached down the stony ravine, so she listened for Rob's footsteps and kept going. His hand grabbed hers, steering her around a mini mausoleum and into a dark recess which was mercifully sheltered from rain and wind.

"Where are we?" she asked.

"Rock Cemetery," Rob answered, as if she should know it. "Let's go in."

She could feel metal rods barring their way. Rob pulled something from his pocket. She could hear a rattle and a click, then the bars swung away.

"You have a key for this place?"

"Sort of," he said, evasive.

"You picked the lock?"

He searched his pockets again and produced a small plastic torch. It looked like one of his winnings from earlier. It gave just enough light for her to see they were in a rough-hewn cave with pillars carved from the same stone. If it hadn't been for the rain and Rob beside her, she would have turned away from the dark confines of the cavern.

"Watch out for sandmen," warned Rob. Anna thought he was joking but he had a straight face. He led them over behind one of the pillars where they found a ledge that would do for a place to sit. It wasn't cosy but it was a refuge from the downpour.

"That was fun," said Anna. "I guess we should have kept the money, used it for..."

"For what?" asked Rob. "A suit? A car? A house?"

"There wasn't enough for any of them."

"But there were enough for fun."

"Yeah, there was. And you shared it."

"Wouldn't be fun if y' didn't share it."

Anna looked at Rob, as if meeting him again. She guessed he must have mixed race parents, his skin tone, hair, and eyes all looked middle eastern. He had a strong Nottingham accent, yet he wouldn't have looked out of place in an Iranian bazaar. She guessed he was about nineteen or twenty, not much older than her. His frame was scrawny and gaunt. His face had high cheek bones and dark brown eyes that drew your gaze.

"Thank you," she said.

"What for?"

"Asking me to come with you."

"Thought y' asked me."

"I suppose I did. But thank you anyway."

"Y' a'right for a southerner," he said, that sly grin reappearing.

"You're alright for a Nott'n'm lad," she smiled, poking fun at his accent.

They sat quietly for a while. Anna tried hard to avoid thinking about tomorrow. She tried to hold onto today a little longer.

"Y' surprised me," said Rob, breaking the silence.

"How?"

"Thought y' were some runaway from rich family, lookin' for attention."

Anna thought a while before answering, she didn't want to say anything to start an argument again. It reminded her of Beatrice calling her a runaway. "I used to be okay. You might have called me and my mum well off. She was a university researcher. We had a nice house in a nice place. But just because you start well, doesn't mean you stay that way."

Rob took time to reply too, seeming to think over what she had said. "What happened?"

"She got ill. Cancer. It takes a long time to kill, so we had plenty of time to lose everything. First, she lost her job, she was too ill to keep working. Because her job was contract, she had no sick leave. Then we lost our nice house in Blackheath. Got moved to a council flat in Catford. Then I lost her. The council put me in care, but I hated it. I ran off. I found a cheap B&B for a few nights, but the place was full of addicts and I didn't feel safe, so I took up the offer of a friend's sofa. Didn't take more than a couple of months for us to get on each other's nerves, so I moved on to strain another friendship to breaking point. Once I'd lost both friends, I came here to search for the only other family I felt I could ask a favour of. I seem to have lost her too."

Rob put his hand on her shoulder. "What were y' mum's name?"

"Eleanor."

"Did y' love her?"

"We argued sometimes, but… yeah. Very much."

"Then y' still have something."

Anna put her head on Rob's shoulder. "She was my family. Just the two of us," she said quietly. "I felt so lost when she died. I felt homeless long before I was sleeping on a pavement."

After a while she noticed his shoulder getting damp with her tears, so she sat up again.

"Do you still have family?" she asked, cuffing her cheeks.

"No. Mam were addict. Died of overdose. Never really knew her. Dad brought up brother, Will, and me. We had to move to council flat in St Ann's." There was a long pause. "There were a fire," he said. Anna sensed that he rarely told anyone this much. "Dad and Will died. I got away."

Now Anna put her arm around Rob's skinny waist. "What was your dad's name?"

"Mamsūh."

"Is that Arabic?"

"Yeah, but he were Christian. Refugee from West Bank. Them who torched our flat thought he were Muslim."

"Bloody hell! What kind of people would...?" her question trailed off. There were no words.

"It were after London bombings. Anyone who looked Muslim got spat at. Or worse."

Anna couldn't comprehend what drove people to burn a single father and his boys. The London bombs happened about fourteen years ago, thought Anna. "What age were you?"

"Six."

Even younger than little Beatrice. She gave Rob a squeeze. It was his turn to cry.

Little by little the torchlight faded. Anna's eyelids started to droop but she fought against the urge to sleep. Without really meaning to, she drew her mind across the memories that had accumulated like sediment in the cave. She thought she caught a glimpse of someone carrying a cross and looked as if they wore medieval leggings and a cloak. Then another, more recent, of a man digging a grave. She saw a glow coming from deep within the cave. Shadows reached across the ceiling and down the wall behind them. Voices muffled by distance but growing nearer. Rob tensed and gripped Anna's hand. She could tell he was ready to run.

"Sandmen!"

Cemetery Mine

They ran for the gate. Ahead the cave walls flickered with reflected light. They weaved around stone pillars, more of them than Anna remembered passing on the way in. The light grew stronger, and Anna hoped it was coming from outside, but it glowed and flickered like flames not daylight. Sand fell from the ceiling onto her hair and face, following a muffled crack. She saw flaming torches in niches cut into the sandstone, like an Indiana Jones film.

"Where are we?"

"I... I don't recognise this," said Rob, a frown creased his forehead and he backed away from the torch flames. He turned to search for an exit then froze. A pair of men were walking towards them, pickaxes over their shoulders. Candles stuck to the brims of their hats gave their faces an eerie wash of light. Miners? If they were, they weren't twenty-first century thought Anna. No safety helmets, no electric lamps, no high-vis and no machinery. Nothing but a candle and a pickaxe.

"Ay up! Y' lost?"

"We just wanted shelter from the rain," explained Anna.

"We didn't disrespect any graves," added Rob.

"Graves?" asked the first miner, putting down his pickaxe.

"The cemetery," said Rob, his face screwed up with confusion.

"Graves are near top of hill," said the miner.

"Ay, there'll be another today," said the other, grim. "Hanging day. He only stole a pheasant off Baron's land at Wollaton. He were hungry. Won't be hungry no more."

"If Baron en't killing foxes he's killing paupers," said the first. "Both vermin in his eyes."

There was another crack. Louder this time, and more sand fell as if poured from buckets above.

"Get thisens out!" the second miner jerked a thumb over his shoulder at the way they had come.

"Ed an' Will en't out yet," said the first. "We got t' warn 'em." He grasped his pickaxe and ran on into the cave, calling the names of his friends. Anna and Rob wavered, not knowing if they should help or run. There was another explosive crack, and they could see one of the thinner sandstone pillars trembling, shaking a cloud of sand from it.

"COME. NOW!" roared the second miner. They could see shadows dancing on the walls and ceiling. The sound of people running towards them. A low rumble shook the whole cave, even the ground they stood on felt alive. Two men emerged from behind the pillars.

"WHERE'S ED?" called the second miner.

"JUST BEHIND," shouted the new man who must be Will.

Another figure now appeared from behind the pillars, presumably Ed. He was struggling, half limping, half jogging. Just as the lead two were getting close there was a rumble as if a mighty storm were breaking. The thin pillar split with the sound of a canon shot. Rob flinched and crouched, but the two running miners each grabbed an arm and dragged him. The other miner took Anna's hand, and everyone was running.

Chunks the size of footballs fell from the ceiling and it rained grit. The rumble escalated to a roar and Anna could hear the impacts of far larger rocks on the ground behind. The miners steered them in a zigzag around standing pillars until they fell headlong onto mud, in cold leaden light at the mouth of the cave. The thunder grumbled into silence and they sat panting for breath.

"Where's Ed?" asked the first miner.

Will was sitting with his elbows on his knees and his face in his hands. "Back there," he nodded. "'is joints were stiff from digging on 'is knees. Could never run fast."

"What'll we say t' Missus Hughes?" asked Will, a tear streaking the dirt on his face.

"That she don' need t' pay no burial fee," said the second. "They'll prob'ly pull rest of mine down now. En't safe." He looked at Rob, who was still shaking, "Like y' said, only good for graves."

A soft drizzle floated on the breeze. Anna helped Rob onto his wobbling legs and walked him up the hill, where she thought the Mansfield Road and the route back into town should be.

"Sorry," muttered Rob.

"What for?" asked Anna.

"I'm no good for stuff like that."

"What do you mean? We got out alive, unlike poor Ed Hughes."

"No thanks to me."

"How do you think you'd have helped? Hold the mine up with one hand and pull him out with the other?"

Rob looked at her sourly. "I'm no hero is what I mean."

Anna stopped suddenly, looking at the brow of the hill. The silhouette of a gallows stood stark against the grey sky and a limp figure swung in the breeze beneath. The Baron of Wollaton had his justice for the stolen bird and the pauper had no more need of food. Rob stared. Anna could see a cold fury growing in his eyes, his teeth grinding.

"Bastards," he muttered. "World is full of evil rich bastards who'd sooner hang us 'n hand us a slice o' bread."

There was a time when Anna might have argued that those with money are no more or less evil than anyone else. She had been 'rich' in some people's eyes. But more and more she found herself on the wrong side of a system, an attitude, a gulf between the haves and have-nots. Now she started to wonder whether the poor would always be seen as vermin. Did the haves feel threatened by the have-nots? Were they embarrassed? Or were they too busy looking after themselves to remember to be human? How could anyone hang a person for being hungry?

"Where the hell are we, Anna? What's going on?" He looked angry and scared.

Anna had returned from her previous visits to the past simply by opening her eyes, because she had been fully aware of her presence in the modern day. This was different. Her eyes were open to a past world and when she tried to sense her body in the modern day, she simply couldn't do it. What if she were to reverse the process?

"Close your eyes," she said. "Hold my hand." After some hesitation he did as she asked. "Can you remember the taste of that sticky bun you had from Tina's?" Rob opened one eye to look at her suspiciously, sensing she was winging it. She was.

Anna tried again. "Close your eyes, just focus on that taste. Remember our carousel ride at the fair." Anna had no idea if what she was doing would work, but she wasn't panicking yet. She had always returned before. "Remember hitting the bullseye at the archery stall," She continued, trying to focus her own mind on recent memories of the present, as well as Rob's. "Remember winning the yellow bears." On an impulse she tried another way. "Sit down. That's right." She put her arm around his waist, trying to recreate the moment they had entered the past. "Remember sitting in the cave. Keep your eyes closed and put your head on my shoulder."

Anna's mind seemed to lurch upwards and she felt an absence, as if something were slipping away beneath her. Yet she also felt the presence of Rob, both physically and in her mind, and she clung to him as the old world fell away.

Rock Cemetery, Forest Fields, Nottingham, October 2019

A dim light crept across the ground and somewhere beyond she could hear the dawn chorus. Rob sat up with a start, then stood. Anna stood next to him, still holding his hand. They were on the other side of the Rock Cemetery, beyond the iron railings where the cave was. Trees swayed slowly in the breeze and a soft rain made the gravestones glisten. The hum of traffic and a remote siren reassured them they were standing near the Mansfield Road in twenty-nineteen.

"What did y' do?" asked Rob, tone neutral yet the question was threatening.

Anna didn't know where to start. She had spent so long trying to hide what she did that she couldn't begin to explain. Nor did she understand how she and Rob had both gone back in time together. Instead, she asked another question. "Why did you warn me about sandmen?"

Rob looked away, silent.

"You'd seen those miners before, hadn't you," said Anna.

Rob shook his head, frowning. He looked close to tears again.

"You've been in that cave before and you saw miners coming up through the tunnels," asserted Anna.

"Thought I were dreaming."

"Why did you take me to the cave?"

"It were wet. Cave were close. I knew how t' get in."

"Why risk seeing the sandmen again, Rob?"

"I thought..."

"You thought if I saw them too then you weren't dreaming. That's what you thought."

Rob hung his head and gave a slight nod. "Sorry." Then he looked up again, confused, still angry. "But they never stopped. They never talked. An' the cave never fell in, an' no one got killed, nor hanged. What happened back there, Anna? That were no dream, that were... that were bloody weird!"

"You can do what I do," murmured Anna.

"What?"

"What were you doing when you saw the sandmen before? What was happening in your head?"

Rob searched her eyes as if looking for some sign this was all a hoax, but Anna was serious. If he could see the ghosts of the past as well, then she was not alone with her curse-cum-gift. "I... I thought I could feel something... at edge of my mind."

Anna's heart leapt with a mad mix of joy, vindication, and relief. "You could sense a memory?"

Rob looked utterly baffled. "Yeah, s'pose. But I could see it."

"That's it! That's what I do. You can do it too I know you can."

"I don't understand."

"You can lift memories from the past in your mind and look at what happened."

"Ghosts?"

"That's one way of looking at it, but they don't feel like ghosts to me."

"Them miners weren't ghosts. They grabbed my arms and dragged me out that cave, or I'd be dead an' buried like Ed."

"All I did before was watch, but a couple of days ago it all changed. I spoke to a little Victorian girl. She took me by the hand and showed me a riot."

"A riot?"

"They were burning down the Duke's mansion."

"Should have brought me, I'd have helped," he said dryly.

Anna laughed. "I believe it!"

"How're you doing it?"

"I don't understand how it works, any more than you. This is only the second time I've... taken part. Talked, held hands, felt the sand on the cave floor, felt the heat from the castle fire," she rubbed the back of her head, "felt a hussar try and take my head off."

"'oozar?"

Anna laughed again. "Come with me," she took his hand firmly and led him up the Mansfield Road.

"Where are we goin'?"

"The library."

"Can we go to Tina's first?"

His Will

Central Library, Nottingham, October 2020

Rob looked uncomfortable. Anna felt frustrated because she was more relaxed in the library than anywhere else in Nottingham. She had shown Rob the articles on the Reform Riot of 1831 and duck 'enry. He showed little interest, fidgeting, looking around to see who was watching. Finally, she found what she was after and turned the screen towards Rob, pointing triumphantly.

"There," she declared.

Rob squinted at the screen and nodded. "Hmm," was all he could manage.

"Well?" asked Anna.

"Well, what?"

"There he is! Edward Hughes: died 1806 in a sand mine cave-in. And, just like the other miner said would happen, they closed it all down in 1811, collapsed most of it to stop it falling. The bit we sat in must be the last remaining part of the sand mine."

"Oh!" Rob's eyebrows went up, she could almost hear the cogs turning. His deep frown returned as the truth of their encounter dawned.

Another thought occurred to her. "How much time did you get in school, Rob?"

He looked down at his feet. Anna was worried she had asked something he might be ashamed of. "I were in an out a lot of schools. Don't think they knew what t' do with me."

"I guess you had a tough time. You'd lost all your family by the time you were eight."

"Didn't help. Neither did dyslexia."

"Oh, Rob!" She knew that schools knew what to look for and how to help, which was a world of difference from a couple of decades ago. But if he'd been passed between schools like an unwanted parcel then none of them would have had time to help.

"Didn't help when I were trying to sign on. All benefit forms are on-line. Kept messing 'em up."

Anna felt she could cry. Who would design a system that was supposed to care for the most vulnerable that ended up excluding the most vulnerable?

"Wasn't there someone in Loxley House who could help?"

"Some tried. Most were too busy. Kept telling me t' come back when someone's available'" he mimicked an official sounding voice. "They're not homeless, they're alright."

"Not everyone's like that, Rob."

"When it comes down to it, y' put y'usen first. We all do."

"That's bleak."

"It's true though," he said, getting angry.

"You didn't at the fair. You shared those coins with me and the boys."

"So?"

"So even though life keeps dealing you shit, you still take time to think of others."

"Like, I said. I'm no hero." He hunched his shoulders and turned away from her.

"No one said you need to be a hero. You just need to try thinking of others once a while. Share a little, listen a little. And you do."

Rob sat with his face buried in his hands, as if trying to shut the world out. "This is all messed up," he muttered. "Sandmen, ghosts, memories. It's all a joke." He got up suddenly.

"Where are you going?" asked Anna

"I've had enough."

Anger rose swiftly: he was walking out on her. "Well sod off then!" and she waved him away, turning back to the screen.

"Yeah, I will," called Rob over his shoulder and stomped downstairs.

Anna was alone and in shock. Had she gone too far? Had she pushed him again? She could understand why touching ghosts would frighten him and why he would reject it, but why was he rejecting her?

Anna shed an angry tear and gritted her teeth. She picked up her oversized coat and shrunk into it to keep the world out. Just for one day she had been allowed to feel good. She had gone to Goose Fair, forgotten all her troubles, and she had shared it with a new friend. More than a friend, he was the only other person she knew who could shake hands with the past, let alone see it. Anna felt utterly abandoned.

She emerged onto Angel Row and walked downhill with no idea why or where she would end up. It was raining again. Puddles reflected the grim concrete blocks and metallic sky. Everything seemed pointless. No point going back to Hope House, no point looking for Rob and no point searching for Jane. She just walked and got wet.

She passed the Bell Inn and closed her eyes, idly flicking at the past it had seen. Ghostly revellers rolled in and out of its narrow lobby, overlapping and walking through each other as memories coalesced. She opened her eyes again and walked on.

At the corner of Long Row and King Street she paused by an ornate confection of Victoriana and closed her eyes to see a dandy in a bow tie and top hat step out of the door, followed by an office boy who carried a roll of drawings under his arm. She turned south, across the front of the Council House, watching some present-day worthies being ushered up the steps into the hall to the grand stair beyond. She wondered how many rough sleepers had been told to clear off before they arrived.

On Cheapside a highly decorated half-timbered building leaned over the street on a trio of carved columns. Discreet designer labels edged the leaded windows promising a superior experience for those who didn't look for price tags. Anna turned down Flying Horse Walk, not because she could afford anything in the arcade, but because it took her out of the rain. She caught a glimpse of her bedraggled hair and dirty sodden coat in the shopwindows. The looks she got from the women carrying Gucci bags and the men dressed in Burberry didn't encourage her to stop.

She emerged onto St Peter's Gate, passed a stand of trees in front of the church, and crossed into Hound's Gate. This street was much narrower and reminded her of the ones she had walked with Beatrice. There was a bridge high up that spanned the street and linked two old red brick buildings. It looked like a picture she had seen of a bridge in Venice. Maybe the person who designed it had gone there. She turned at random into an alley called Truswell Yard, so narrow she could touch both sides without even stretching her arms. There were old fashioned gas lamps at the end, and it reminded her of the darkness of Victorian Nottingham. That in turn stirred memories of hurrying from one streetlamp to the next while the man in the jacket and tie pursued. Suddenly the alley felt dark and oppressive, and she started running, even though she couldn't see anyone. Especially because she couldn't see anyone.

Anna burst into the daylight at the end and found herself on Castle Gate. There were a few couples sheltering from the rain in doorways. She calmed herself and walked on towards the castle. Near the top of the street a blast of wind drove raindrops at her face as hard as bullets, forcing her to pull her hoodie across and veer away. She peered out and found herself in a graveyard (again, she thought sourly). To her right was the old Salutation pub but she had no money. To her left was an ancient red brick church. The weather had turned so foul she slipped in through the old timber door and found a cushioned seat near the back. The church was empty. Tall white columns stretched up to a forest of white trusses. A wide white arch reached across the altar. She felt a warmth from the pale timber floorboards and the red cushions on the chairs. The place felt friendly. Hopeful. Not what she had been expecting when she saw it from outside.

Anna was not religious, nor did she have any strongly held beliefs, but she was content to sit quietly in the church and feel some measure of peace. Was that what churches should offer, she wondered, a space to be at peace for those who were in need? She needed it. If she couldn't keep her friends, then perhaps she could find some calm and strength within. She had done that many times before. Again, she wondered if the time spent in the past, had cost her friends. Again, she felt her skill to be more burden than support. Even so, it was a refuge. Like this church, it was there for her when she felt alone.

Her coat dripped, making a puddle on the pew she sat in. She tried wiping it with her sleeve but it just pooled on the floor. The wind battered at the tall arched windows, yet it seemed faraway, shut out. She looked at a random gravestone set into the wall: 'Rev. Johannes Aysthorpe, d. 1665'. Slowly she closed her eyes. She felt weak for praying to someone she didn't believe in, but the calm of the church made it feel okay. *Dear God, she asked silently, if you are as real as my ghosts then tell me what I should do. Tell me where I should go, because I have no idea who would want me, or need me. Tell me, why am I here? Why have you given me this... sight? What is your will for me?*

She could feel her mind slip and something shifted beneath her. When she opened her eyes, she was sitting on a timber pew battered by time and wear. Looking up the church was wholly different: bare stone rather than white walls, thicker columns, and much narrower windows. A priest knelt at the altar and prayed, mumbling to himself in a strange language. She had a hunch it might be Latin.

St Nicholas Church, Nottingham, 1643

"Reverend Aysthorpe!" called a deep, well-spoken voice from behind Anna. "It be time." She squirmed to look behind her and saw a tall man with a narrow face, pencil moustache and a wig with long black curls. He wore a steel breast plate, polished to a blinding shine, and carried an ornamental sword. Anna edged back to the far end of the pew. She didn't like swords.

The priest stood and turned to face the other man. "Colonel Hutchinson, may I ask ye to reconsider?"

"Nay. Clear the church and tell this beggar to leave," he gestured casually to Anna as if she were a sack of dirt that needed taking outside.

"This is a house of God, sir, and I am praying for your soul."

"No need. I have no soul."

"These are evil times indeed, yet we all have a soul, sir. We may bury it deep, but it be there."

"Be gone. I have no wish to bury a rector in the rubble." The colonel turned on his heel and left.

The rector walked over to Anna and regarded her. "Ye have strange garments."

She looked down at her oversized coat and hoodie and realised they weren't very seventeenth century, as she guessed that was probably when she was. Anna was getting the hang of this now: when not where. "They're warm. Why does he want you to leave your church?"

"Ye do not know? Royalist troops seized this church tower as a platform for their bombard in June," he pointed above them. "They blew half the castle walls to smithereens. The other half were in ruins already. Colonel Hutchinson does want this church gone, should the Royalists return and be tempted to use it again."

Anna didn't know whether to rush out and gawk at what was left of a real castle or take the rector's hand and offer him some tea and sympathy. "What will you do?" she asked.

"God's will," he answered simply.

Anna couldn't help herself. "What do you think that is?"

"Only God knows," he shook his head, "but I doubt it involves a young pauper woman dying in a church. Follow me, dear. Perhaps he may grace us both with His will in due course."

Anna took some small measure of comfort that the rector had no more idea of God's will than she did. She followed the Reverend Aysthorpe down the aisle and into his vestry, where he placed a few precious items into a velvet sack. A chalice, a silver jug and a cross. The essentials for holy communion she realised. Then he reached for a pot and shook a few old coins from it.

"This is our last collection for the poor. Please take it."

Anna felt humbled. She didn't know what to say but managed a smile and a nod.

"We must go. The sappers will be laying charges."

She followed him out through a heavy wooden door to see men in long red coats and breeches rolling barrels up against the walls of the church and attaching them to reels of chord. Soldiers stood watch wearing wide brimmed steel helmets, brown coats and breast plates, though not nearly as shiny as the colonel's, she noticed.

Looking around she felt oddly exposed. There were far fewer buildings than she remembered. All the Victorian and modern piles were absent. To the south were open fields and boggy ground around a small meandering river. The Broadmarsh, she wondered? She guessed that was where the modern shopping centre of that name would be, so it started to make some sense.

Above her, up on Castle Rock was a ragged wall punctuated by crenelated towers that had seen a little too much glory. One tower was split from top to bottom, another was missing a top altogether. She could see people hauling stones up to the walls for rebuilding, watched on by more soldiers with swords and pikes. She doubted these amateur builders were being paid for their labours. Perhaps they might be lucky enough to take shelter when the royalist troops returned. Perhaps they just hoped if they kept their head down and hauled stones then no one would skewer them with a sword.

"STAND AWAY!" yelled a soldier with a shinier breast plate than the others. Must be their commander thought Anna. The brighter the shine the more they got to yell at people. She hurried back behind a stone wall that joined a pair of old half-timbered houses, only her eyes peeked above it. The rector stood beside her observing calmly, not cowering. "READY," called shiny breast plate, "NOW!"

The sappers lit the fuse chords and stepped back into cover with the soldiers. The sparks fizzed and spat, chasing down the fuses towards the barrels: it reminded Anna of some cartoon caper and half expected to see ACME written on the barrels. The detonation deafened. Anna flinched. Ground shook as the heavens rained chunks of stone.

When Anna risked raising her head above the wall, she saw a smoking ragged ruin where the church had stood only moments before. "Fare thee well Saint Nicholas," said the rector sadly, still standing and miraculously unscathed.

On the order from shiny breast the sappers ran forward again with carts and shovels. "Take the stone to the castle," he commanded. It seemed the notion of recycling was not new. Ironic that one of God's houses should be taken to rebuild a place of war.

"Look after yourself," she said to the rector, who turned to look at her as if he had forgotten she was there. She wondered if he was just as homeless as her now. Likely he had a rectory to go to, but she could see how lost he looked without his church.

His recognition returned as he looked at Anna. "God be with ye."

The clouds were thinning. A hint of blue sky promised some respite from the grey. Anna walked along the edge of the marsh, towards the river and saw cows grazing in the fields beyond, oblivious to civil wars and the passing of St Nicholas's church. She found a wooden fence and sat against it, looking out across the peaceful rural landscape that seemed so alien to central Nottingham. She hardly recognised the place. There were two clusters of buildings: one near the castle and the smoking remains of St Nicholas's church, another further east along a rocky escarpment. The escarpment itself appeared a hive of humanity with hovels that seemed to grow out of the sandstone like mushrooms from a tree stump. She wondered if the cliff edge might be riddled with caves dug by the locals. If so, she was only looking at the edges of their homes.

Further downstream from her she saw people wearing dark stained leather aprons washing skins in the river and hauling them back to open mouthed caves at the bottom of the hill. A tannery perhaps? The people of Nottingham did not look wealthy. Nor did they seem to care who was winning: royalist or roundhead. They seemed more interested in surviving the day.

Anna looked back across the fields to the south, away from the madness of exploding churches and civil war. She was tired. She wandered back to sit among the ruins of the church and rest. A little sunshine broke free and warmed her face. Her eyelids drooped.

St Nicholas Church, Nottingham, 2019

"Can I help you?" Anna jerked awake to see a woman with a dog collar smiling at her. The church had white walls again, with broad arched windows to let the sunshine through. She looked at the memorial stone set into the wall. The Reverend Aysthorpe would be pleased with what his descendants had done, she thought. Perhaps he would have been surprised to see that the present incumbent was a woman, but she suspected that he of all people might cope.

"Sorry, I... I just wanted to get out of the rain." Anna reached out to wipe the puddle she'd made and found it gone. Her coat was only slightly damp, as if it had been dried in the sun. She frowned, confused.

"That's okay. You look like you could do with a cup of tea. We're about to start our drop-in session and it seems you've already dropped in. Come join us."

Looking around she saw a table had been set up with urns, mugs and plates piled with biscuits. She was hungry enough to eat a whole plateful but tried to stifle the dull empty ache. She nodded thankfully and followed the rector over where another friendly face greeted her and handed her a steaming mug.

"Are you okay?" the reverend asked her.

"No," she answered with feeling. After a deep breath, between many gulps of tea and digestives, she told a perfect stranger the story of her mother and the search for her aunt. She carefully left out any references to historical memories, ducks, riots, or shiny breast plates. It was only when she finished that she realised the back of the church was now full of other people who seemed every bit in need of help as her, if not more, and she felt guilty for hogging her attention.

"Do you mind me asking your aunt's name?" asked the rector.

"Originally Jane Fitzwalter, but she divorced. I don't know if she took her ex-husband's name or what that was."

"Fitzwalter, that's an unusual name, I think I heard of a local family by that name. Did she come to church at all?"

"I think so, but I don't know which church," said Anna. "All I know is she used to live in Hermitage Court, on the south edge of The Park."

"It's possible she came to St Nicholas then. I'll ask my team to have a look through recent parish records and we'll ask the other churches nearby. Someone may know her and tell us where she's gone. It's possible she might still live close by."

"Thank you. Thank you so much." Anna felt pathetically grateful. All it had taken was for someone to listen and take a little interest.

Anna didn't understand why she had gone back in time to meet the Reverend Aysthorpe. Perhaps it was because she was in his church and she needed to talk to someone? Perhaps he needed someone to be with him when he lost his church?

As she left St Nicholas's she dug her hands in her pockets, bracing for the cold October day. She felt some coins rubbing together in the fold of the right pocket and wondered if they were what she had left from her night at Goose Fair with Rob. Drawing them out on her palm she saw an assortment of old copper coins mottled with a green patina. She turned them over and saw various depictions of a king's head on them. Not one picture of Queen Elizabeth.

The Park

The Park, Nottingham, October 2019

The Park is the posh part of Nottingham. It has elegant tree lined streets atmospherically (badly) lit by original gas lamps, generous gothic mansions individually designed for each of the original owners, and gates intended to keep out the riff raff. Anna trudged around the gracious curved crescents in her tatty boots and grubby overcoat. The gates had failed.

Fortunately for Anna the estate was quiet. Not many around to stare at her and make her feel unwelcome. She had a vague notion she might just bump into her aunt if she kept wandering the area where she used to live. Jane might even have moved to another part of The Park. Anna had started the search late morning, at the relatively ordinary house which Jane had lived in on the southern edge of the estate. She took a moment to peer at the view from the edge of the escarpment. The industrial parks and housing estates of Nottingham spread out to the south, though she caught a glimpse of fields beyond. It reminded her of the view across seventeenth century fields. She remembered looking back at escarpments which had been stacked full of ramshackle houses cut into the rock. She wondered whether anyone had lived at the foot of the drop beyond Hermitage Court.

Anna walked on, circling around generous streets towards the mini mansions that rose among the flower beds and cast-iron railings. By now the sun had set and the rain had returned. Her feet hurt, her empty stomach ached, and the raindrops were soaking through her hoodie. Whatever respite the church had offered seemed a distant memory, along with the dreams of friendship at Goose Fair. Anna was too tired to feel angry with Rob and too empty to think about looking for him. The thought of returning to the refuge at Hope House depressed her. More forms. More questions she couldn't answer.

She found a hedge by the side of the steep street and slumped into a gap, thinking she would just sit for a moment and gather her strength. The rain was getting heavier, so she wriggled deeper into the hedge for cover. Leaning back out of the wind she noticed a sandstone outcrop behind her. Surely the owners of this huge garden wouldn't notice if she took shelter under it for half an hour or so, until the rain eased off.

The outcrop turned out to be a cave, dug deep into the sandstone. She fumbled towards the back of the cave searching for an alcove to curl up in and started to wonder just how far it stretched. She could feel the edge of a carved stone staircase rising to her right. To her left she could hear the echo of a larger space, though it was too dark to see. As the stair rose it formed an alcove beneath and Anna got down on her hands and knees to crawl into the gap. Drained, she lay back against the stone wall and closed her eyes.

The Park, Nottingham, 1870

Laughter woke Anna. Hilarity, chatter, and the clink of glasses. Peering out from the edge of her hiding hole she saw the cavern beyond, a forest of elegant stone columns each lit by a pair of flickering candles. The columns fanned out overhead into a succession of hand carved vaults, as if she had stumbled on a dwarven throne room. Between the columns was a long dining table laden with fine chinaware, wine glasses and silver serving platters, all lit by tall candelabras. Around the table sat a dozen smartly suited gentlemen who slapped each other on the back and told stories that were hilarious to each other but meant nothing to Anna. The sound of footsteps echoed over her head and she ducked back into the shadow. The stone stair must have been a long one because the steps seemed to echo towards her for a long time. Finally, a young woman in a nineteenth century scullery apron appeared from the bottom of the stair carrying another platter filled with chicken drumsticks. Anna's hunger returned with a cruel stab of pain. The woman served the platter to the table and as she turned to go one of the men gave her a casual slap on the bottom. The woman grimaced and walked back to the stair. Anna fumed. Images of shadows under streetlamps and the smell of boozy breath haunted her again.

As the woman got close to the stair Anna caught a glimpse of her face. There was the same weird tingle of familiarity she'd had when standing beside Beatrice's mother. It was a different woman, yet she wondered if there might be some family resemblance between them: a thin face with well-defined features, intelligent eyes and an air of quiet determination.

The woman looked towards Anna's hiding place and hesitated. Their eyes engaged. She had been seen. Anna's mouth opened but she didn't know what to say. The woman regarded Anna with surprise which quickly turned to shrewd assessment. She took one hand from beneath the empty platter and put a finger to her lips, winked, then surreptitiously tossed a drumstick to Anna. The woman was gone from sight, up the stairs before Anna could say thank you.

Anna sighed her relief and slumped back against the wall, into the shadows to gnaw at the drumstick. For a while she wondered who the woman could be and why she seemed so familiar, then her thoughts were interrupted by the dinner conversation.

"Have you read the news?" asked the man who slapped the serving woman's bum. "School for all children from five to twelve years old! Why on earth would they want to school every urchin and tearaway? Better for their souls if they did some useful work if you ask me."

There was a mix of 'hear hears' or jeers from the others.

"Oh, do come along, this is the nineteenth century and all that," said one.

"Have you any idea how much it will cost me to replace all those children in my lace factory, Herbert?"

"Well, I must say you seem able to afford it," answered the man called Herbert. That caused a gale of laughter from the others.

"It is not just the money, it is the dangerous precedent set," warned the bum slapper, waving away Herbert's retort.

"Ay, if they learn their numbers, they will get ideas," said another portly man with a colourful variety of gravies dribbled down his shirt. "They will be asking for higher wages you mark my words."

"Perhaps they may deserve it," said an older man with a tired yet kindly face, "knowing how you drive those poor souls!" Another shout of laughter, this time at the portly dribbler's expense.

"Education should be the responsibility of the church and the private schools, Adams," argued a man wearing a dog collar. "I don't see why more tax should be levied than there is."

"Frightened of a little competition, are we?" asked the tired old man called Adams, "Half the liberals I know are afraid their extra taxes will end up in your church schools anyway." A few 'oohs' and muttered reproaches circled the table.

"I agree with the reverend," said the bum slapper. "The church and the private schools do a splendid job for those who are born with potential. I know this Forster chap who started it all. He is a well-meaning liberal, yet frankly we are in danger of wasting our efforts on those who were never born to achieve."

Anna fought a growing urge to go and slap the bum slapper.

"Hear, hear!" added portly dribbler, sloshing a glass of red wine and adding to the colour collage on his shirt.

"If I did not know you gentlemen better," said Herbert, "I would say you were afraid of a little education for the poor."

"Poppycock!" exclaimed portly dribbler. Anna stifled a snort. Surely no one said poppycock, even in Jane Austen novels.

"It is a threat," said Adams. His voice was quiet, yet he commanded their attention. "Education is an escape from poverty. If everyone were to escape then no one would work the lace factories, mills, or mines. No one to make us factory owners as rich as we are." Adams paused, letting his words sink in. Anna held her breath.

"Then why permit such nonsense?" demanded the bum slapper. "Why have you already given away so much of your hard-won fortune to schools for the poor? Why lavish so much on your own molly-coddled lace factory workers?"

"Because we seek to be civilised human beings, sir," answered Adams. "As Mr Dickens suggests, we can no longer live with ourselves if we continue to live as two cities, one for us and another for the less fortunate."

"Please, Thomas, show some pragmatism," said bum slapper. "We cannot risk making everyone equal without the collapse of our economic society."

"Mm, I suspect there is much we must risk in order to advance our journey through this world together," said Thomas Adams, as if musing to himself. "Perhaps we must be prepared to lose much in order to gain more."

"Hah! Now you sound like the reverend," laughed bum slapper. But no one else was laughing.

The mood of the table shifted subtly after that exchange. Other topics aired and floated away. In time so did Anna.

The Park, Nottingham, October 2019

A familiar and unwelcome shove against Anna's side jarred her awake. The long leg of the law, with a uniformly booted size ten at the end of it. "Up you get," said the officer, "you're being charged with breaking and entering."

"You do not have to say anything..." started the WPC beside him.

"What would you say if someone shoved you in the ribs with their boot?" cut in Anna.

The WPC ignored the outburst and cited Anna's rights in a monotone. Her expression didn't appear totally devoid of feeling, though whatever sympathy she might have was hidden behind the professional façade. "The owner alleges trespass with intent to steal."

"Steal?" Anna scowled mutinously at the WPC. "What would I steal from their back garden? A gnome? A dahlia?"

"I need to remind you that you're..." started the PC.

"What?" Anna struggled to her feet and pulled the inside of her coat pocket out for inspection. The only thing that fell out was an empty Mars bar wrapper from when she'd stuffed it full at Hope House. It fell across a small bone on the ground and she paused, confused before resuming her fury, "What am I supposed to have taken? A nap? No chance of that with you lot!" She threw a glare that slapped the PC back a step.

"The owner alleges intent to steal," he insisted, examining his boots.

Anna opened her mouth to protest and closed it again, shaking her head. Arguing was pointless. Besides, what was the difference between one institutional bed and another? She was beyond caring whether she had a criminal record by now.

Anna lied about her age again to avoid being put back into care. It was almost a disappointment when they released her after a minor caution, on the basis it was her first 'offence'. They'd only offered her a cup of lukewarm water. She'd been hoping for a cup of tea and a sandwich at the very least. Anna reflected that only a couple of years ago she would have been mortified at the idea of being arrested. Now she just felt cheated. Worse than cheated, she had been discarded again: someone else's problem. The WPC suggested Hope House. Anna said she knew the way.

She felt weak from hunger so she trudged up to Trinity Square to see if Tina's Pantry might be open. It was too early for the volunteers; they were probably still picking up supplies from the generous donors dotted around the city. She was not the only one waiting.

Robin of Loxley

Trinity Square, Nottingham, October 2019

Anna was torn. She didn't know whether to say hi to Rob or turn her back on him, as he'd done to her. Before she could do either, his dark brown eyes found hers. She thought he might flee, like a hunted hare, but he continued to watch, waiting for her to make the first move. She couldn't tell whether he wanted to be caught or hoped she might ignore him. Anna couldn't ignore Rob, so she walked forward slowly, as if trying not to startle him.

"Hi," muttered Rob. He sounded ashamed.

Anna put her hands on her hips. "What did I do?" she asked, tired. "What did I say to make you clear off?"

Rob looked away. "Sorry," he muttered.

"If you can't handle it, go. If you want someone to share it then stay and talk."

"It... it's a lot to deal with."

"That's a bloody understatement!" Anna pulled the ancient coins from her pocket and spread them out on her palm in front of Rob.

"What are they?"

"Take a look."

Rob picked one off her hand and turned it over and over, as if searching for some conjurer's sleight of hand. "It's old," he said.

"No shit, Sherwood!"

"Very old. Date says sixteen something, rest is all scratched and covered in green stuff."

"I've had people toss me all sorts: cents, washers, car park tokens, but not antiques." Anna still had the other hand balled in a fist on her hip. "Tell me those coins and the seventeenth century rector that gave them to me were all in some stupid dream as well."

Rob looked from the coin to Anna. "I didn't think we could take stuff with us, from the past."

"A few days ago, I didn't think I could talk to people in the past, let alone take their charity."

"I thought…"

"What? That I was some time traveller? That I was Doctor Who? I don't even look like her."

"Y' could have regenerated," suggested Rob, a sly grin creeping into the corner of his mouth. It died on his lips as Anna gave him a look that could peel the paint off a phone box.

"This is no game, Rob. It doesn't feel like a super-power, it feels like a hole in the bottom of my world, and I keep falling through it."

"Yeah, an' y' pulled me in after. More like white rabbit y' are."

"You pulled me into that cave full of sandmen, Rob!" her voice was rising, and her fists were clenching.

"I told y' why, it were raining." He backed away from her, as if she were in danger of exploding or regenerating or whatever it was that time travellers did.

Anna was about to let fly again then saw him hang is head like a whipped dog. It seemed like a learned response, like something he always did when yelled at. She weakened. She could tell he felt as messed up as she did. She realised she was just taking out her frustration on him, though a part of her felt he deserved it after walking off and leaving her.

"I'm starved," muttered Anna.

"It'll be an hour before Tina comes," said Rob. "But I know another place."

The other place turned out to be the bin store behind The Road to Arabia. Not the best side of one of the best-known pubs in Nottingham, but Rob knew one of the cooks.

"Thought I told y' to keep it quiet," said the young chef, wiping his hands on his apron and looking pointedly at Anna.

"Please Jamaal, we 's starving," pleaded Rob. "Promise we won't come bother y' again... too soon."

Jamaal shrugged as if knowing he was easy pickings for these two scavengers and disappeared into the kitchen. A few moments later he reappeared holding a stack of choice steak doorstop sandwiches. "Customers said they ordered chicken," he announced. "They'll only go in the bin."

Rob's eyes widened. Anna felt a little dribble run down the corner of her mouth. "Thanks mate," said Rob.

"Thanks," echoed Anna.

"Go on, piss off," Jamaal said gently, "pair of y'." He turned and went back inside, shaking his head as if to say what a fool he was. Soft as butter.

Rob and Anna devoured the sandwiches and took a walk around the base of the Castle Rock. They found an arched doorway in the base of the castle walls and huddled into the recess, licking the butter and juices off their fingers. She could just see the top of St Nicholas' church tower, above the concrete barrel vaults of the building opposite. "Last time I was here that church got blown up."

Rob looked at the tower, then her. "What d' y' do that for?"

"I didn't do it, did I! It was the Roundheads. Well, it was Royalists that used the church to bombard the castle and the Roundheads got hacked off and blew the church up to stop it happening again."

Rob looked up at the castle wall above, then back at Anna. "So, y' time travelled without me. 's not me that starts it, 's you."

"I don't start anything, it just happens. And it's not like time travel it's like... finding a thought, feeling for it in another time in the same place."

"What's the difference?" asked Rob, reasonably.

"I'm looking for something that's already there, I'm not travelling to find it. Usually I just look, that's all."

"Where are y' when it starts talking back?"

Anna hadn't thought about that before. It was a good question, possibly a relevant one. "First time I fell into a cistern. A cave with a well. Second time was with you in a... cave."

"Better keep out o' caves."

"But they haven't all been caves, I got the coins from the rector in that church over there. Well, not that church, the one before that."

Rob stroked his chin. For a moment Anna thought he looked like a wise old man pondering the mysteries of the world. "Stone has memory," he said.

"Don't be daft, stones have no mind to remember anything."

"Not literal. But things people do lie on t' stone and maybe it leaves mark. Them marks might get rubbed off if too much happens, but caves and churches, they're quiet places. Places where you see marks if y' know how to look." Rob paused. Anna was looking at him hard again. Not the evil eye but concentration, analysing every word. "I'm guessing, but that's what I think," he added.

Anna nodded. Then she craned her neck to see the castle walls that soared over them. If she could look into the past at will, then maybe she could engage with it at her will, rather than rely on falling asleep or falling down wells. She wanted to find out and the castle had seen more than a little history. "Good place to test your thought. Plenty happened here."

Rob looked uncertain. "Will they have guns? Them Roundheads and Royalists?"

"Depends on which marks we find. Could be torch waving rioters and mounted soldiers with swords."

Rob recoiled. "Couldn't find someone waving sticky buns could y'?" Anna remembered how he had flinched at the torches in the sand mine.

"I'll try," said Anna. She led Rob up the road towards the main castle gates. "If we're going to find something interesting it'll be here."

Rob eyed the plywood hoarding and safety signs around the gatehouse sceptically. "What, in a building site?"

The Castle Refurbishment Project had been going several years, causing double disappointment for tourists: not only had the medieval keep been pulled down in the seventeenth century, but now they couldn't even get at what was left. Anna gave Rob a look. "I didn't see any signs saying I was entering a hard hat zone when they were rebuilding it in the civil war."

"Bet they wore helmets."

Anna rolled her eyes. She grabbed Rob's hand and led him around the corner where the castle wall started to merge into the sandstone on which it had been built. They found a hollow in the rock and settled into it. This was going to be her first deliberate attempt at finding past lives and talking to them. She had no inkling whether it would work, but if what Rob said held any truth then at least they were in a place that might make it easier. Anna told Rob to close his eyes and silenced her thoughts so she could focus on the Castle rock. She searched with her mind's eye looking down, or so it felt, reaching downwards through time. As usual she felt that small lurch of vertigo.

Almost immediately she felt a presence on the borders of her consciousness. People flickered in and out of her thoughts: builders, soldiers, cooks, brewers, tanners, farmers, the whole of Nottingham had come to the foot of Castle Rock at some time in their lives. As she searched, she felt another presence beside her, not flickering but constant.

Rob.

Finally, her attention was drawn by a straggle of people coming down a muddy street towards them. Old and young, tall and small, some dragging carts, most laden with sacks or bundles. They stood out against the other marks of time like an illuminated page against black and white print.

Castle Rock, Nottingham, 1194

A woman clutched a girl of about three to her chest while her man carried a pair of hessian sacks that might have held all their belongings in the world. Behind them staggered a small boy, perhaps no more than about five or six, it was hard to tell for the child was so thin. He wavered and dropped to his knees.

Anna rushed forward and lifted him up in her arms. He was so slight. Rob offered to carry one of the man's sacks and he muttered his thanks. The mother managed a half smile as Anna walked beside her, the weightless scrap of child cradled to her.

"What happened to you?" asked Anna.

"War," said the mother. "King Richard has returned, and he wants blood."

King Richard. The Lionheart. Anna was starting to understand just how far back in time she and Rob had gone and it shocked her. Almost as much as the plight of the king's people.

"His men robbed our village, took everything," continued the mother. "We be looking for shelter in Castle." Anna looked up to see Nottingham's castle in full medieval glory: fortified walls lined with soldiers and a tall keep flying red flags, each embroidered with three yellow lions or leopards.

"Whose blood does he want?"

"Have ye not heard?" The mother seemed surprised as Anna shook her head. "His brother, Prince John. This here be John's castle," she nodded at the walls above them. "King has taxed us all for his crusades 'till we can barely feed ussens. He hardly seems t' care if there's no one left to be ruled."

Anna looked at the starving boy in her arms. It dawned on her that those fighting for power rarely seemed to care how many suffered for them. The Royalists found the church expendable. The Roundheads found expendable people to rebuild the castle. If she remembered her history for King Richard, these miserable refugees had been taxed to starvation to pay for the Crusades. A war against those in a different land whose only crime had been to believe in a different god. Now Richard's subjects were fleeing for their lives.

Rob put a free hand in his pocket and looked surprised. He pulled out the last couple of sandwiches they'd been given by Jamaal and offered them to the man. He smiled, broke off chunks and shared them with his family.

He chewed on a generous bite and raised his eyebrows. "A cow cob!"

"Yeah, beef sarnies," said Rob.

"Boeuf? Ye be Norman?" he asked.

Rob was confused, but Anna stepped in with a quiet prompt. "He thinks you're speaking French. I guess we've gone back so far, the Normans and Saxons are still speaking different languages. Weird we can understand them though."

"Oh!" Understanding dissipated Rob's confusion like sun on an early mist. "Er, no. I'm a local lad," Rob said to the man.

The man seemed to relax a little and offered his name, "John the nailer of Hathersage."

"Rob..." he hesitated, perhaps wondering how to introduce himself, "from Loxley."

"Thank ye, Robin of Loxley," said John, shaking Rob's hand.

Anna suppressed a snigger. Rob turned and dared her to contradict him. John looked puzzled but nodded to Anna, inviting her to name herself. As often happened, she wondered how best to answer, whether to give her mum's maiden name or her actual surname. In the confusion she muttered her other names.

"Mary Ann."

"Marian? That be a fine lady's name. Here be my fine lady, Sarah," the mother smiled in response, "my fine lass be Lizzie, and that be little John." He looked proudly at the child in Anna's arms, chewing slowly but determinedly on a corner of his bread.

Anna's head swam. Surely this was an elaborate practical joke. She and Rob had just been named as two of Nottingham's most famous folk heroes and she was carrying the third one in her arms. All she needed now was a quiver full of arrows, and that made her remember the archery stall at Goose Fair.

"Bloody hell!" she muttered under her breath to Rob. He turned a questioning look at her. "Where did you learn to shoot a bow?" she whispered.

Rob frowned, no sign of understanding. "Youth centre. Sod all else worth doin' there but they took us on a free course an' it were only thing I were good at."

"You didn't have a forest full of merry men to help did you?"

A carnival of expressions ran riot across his face before he threw his head back and made a sound like a donkey braying. It was a moment before Anna realised, he was laughing. She hadn't heard it before.

The castle gatehouse no longer looked like a picturesque folly. It had a business-like portcullis made of iron which was half lowered over hefty oak gates. A dozen soldiers in red tunics and iron helmets stood guard, holding equally business-like spears and swords.

Rob nudged Anna. "Told y' they'd have hard hats." Anna gave him another look that could corrode copper. "Told y' they'd have swords an all. Not a bun in sight."

The soldiers made it plain there was no room for refugees, by order of the bailiff. As John and Sarah stood bewildered and abandoned, wondering where they could go, there was a shout from the gatehouse towers above them and a soldier pointed out across the fields. Anna and Rob followed the direction of his outstretched arm, squinting across the fields to the south, looking for the source of the alarm. A thin silvery line caught the rays of a weak winter sun and glittered. It looked like the reflections off a distant river, and yet it was edging slowly across the fields towards them.

"Richard's men," said John.

"God help ussens," said Sarah.

Neither Anna nor Rob had a clue what to suggest and were starting to wish themselves back on the streets of twenty-first century Nottingham when a young man with a mop of blonde hair and a grey monk's habit walked towards them.

"Come," the monk beckoned. "Follow me."

Sarah and John looked at each other, then trudged after the monk, the other refugees following like lost sheep. Rob and Anna felt they had no choice but to follow too. They walked east down a street of half-timbered buildings with a mix of thatched or tiled roofs. At the far end they found a broad market square with a shoulder height brick wall dividing it lengthways. People were hurrying to clear away stalls from both sides of the wall, herding sheep out of pens and chasing chickens, no doubt warned of King Richard's vengeful approach. Anna was curious about the wall but didn't think it the time to ask.

They passed a strange building which was all timber columns and roof, but no walls. She guessed from the number of people packing away scales and purses that it might be a market hall where the buying and selling of stock was done. Past the hall was a narrow street with upper floors jettied out over it so she could barely see the sky. Hammers rang out from several of the doorways and peering into one she could see a man in a leather apron striking an anvil, backlit by a roaring furnace. She paused while a mix of familiarity and utter strangeness fought for control of her mind. She guessed she was standing in Smithy Row, just to the north of where the modern Council House would stand in another eight-hundred years. She was surrounded by blacksmiths: no wonder it got called Smithy Row.

Little John wriggled in her arms. "C'mon, let me take him a while," said Rob and swapped the boy for the sack which felt a little lighter. Anna didn't know which to feel most sorry for: the Nailer family's lack of possessions or little John's lack of feeding. They walked on down a street that Anna thought might become Pelham Street, then turned off north. Eventually they arrived at a gap in a great ditch that seemed to stretch along the whole northern edge of the town, like a long dry moat.

John Nailer hesitated and called after the monk. "Hey! Why leave city walls?"

"It be safer," the monk reassured them. "Come."

Beyond the ditch, beside the track was a field where scores of people milled around a huddle of tents and open fires. To one side stood a chapel built out of logs with a cross at the ridge. On the far side of the field the ground sloped away to a narrow river, perhaps no more than a brook. A second monk was carrying a pair of leather water buckets back towards them.

"Please," said the first monk to the weary stragglers, "take some water from the well and a blessing from Saint John the Baptist." He pointed to the small statue of a holy man beside the wooden chapel.

Anna could take or leave the blessing, but she was as thirsty as the others, so queued up for a cup full of clear cold water. A third monk came offering bowls of something grey and steaming. Anna took a sip. It was a watery mix of oats that might have been an attempt at porridge. At least it was hot. She was still hungry, so she drank it all down, just like the others around her.

"Welcome, my name be Brother Tucker, but most here call me Tuck."

Anna was aware that her mouth was hanging open again.

"We've found y' merry men," grinned Rob. "All we need now is Sheriff!"

St John's Chapel, Nottingham, 1194

Tuck was fascinated by Rob and Anna. He found their accents strange and their clothes even stranger, especially their shoes and the popper buttons on Anna's oversize coat. Rob caught Tuck staring at his crotch and was starting to get uncomfortable, only to find out he'd never seen a zip before. Anna wanted to avoid awkward discussions about time, so diverted Tuck with questions of her own.

"Why did you take us all here, outside the city defences?"

"King Richard wants yonder castle, and his men will plunder the town, but they will have no care for a few paupers and a wooden chapel in a field. We be safer without than within. In time we hope to start a hospital here."

"Are y' doctors?" asked Rob.

Tuck looked puzzled. Anna realised they might be using words which had different or no meaning to him. "Are you healers? Is it your calling to care for the sick?"

"We care for the poor. Many are also sick so we do what we can, but a hospital would give succour to all in need." Anna made a mental note that a hospital meant something different in medieval England, perhaps more like Hope House. Tuck went on, "when we arrived from the Fountains Abbey, we pitched our tents here, beside the York Road. It be humble, but all great things must start so."

"Better hope Sheriff don't come taking tax off y'," warned Rob.

"Sheriff?"

"I think the soldiers called him a bailiff, Rob," said Anna.

"Which one?" asked Tuck.

"What? There're two sheriffs?" asked Rob, "bailiffs I mean."

"The Norman bailiff and the Anglish bailiff, of course," said Tuck. "It would be Norman bailiff if ye were talking to soldiers at castle, he be in charge there. The Anglish bailiff enforces the Anglish law on this side of the city: the Anglish Burgh."

Anna frowned. "Does that have anything to do with the wall down the middle of the market?"

"Aye of course, dear Marian." Tuck had been introduced to Anna by John the nailer before she had a chance to put either of them right. She felt it was getting out of hand. "Ye would not want to try a man under Norman laws if ye were standing on Anglish soil," Tuck explained patiently.

Anna guessed it was only about a hundred years or so after the Norman conquest and it would take longer for the two peoples to merge their laws and leaders. Maybe even longer to merge languages.

She noticed that Tuck and the others were speaking a strangely accented English and Tuck's sounded slightly less coarse than the others, perhaps because of a Norman clergy education. Apart from odd words and alternate meanings, she and Rob had no especial difficulty understanding which seemed unlikely. She wondered if this was a perk of being a ghost in their time.

Anna may have lost herself in questions about her time travelling ability if it were not for a small hand placed in hers.

Little John and Brother Tuck

Outside the Anglish Burgh, Nottingham, 1194

A straggling crop of fair hair parted over the boy's face, looking up at Anna. Expectant. Trusting. It was little John.

"Ye have an admirer!" smiled Tuck.

Anna's heart lurched. The boy had sought her out among the crowd of refugees and clasped her hand as if she were an anchor of stability and safety. If only he knew. She barely knew how to look after herself, let alone the boy. She opened her mouth to say she could not offer what he needed then pressed her lips tight when she saw Rob looking at her. His expression seemed envious of little John's hand in hers, as if longing to be him. Perhaps longing for someone to look after him too. Give him a chance to relax for once, knowing someone had a plan for him and that he would not have to fight for his next meal. Anna longed for that too. Strange how the lost gravitated together.

"Ye are not from this shire, are ye?" said Tuck. It was a statement more than a question.

"No," admitted Anna. "We've travelled a long way." In time, not space.

"Abroad?"

"South of the River Thames." Blackheath was indeed south of the river, reasoned Anna.

"They say Kent seems a foreign land yet your speech and attire appear stranger still."

Tuck was not going to be fobbed off with glib statements. He had a keen enquiring mind. "Rob and I have travelled much," she offered. She had taken holidays in France and Spain when young, though she was only guessing at Rob's past.

"Ay," agreed Rob. "Seen more 'n my fair share of desert sands." Anna guessed there may be more to that statement. She made a mental note to ask later.

"Ye have taken part in King Richard's Crusades?" asked Tuck.

"Wouldn't call it a crusade," said Rob, looking at his feet. "More a death trap."

Tuck gave Rob a long look, "Our knights of the realm would have us all believe that glory and riches await those who fight for King Richard in yonder Holy Lands. Yet I have heard tell that the Saracens are fierce enemies, not to be underestimated."

"Wouldn't underestimate anyone defending their home," said Rob. "Nothing more precious."

"Mm," agreed Tuck. "And they defend their own faith. People will die for both."

Rob and Tuck held each other's eye and understanding seemed to pass between them without further words.

"What brought you to Nottingham, Brother Tuck?" asked Anna. "Was that faith too?"

Tuck nodded, "The Lord sends me where I may serve him. There are many here who seek sanctuary from war and failed harvests. My brothers and I do our best to help." He paused, allowing a lopsided grin to spread, "I also find the Nottingham ale most agreeable."

"So good you thought you'd build a chapel here?"

"The Lord moves in mysterious ways," he beamed.

Anna felt a tug on her hand and looked down. Little John wanted her to follow him.

She allowed herself to be led through the throng of refugees until they reached a camp fire where Sarah sat with his little sister Lizzie on her lap and John the nailer fed the fire with scrounged brushwood. He offered Anna a shawl. She took it, hesitated, then wrapped it around little John's shoulders and sat him beside her while she pulled her overcoat tight. The fire warmed her face and she watched while the flames fluttered and spat. Rob joined them, sitting the other side of little John, sandwiching him between them to shelter him from the wind.

"Story," demanded little John, looking up at Anna.

"Now John," admonished Sarah. "Don't ye go bothering Marian."

"It's no bother," said Anna, surprising herself. "I like stories." She hadn't thought of herself as a storyteller, yet she had often made up her own about the people she had seen from the past. Trying to make sense of the glimpses she had of their lives. One such life floated to the surface in her pool of memories.

Anna told little John about a young man in Victorian flannels she had seen hovering by a small pond in the middle of the heath near her home as a child. He would spend hours watching the creatures who inhabited the pond. He carried a net in one hand and a notebook in the other.

"What's a notebook?" asked little John.

Anna paused, derailed. Her story might be more difficult to tell than she had imagined. "A kind of scroll. Small, lots of sheets packed together. He made drawings in it, of what he saw among the rushes at the edge of the pond."

"What did he see?"

"Lizards, dragonflies and toads. Natterjack toads, I believe."

"Natterjack," little John smiled, enjoying the sound of the unfamiliar name. "Natterjack, natterjack, natterjack."

"He drew them all, very carefully in his notebook. Beautiful drawings, very detailed and life-like."

"Why?"

"Because the creatures he found fascinated him. He watched how they moved and fed and where they made their homes." Anna did not know this for sure, yet she had watched the young man return to the same pond over and over, so she felt she understood him. She embellished for her listener. "He came every day, early morning and late afternoon, after he had finished his work as a... scribe. He liked to listen to the dragonflies buzzing and the toads nattering. It made him happy. One day men with horses and spades came to widen the road nearby."

"Why?"

Anna thought for a moment and improvised, "Because the road was becoming very busy with more horses and carriages. Because the road led from the coastal ports to the centre of London and many people came to work there. The young man... Cecil, stood in front of the pond and spread his arms wide saying, 'You mustn't dig here, or you'll destroy this home for the lizards and dragonflies and toads.' The men with spades didn't much care for lizards or toads and told him so. But Cecil was determined. He took a spade and started digging on the far side of the road, away from the pond. 'It's flatter here,' he said. 'Easier to widen the road. You don't have to touch the pond.' The other men watched him, shaking their heads. Eventually one shrugged his shoulders and joined Cecil, digging. Soon all the others followed. Cecil helped widen the road and saved the pond for the natterjack toads."

"Good," nodded little John, satisfied with the outcome. "Another story."

"Er..." Anna caught Rob out the corner of her eye. She wondered if he was concealing a smile. "Your turn," she suggested.

"Not much good at stories," Rob grimaced. "None as would be right for little 'un."

"Perhaps John knows one to tell us?" asked Anna.

"When will we go home?" asked the boy with skilful evasion. It seemed he'd made the connection between the toad's home and his own.

"I don't know," answered Anna truthfully. It occurred to her that she and Rob could return to the twenty-first century when they chose. Or at least try, since she was still trying to understand how that worked. But travelling forward in time would not be the same as going home. She and Rob felt as displaced as little John and his family.

Little John turned to Rob again, "Game!"

"Game?" Rob he repeated as if the word were unfamiliar to him. He looked awkward, "Don't know any."

With a twist in her gut, Anna wondered when the last time was that anyone had played a game with Rob. For fun.

Then the boy looked at Anna. "Play," he demanded, undeterred.

The memory of a silly game she used to play with her mum came back to her and she put her hand palm down on her knee. "Put your hand on top," she said to little John who did so without hesitation. "Now you," she said to Rob.

Rob looked at her, confused.

"It's a game. Go on, just put your hand on John's."

Rob reached forward and placed his palm gently over the boy's hand. It was longer but almost as slender.

Anna placed her free hand over the hand Rob had just placed. It was cool. Slight yet strong and tensed. She nodded at little John who seemed to guess the game instinctively and placed his free hand on top. Now Rob placed his.

All six hands, one resting on top of another.

Now Anna gently slid her hand at the bottom and placed it on top, over Rob's.

Little John pulled his hand out and put it over hers. Then Rob followed.

Now Anna took her hand at the bottom more quickly and slapped it on top. Little John pulled his faster and gave hers a playful slap. Rob followed, faster still then suddenly the three of them found themselves flailing and slapping each other's fingers, all looking for the top of a vanishing pile of hands.

Little John giggled, "Again, again!"

Anna placed her hand down again and instantly the boy's laid on top. Rob followed quicker this time, grinning and he caught her eye as she placed her other hand on his. She flushed slightly and looked down at the growing pile of hands. All too soon their hands were flapping wildly in the air and little John shrieked with laughter.

Anna saw Sarah and big John smiling at them. Lizzie watched with large round eyes.

Tuck found them a little later, by the fire. He carried a basket heaped with bread and offered it to them.

Rob stood and pointed to the bread "I can help."

"That would be most welcome," said Tuck, handing him the basket. "There is more to be given out."

"Then I'll help too," offered Anna.

Together they wove between the campfires handing out small loaves. The encampment sprawled across the field north of the city walls and some were erecting make-shift tents or carrying loose stones to build a low wall to shelter against. More people were evacuating the city and joining them.

"Not much faith in the city walls then, observed Anna. "And no room in the castle."

"Only care about thesens," muttered Rob.

"We don't know that."

"Nothing changes. Them with power get shelter while them without stay out."

Anna could hear the bitterness in Rob's voice. She used to consider herself an optimist, but after many months seeking help she had to admit that it was hard to find. Yet despite his bitterness he had been first to give a hand. "Is that why you offered to help with the bread?"

Rob looked away from her, giving the last few loaves to a family huddled beneath a hessian sheet strung between loose branches. "Just want to feel useful is all."

They returned to Tuck's log chapel where the monks were busy making more. The aroma of baked dough drew Anna and Rob close. Tuck saw them and handed them a pair of pale loaves.

"A little under baked, but edible," he said. "Only way to see when they are ready."

Anna didn't care. She broke her loaf and ate greedily, savouring the freshness. She glanced to her side and snorted with mirth.

"Wha?" mumbled Rob, cheeks bulging.

"You look like a hamster stuffing himself for hibernation."

He brushed a spray of crumbs off her coat, "Y' no dainty eater y' self!"

Tuck stared over their heads. They turned to see plumes of black smoke rising from the far side of the city. "Follow me," said the brother, walking parallel to the walls.

Anna and Rob hastened after him, wondering what was going on. Tuck led them around the eastern side of the city, towards the top edge of an escarpment. From there they could see the shimmer off the marshes and a pall of black cloud over the fields beyond. As they turned back towards the city walls they saw a dark mass of bodies caught in a bottleneck at the river bridge. Many had already arrived beneath the city walls and were busy erecting large wooden shields. Pavise was the word which floated into Anna's mind. Behind each pavise a pair of men tended a metal brazier which threw thick smuts of smoke into the air that rose in lazy spirals to join the charcoal clouds overhead. So these were the sources of the plumes Tuck had spotted from the far side of the city.

"Behold the avenging army of King Richard," said Tuck, waving an arm across the vista.

"What are they doing?" asked Anna, pointing to the braziers.

"I hoped Robin might enlighten us," said Tuck. "He is the man with some military experience."

He is, wondered Anna? Perhaps Tuck gleaned more from the short exchange with Rob than she had.

"Flaming arrows," muttered Rob, staring at the braziers. The daylight was starting to fade, which made the flames easier to see, yet harder to pick out any other details. He pointed, "Look at them quivers."

Anna squinted into the gloom. Now she'd been told what to look for, she could just make out shadowy stacks lined up near the braziers. Bless Rob's eyesight, she thought. "They'll shoot flaming arrows at the city walls?"

"Over them." Rob's jaw was clenched, "Set the roofs alight. Burn 'em out." His eyes narrowed as he searched the mayhem below the walls, then he pointed, "That there's a siege engine."

Tuck and Anna leaned to follow the direction of his finger and saw a large mass of cross-braced timbers with a growing pile of stones beside it, fed by a long line of men. She could see them loading the stones into something that looked like a huge sling.

"They'll toss that lot at the castle," said Rob. "Break stones and bones alike."

Anna realised that Rob did indeed have some understanding of military tactics. Everything he said made complete sense and it overlapped with what little she had heard about castle sieges. He seemed too young to know such things and yet she knew that soldiers were never too young to serve. And die.

Tuck looked on, his face grim. "Thank ye, Robin. Ye have confirmed my suspicions. We had better return to the encampment as I am now of firm belief that we are safer without the city walls."

Anna was about to ask more but she was interrupted by shouts from below. She watched as hundreds of archers stepped forward to take arrows from the quivers. They gathered in knots around the braziers. When all the tips were alight they spread out in a ragged line beneath the steep escarpment and raised their bows. There was an unearthly whickering sound followed by a low whoosh. The sky blackened with blazing arrows each tracing their own arc of smoke.

Then all fell silent.

Anna found herself holding her breath.

The whooshing sound returned as gravity overtook the upward flight of each arrow and pulled them down towards the houses of Nottingham. There were scattered screams and shrieks, then more black plumes spiralled slowly from the rooftops. Just like the smoke from the braziers below.

"Run!" called Tuck. "The siege is begun."

The Bailiffs of Nottingham

They returned to the chapel, sweating and panting, in time to see a short stocky man in a fur edged cloak appear at a gap in the ditch and call out to the monks in a deep guttural accent. "Last chance! In or out?"

"Thank ye Bailiff, we take our chances out here," answered Tuck. The Bailiff made a curt nod and signalled to some men behind him, who came forward with carts to block the track where it crossed the ditch. The smoke rising from the far side of the city was now joined by a low intermittent thunder from the direction of the castle.

"Which one were that?" asked Rob, pointing to the man Tuck had addressed.

"Bailiff Henrik, our Anglish Bailiff. He may not be one for lengthy discourse, but he be fair, and I have respect for him."

"What about Norman Bailiff?"

Tuck hesitated. "May God and King Richard forgive him." He looked across a low cluster of medieval rooftops to where the castle stood above all, on its sandstone plinth. A plume of dust erupted from one of the towers as a stone hurled by Richard's siege engine struck it. "He hath done much that needs forgiveness."

Rob and Anna tried to draw Tuck on what the Norman Bailiff had done. Tuck would say no more, as he was busy helping those who had not been helped at the castle. It seemed the Norman bailiff now found himself caught in a fight between two brothers at war: King Richard and his younger brother Prince John. Anna's memory of late twelfth century history was hazy. She remembered more of the popular tales than fact. Tales of evil Prince John, taking taxes from the poor and noble King Richard returning from his crusades to put John in his place. She knew enough about history from her mum to realise that this was popular perception, without hard facts. But here she was outside the city of Nottingham while the frighteningly real army of King Richard laid siege on the people who supported Prince John. All they could do was huddle around the campfires and wait.

As night fell, they saw the fires burning within and outside the castle walls. The flaming arrows crossed the sky like a rain of shooting stars. Rob looked more and more uneasy in the red glow. Slowly the fires crept outwards across the edge of the city and they began to hear cries from the town folk, panic rising like a tide.

"You were right," said Anna to Tuck. "We're safer out here."

"But am I right to ignore those who plead for help?" he replied, looking as uncomfortable as Rob.

"What can we do against a king's army?"

Tuck stood up; his fire-lit face had lost its kindness, transformed by angry frustration. "We must try to bring them to safety." He stalked off to find his two brother monks, leaving Rob and Anna to sit and feel helpless.

John the nailer stood up too. "I will go with Brother Tuck," he said to Sarah, "Keep our children safe."

Anna looked at Rob to see if he might come with her. He was hunched forward, head down so he didn't even have to see the campfire flames. "Rob?" He pulled his hoodie up and shrank into it. "Are you okay?" she asked.

"Can't go," he said quietly.

Anna remembered what he had confided at the Rock Cemetery cave. "Your brother and father," she put her hand on his shoulder, thinking how frightened he must have been when he lost them in the fire that destroyed his childhood home. "It's okay. Stay here with Sarah and the others."

She got up and followed John and the monks, who were already heaving the carts away, clearing the gap in the ditch. The priority had changed from keeping soldiers out to letting the town people escape. Tuck paired the helpers to go searching for those who might be trapped. Anna went with Tuck. They ran from door to door on opposite sides of the street, banging until they replied. If the families emerged, they were sent back up the street to what Tuck called the bar, the strip of track that crossed the ditch.

Anna hammered on a door where she could see candlelight from within but got no answer. She expected it to be bolted but all she had to do was lift the latch. It seemed that locks were a luxury for those who had something worth stealing. She was in a small parlour with a wooden table and chairs, a copper pot, sacks of flour and a strangely large oven in one corner. The candlelight was coming from a doorway at the back of the room, so she hurried to it. "Hello! Anyone there?" No answer. There was a cramped landing and stone steps leading down to a cellar that seemed to have been hand carved out of the soft sandstone. "Hello!"

She heard a whimper coming from under a sack cloth in the corner of the room. A candle stood in a niche cut into the rock and straw littered the floor. This must be where the family slept, thought Anna, and the whimper sounded like a child. She knelt by the sacking and lifted it gently making soothing noises. Underneath were two girls, barely older than Lizzie Nailer, holding each other tight.

"Where are your parents?" asked Anna. They just shook their heads, too afraid to answer. She put her hands out and asked, "Would you come with me and look for them?" One tentatively put her hand in Anna's then looked at her sister, who reluctantly wriggled forward to take the other outstretched hand. "Come on, I have a friend who'll be searching for them too."

They could feel the heat of the fire at the front door. It was spreading fast among the houses, which would have been dry as tinder, especially the thatch. Anna saw Tuck in the street waving refugees towards the bar. He signed to her, urging her to take the girls back. They clung to the doorposts, afraid to go out so Anna lifted each up onto her hips. Half jogging, half stumbling, she tried to remember nursery rhymes that her mother had told her as a child. Anything that might distract them from the flames and the panic.

"Ride a cock horse to Banbury Cross,

To see a fine lady upon a white horse,

Rings on her fingers and bells on her toes,

She shall have music wherever she goes."

She stammered out the rhyme and jigged the girls up and down in time, as if they were riding a horse. The whimpering abated long enough to reach the camp and she set them down with Sarah and Rob beside the fire. Rob looked at her in a way she didn't understand. Sarah turned the two fair-haired little girls towards her and started another familiar rhyme.

"Pat-a-cake, pat-a-cake, baker's man

Bake me a cake as fast as you can..."

"Mammy, daddy bake," said one of the girls.

The sacks of flour, the big oven... their parents were bakers. Anna ran back into the rising flow of people escaping from the conflagration. "HEY! WHERE ARE THE BAKERS! BAKERS!" she shouted. Some looked at her as if she were mad, calling for someone to bake them bread while the city burned, others just ignored her and ran past (she was used to that). "BAKERS!" she persisted.

Finally, a dusty haired man and woman stepped aside from the throng, wild eyed with worry. "We be bakers," he said.

"I've two small girls crying for their parents and they say they're bakers."

"Mercy!" the woman cried. "Fair hair? Three and four years?"

"Yes, come with me."

Mother and father hugged their children, tears running down their faces. "How can we ever thank ye?" the mother kept asking Anna and Sarah.

Anna resisted the urge to ask for a sticky bun for Rob, smiled and went to find them some hot porridge. When she returned, Rob had disappeared. "Did you see where Rob went?" she asked Sarah.

Sarah pointed at the bar over the ditch where the last few evacuees were emerging.

"Oh no!" groaned Anna and ran back towards the fires that now raged through the streets of Nottingham.

The heat was now intense, the burgh was alight. She staggered, clumps of burning thatch dropping around her. "ROB! ROB!" she screamed. A wall collapsed behind, erupting sparks and embers. Where was he? Distant shouts. She ran on, eyes streaming, smoke stinging. "ROB!" Blurry outlines of figures in red and yellow. More shouts, nearer to her. "ROB!"

"HALT!" yelled a command through the smoke.

Something whipped past her ear. Soldiers with bows, firing at her.

"STOP!" A voice beside her, deep, guttural. "STOP FIRING! She be from hospital."

The soldiers lowered their bows. Anna turned. The Saxon bailiff, Henrik, had his palm out to the soldiers and waved her back with the other. She stumbled away. A tall thin man in a fine cloak stepped beside the bowmen and replied, "Be this treachery, Henrik?"

"Nay," Henrik stepped forward to face the other man. "This be your war, not ourn. Leave us, we will have nothing to do with it."

"If I find ye sided with Richard…"

"Richard, John, 'tis all same to me, de Wendenal. Let us be."

The man called de Wendenal spat on the ground and led his bowmen back through the smoke towards the castle.

"Come," Henrik gestured for Anna to follow him.

"But my friend…" she started.

"Anyone alive be outside by now. Come."

Anna was terrified for Rob but had no idea where he was. Another clump of flaming thatch slid into the muddy street, forcing her to hurry after Henrik. What had happened to Rob? Then she started blaming herself: why had she taken him here?

"ANNA!" a familiar voice was calling from the bar over the ditch. A young man straining to see. "ANNA, OVER HERE!" It was Rob.

She ran to him. Hugged him fiercely then stood back and slapped his face.

Rob staggered back holding his cheek, "What d' you do that for?"

"Where the hell did you go?"

"To bring food for folks escaping city."

"I thought..."

Anna's shoulders sagged. She sagged and her knees gave way, overwhelmed by relief and exhaustion. Together they retreated to a low stone wall where they slumped. The city burned. The refugees around them huddled together to watch, mesmerised by the flames. So it was unlikely they would have noticed the pair of them behind the wall, closing their eyes.

Clare Street, Nottingham, October 2019

The smell of smoke woke her, tickling her nose. When was she? A rumble of traffic from the end of the street. Streetlamps threw a harsh sodium glow across a back yard and she could see the neon sign of a shop on the opposite corner. A trio of guys, maybe students, walked past debating whether it would be Ocean or Rock City. The smoky air reminded her of burning houses and flaming arrows searing the night sky. She tried to relax and picture bonfire parties and fireworks, but the siege of Nottingham had been brutally real for her. She had nearly been shot. She had nearly lost Rob.

"What... what happened? Where are we?" asked Rob.

"No Rob, when. We were in medieval Nottingham, now we're back in twenty-nineteen." It was a shock after spending so many hours in the past. It seemed they had slipped back to the present as soon as they fell asleep. Had they lost their focus on the past? Was that why they had come back?

Anna rubbed her face and her palms came away covered in soot.

"Are you hurt?" asked Rob. His face and hair were sooty too.

"No. I'm okay."

"You'd just..."

"Been searching for you in a burning city. Yes, I was there with you. We're both safe now." She brushed the ash from his hair.

"No thanks t' me."

"What? No, it was my fault, I just thought..." she looked at his miserable face. "Never mind what I thought. I shouldn't have taken you there. It was a war zone."

"Yeah, it were." Rob slumped forward and hung his head.

Anna looked carefully at Rob. His agreement seemed heartfelt. She remembered what he had said about deserts and death traps. His confident military knowledge. "You've been somewhere like that before, haven't you." It wasn't a question.

"Afghanistan."

"You were a soldier?"

"What else were I t' do? I weren't top of class."

Anna opened her mouth to challenge him, to say something positive, but stopped. She had a good education, until she had to start caring for her mum, yet she was struggling to find work. How much harder must it be for a dyslexic orphan with more changes of school than clothes? "What did you do there?" she asked instead.

"They called us peacekeepers," Rob shook his head and hugged his knees to his chest. "There were no peace. It were war zone."

"What happened to you?"

"I survived. Seems I'm always one who walks away," he added bitterly.

Anna guessed he may feel guilty that he survived while others did not. "Did something happen to a friend?" she asked quietly.

"Yeah." He paused. Anna waited. "Mate stepped on IED. Never seen so much blood."

"Did he die?"

"No." Rob covered his face with his hands as if trying to stop seeing it all again. "He wishes he did though. Never walk again. Never be a father. I never felt so useless."

"I'm so sorry. How old were you?"

"Eighteen. Both of us."

As a teenager, Anna felt too young to be dealing with her mother's death and her own homelessness. She tried to imagine what it would feel like to be given a gun at eighteen and taught to kill. To see a friend mutilated by a bomb. Not just a friend, a close mate. Someone who had your back under fire. "You left the army after that?" she asked.

"More or less."

Anna sensed there was rather more than less but could see by the way he was hugging his knees tighter that he didn't want to relive it all now. She changed tack. "What did you do next?"

"Been trying to find work, but I'm no use to anyone. Not a soldier, not a civvy, not a…"

"Stop!" Anna pulled him up by his hand and led him slowly back through town, ending up at Tina's Pantry. There was a tray of newly donated sticky buns. They each ate four.

Folktales

Central Library, Angel Row, Nottingham, November 2019

"Look, this says William de Wendenal was a Norman baron, and what we would call the High Sheriff of Derbyshire and Nottinghamshire. Says he disappeared in 1194, replaced by William de Ferrers, Earl of Derby. That sounds sinister, I wonder if Richard got hold of de Wendenal after the siege," Anna drew a finger across her throat.

"Sounds like he deserved it," said Rob, "if Tuck were right."

"I don't think Tuck wanted anyone dead."

"He didn't like de Wendenal."

"Don't think I do either, he nearly had me shot. Perhaps de Ferrers was an improvement?"

"Doubt Tuck would have thought so."

"Did we really meet Friar Tuck?"

"He weren't Friar, he were Brother."

"Says here Friars weren't a thing then. Maybe he got called a Friar later. What about Little John?"

"Didn't knock nobody into a river with a staff."

"Well, I did meet Robin of Loxley."

"Nah y' didn't. I met Maid Marian though."

"They misunderstood what I... never mind."

Rob gave Anna a sly look and she rolled her eyes.

"Does it say anything about Nailer's?" he asked.

"I doubt it, Rob. History is written by and about people with power. They hardly bothered with everyday people, trying to keep their heads down and stay alive."

"Go on, have a look."

Anna shook her head but made some searches anyway, just to prove her point. She was ready to say 'I told you so' before she came across some folklore references. "This is weird," she said. "Some folktales say Little John was also called John Naylor. Like the son of John the nailer."

"See, they do have stuff on ordinary people."

"These are folktales, Rob, not history, not fact. How can we have met a fictional character?"

"Folktales are spoken history," argued Rob. "Okay, they get a bit carried away like, but they start as facts."

Anna frowned. Her mum had spent much of her life arguing over accepted historical facts and scorned the time some historians spent researching folktales. But Anna had to admit Rob had a point. She also reminded herself she had met plenty of real people from history before. She had looked up the dinner party host and his guests from the cave of columns in The Park and found they were all real. And that reminded her of the serving woman who seemed strangely familiar. Who was she? Was she real, and was Beatrice's mum a real person she should know? Their faces haunted Anna and she needed to understand why.

"Okay, say John Naylor and his family really existed. Say little John, his son who I carried in my arms, grows up and becomes Little John from folklore..."

"Then Robin Hood is real!"

"He's a legend, he can't be real. Historians have examined all the tales and records and they can't even decide if he came from Nottingham or somewhere in Yorkshire, let alone whether he was real."

"Sod Yorkshire! He were Nott'n'm man!"

"Spoken like a true Nottingham man yourself. Where's your evidence?"

"There's statue outside castle."

"That's not evidence, that's tourism!"

"And there's whole bunch of roads named after him, and Tuck, and you," he added with a smirk.

"They all came well after the folktales, most of them were named in the last century. It doesn't prove anything Rob."

"Better go back an' take a look then."

"What? Researchers have wasted ages looking for Robin Hood. It's likely the name was used for all sorts of outlaws from the twelfth to the fifteenth centuries. Where, and more importantly *when* would we look?"

"When Little John en't little anymore. He were supposed to hang out with Robin Hood."

"Even if he were real, and I doubt it, then he was supposed to be pretty good at hiding. Have you any idea how big Sherwood Forest was in medieval times?"

"Bigger than Forest Fields?"

"It covered a fifth of the county, Rob!"

"That's fair big. How about we look for Tuck again?"

Anna paused to think about it. She remembered Tuck was trying to start a hospital, a refuge for the poor, so she started digging through the web again. After extracting herself from a few rabbit holes, she found an old map that showed the site of The Hospital of St John the Baptist, just outside where the ditch would have run, where Lower Parliament Street now ran. The map said it was beside the York Road. The nearest match she could see on modern maps was Glasshouse Street, not far from where they woke up. She noticed it lined up with York Street on the north side of the Victoria Shopping Centre and wondered if the two had once been joined as one road.

"Okay, Rob," said Anna, questioning her sanity. "Let's go look for folktales."

Victoria Shopping Centre, Nottingham, November 2019

Anna stood beside the tide of shoppers ebbing and flowing between the Vicky Centre and Lower Parliament Street. It was getting close to Christmas and the annual scrum had started. Fairy lights hung from every other streetlamp and flickered across the shopfronts.

"Bought these for the kids," announced a young mum to Anna, clutching a box of chocolates. "Poundland didn't have what they wanted," she added and looked down at the box. She seemed frazzled.

"Okay," said Anna, puzzled why she was being told. "Nice chocolates," she added with an encouraging smile.

"They'll be grand," said Rob.

"Thanks," said the mum and wandered off. Her eyes didn't seem to see any of the Christmas lights or plastic elves in the shop windows.

"What was that about?" asked Anna.

"She just needed us to agree," said Rob. Anna was still mystified so he spelled it out. "She bought choccies 'cause she couldn't afford what her kids asked for. But she needed someone to say it were okay."

Anna felt a lump rising in her throat. Despite being homeless the last few months, she was still learning of the heart-breaking impact of poverty on those who hung by their nails. Not quite on the streets yet, but any moment...

"Sorry. I didn't realise, I'd have..."

"No worries," said Rob. "Doubt she heard aught we said."

Anna felt both excluded and relieved not to be part of the seasonal madness and the pressure it put on those who couldn't afford it.

"Little chance of finding anything medieval to focus on around here," she said, turning back to their search.

"Broadmarsh has caves, why not Vicky Centre?"

"If there were any. I expect they got filled with concrete when they built this place," she waved at the teeming edifice in front of them.

"There's car park and service ramp to basement off Glasshouse Street. Got t' be worth a try."

Anna had to admit it was better than being trampled by shoppers and followed Rob around the block. Rob led her down a steep concrete ramp into the delivery bay. There were a few workers offloading trucks, but no one paid them any attention. At the back of the bay was a fire escape door, and just like so many workplaces it was jammed open with a fire hydrant. Anna suspected that defeated its purpose but was grateful it gave them a way in. Rob took her down a long corridor, past the foot of a staircase and on around several twists and turns. Down another flight of steps, at the end of a poorly lit corridor, was a dowdy grey door with 'Keep Shut' stencilled in large unfriendly letters. Rob took something out of his pocket and jiggled it in the lock. Anna looked behind them to see if anyone had followed, but it was quiet.

"Here we go," said Rob, pushing the door open. He fumbled around for the light switch. It didn't work, so they waited until their eyes had adapted, using what little light spilled from the corridor.

The floor was unmade with piles of broken bricks and offcuts of wood. The walls were rough stone, shored up by the remains of old brick cross walls. The place had a musty damp smell you would expect from a basement that had been shut up and forgotten for many years.

"This might work," said Anna. They wedged a loose brick in the door to stop it closing on them and settled into a corner against the rock face. Anna let her mind flow over the sandstone walls, searching for traces of the past. After a while, searching out and downwards, the memories found her. She saw families in gas masks, waiting for an all clear, barmen stacking beer barrels, men huddled together talking and hatching plans while a small boy kept watch from a tiny hole above. So much life had been lived down here, but none of it seemed earlier than the nineteenth century.

Reluctantly Anna opened her eyes, stood, and stretched. "We won't find Tuck or Little John down here. It's too new."

"Bet there are other caves round here."

"Bet you're right, but they'll all be behind private doors, even harder to get at than this one."

"How about back at castle?"

"We only stumbled on Tuck and the others last time."

"Yeah, so can't we stumble back again?"

"We don't want to end up in another war."

"You said y'usen, it's when that counts, not where."

"Okay, let's try." Her underfed belly tried to speak over her, and she placed a hand to silence it. "Would we be pushing it to find your friend Jamaal again first?"

The Road to Arabia, Nottingham, November 2019
"You're pushing it!"

"Just scraps, we don' mind, Jamaal," pleaded Rob.

"Do I look soft?" Jamaal waited. "This is where you're supposed to say no."

"You're a gem, man," said Rob.

Jamaal raised his face and palms to the sky, looking for someone to lend moral support. Nobody did. He went back inside his kitchen and Rob grinned. Jamaal reappeared with two bags of chips. "Now clear off!"

"Thank you, Jamaal," smiled Anna sweetly, "Like Rob says, you're a gem."

Jamaal shook his head, refusing to shine.

"If we go back to gatehouse," said Rob between mouthfuls, "we might end up in war again."

"There are caves all around the rock, including those up there," Anna gestured with a handful of chips at the holes in the rock above The Road public house.

"C'mon then," Rob led Anna to a black railing at the foot of the Castle Rock. It was more a mild deterrent than a barrier so neither had much difficulty in climbing it. Climbing the rock itself was much harder. It looked all ridged and full of holes, as if it ought to be easy, but the soft sandstone crumbled under their grip. Anna felt herself slipping and Rob grabbed her wrist, pulling her up into a crevice beside him.

"I don't think I'll make it to the cave mouth," puffed Anna.

"Course you will," Rob scrambled around an overhang and lay flat, reaching back down for her. "Grab my hand."

Anna clung to the rockface, inching up it. She slipped again and swore she would have fallen if Rob hadn't kept his grip on her. Rob dragged her over the ledge and into one of the open cave mouths. Anna peered back over the ledge wondering how the hell they'd get back down again.

"Will this do?" Rob asked.

"Better had," said Anna, still fighting for breath. "Hope there's steps when we're going."

They sat back into the cave mouth, out of the wind and huddled together. Anna and Rob closed their eyes. Mindful of their precarious ledge, Anna had an extra dose of vertigo when she looked down through time. She could feel Rob at the edge of her mind again and together they scoured the memories that had been laid down around the stone walls of the cave. There was no helpful dial telling them what the date was. Only the way people dressed and lived gave clues to when they were, so they sought out medieval cloaks and leggings, half-timbered houses on muddy lanes and ancient revellers in taverns, searching. Searching.

Castle Rock, Nottingham, 1214

"Bloody 'ell!" said Rob. "Steps!"

An oak boardwalk ran around the edge of the cave mouth, leading to a flight of wooden stairs. These descended towards a long, thatched building, washed by moonlight. Anna could hear voices and laughter below, followed by someone singing and gales of drunken laughter. "Guess we can check on The Road to Arabia's claim to be England's oldest pub," said Anna.

"Wonder if they have a Jamaal?" pondered Rob.

"Well, this is the Nottingham end of the road to Arabia, but there's a chance one of his ancestors might have travelled the other way. Let's find out."

They noticed several beer barrels behind them in the cave when they stood up and several more standing on the boardwalk outside. Anna wondered if the beer was brewed in the tavern and hauled up to the caves to keep cool. Or perhaps it was taken up to the castle for the off-duty soldiers.

The tavern heaved with people. All men. Anna pulled her hoodie up over her head and shrank back. Rob did the same, trying to avoid being noticed, just watching and listening to the conversations. There seemed to be two prevailing accents: one gruff (Saxon?) and one flowing (French?) Anna wondered again how they were they understanding them. She knew enough to realise that old English was very different from modern and it would have taken a long time to assimilate the Saxon and French speech, just as it had done the Gaelic, Latin and Norse before. She realised that English must be a mishmash of all western European languages and wondered why it was that English people continued to think themselves so separate from their neighbours.

Watching a knot of men chatting, she noticed for the first time that their lips seemed to move a little out of synch with some of the words they spoke. Like a film that had been expertly dubbed. Was something happening in her head that filled in the meanings where it had changed out of all recognition?

"… and that be another confounded tax on top of them others!" complained a sandy bearded man with a Saxon accent.

"Each by-Our-Lady king be the same," agreed a dark-haired man with a blue tunic and a French accent. It sounded as if he said 'by-Our-Lady' like 'bloody'. "They leave to make war and tax us all to pay for it."

"I hoped King John may differ from his brother," said a darker skinned man whose accent Anna couldn't place. She wondered if the speaker might come from Arabia because of his white shift and slightly darker skin tone. She was also thrown by his words because the last time they had been here Richard was king, not his younger brother John. "The only difference I see is that he kicks his neighbours and relations, rather than take the long trip to Jerusalem to kick us."

"Hah! That were a fine waste of time," said sandy beard man.

"Not entirely," said blue tunic, "now you trade with Arabia. Their spices almost make the food here edible!"

The white shift man bowed deeply, smiling, "One day Angland may be as civilised as Arabia."

"One day Angland may be as civilised as Normandy," smiled blue tunic.

"If ye think thisens civilised then ye can fetch me more ale," retorted sandy beard with a mischievous grin.

"If ye call this ale," said blue tunic. "However, I will admit that the Nottingham ales are not as poor as elsewhere. Indeed, Godfrey's ales here seem better than most."

"The caves," said sandy beard, "we keep the ale cool there and serve it fresh."

"It may help that Godfrey's brewers are Norman trained," said blue tunic, also smiling.

They were interrupted by a scuffle beside the bar. A huge man with bulging muscles gripped the throat of a much smaller man, pinning him against an oak post. The tavern owner shouted for the big man to stop, then another young man stood up, every inch as tall and broad chested as the aggressor. "Leave him be," he said. Anna had that annoying feeling of familiarity again and wondered who he could be.

The muscle man dropped the small guy and turned to face the newcomer. "Who are ye?"

"John Nailer. Little John Nailer," said the young guy with a wry grin and a strong Saxon accent. Anna's jaw dropped; she didn't think she could hold him in her arms anymore.

"Think ye can take me?" threatened muscle man.

"Take it outside!" ordered the tavern keeper.

Muscle man swung a fist at Little John who caught it and rolled him onto his broad shoulders in one swift motion. He carried the bully to the doorway where he threw him onto the muddy street. Muscle man sat up, looking as if he was trying to work out how he had travelled from the bar to the street in the blink of an eye. Little John stepped forward, "Don't pick on anyone Little."

Anna and Rob craned their necks around the doorway expecting a fight, but the muscle man rubbed his head, got up and sauntered off as if this were a normal night out. Little John turned to come back in and stopped when he saw Rob and Anna. "Evening! Ye dress strangely, are ye here from foreign lands?"

Anna looked down at her oversized overcoat and boots and was forced to agree that she didn't look very medieval. "Blackheath," she said. "And Loxley," she added turning to Rob. He raised an eyebrow.

Little John frowned and searched their faces. "Ye seem familiar. I swear I have met ye before."

"When you were more... Little," said Anna. "I think I told you a story about collecting toads."

Little John's eyes popped wide. "Natterjack!" he muttered in disbelief. "Heavens, ye be Marian! And... and ye be Robin. Hey, Godfrey! Two ales for my friends here, if ye please."

Before they could evade attention, Little John had taken each by hand and led them up to the bar where Godfrey was pouring ale into leather tankards from a barrel. "I guess I owe ye for keeping the peace," said the tavern keeper, and passed a brim-full tankard to Rob, who eyed it warily. "Though women oughtn't to be in here," he gestured to Anna, "even if they dress as a man."

Anna didn't know which part of that comment to take offense at first. Fortunately, Little John spoke before she could. "Marian here picked me up and carried me when I were small boy, falling down with hunger, and Robin here fed me and my family when he had never met us before. Helped save us from King Richard's siege. They deserve hospitality." Then he took a closer look, "The pair of ye have not aged a day. How so?"

Judging by Little John's size he must have been about twenty years older than when they first met him and his family. "Good living," said Rob, deadpan.

Anna looked at him and raised an eyebrow. John laughed and slapped Rob on the back. Anna thought it wise to redirect the conversation. "How are your family, John?"

"My mother passed on six years hence, but my father travelled back to Hathersage to continue his work as nail maker, and my sisters Lizzie and Mary be with him."

"I'm sorry about your mother," Anna paused and looked down. "We never met Mary; she must have arrived while we were away."

"She be youngest. It were her arrival that did for our poor mother. Brother Tuck helped us lay her to rest."

"Is Tuck still here?" asked Anna.

"He builds his hospital with the brothers of his order. Says he may receive formal blessing and assent before long. At least there be some as are doing good here."

"We overheard complaints about taxes," said Anna.

John hung his head. "It were taxes that near ruined my mother and father. Taxes will ruin us all and for what? Another war? I hear the barons plan to rebel, but how will that help? When John resisted King Richard, Nottingham were put to torch." Anna was trying hard to recall her history again, but all she could remember was the sequence of kings and queens. Their stories seemed sketchy. "We were lucky to escape with our lives," continued Little John, "and I know it were the two of ye and Tuck to thank for that."

"It were Anna who helped people from the fires," said Rob quietly, examining some genuine spit among the sawdust on the floor. Anna noticed him pretending to take a polite sip of the ale before pushing it away again.

"And ye who warmed and fed them," said Little John, placing a hand on Rob's shoulder. Rob looked up. He seemed unsure what to say. "Some of them folk returned to rebuild," continued John. "Some stayed to help Tuck build his hospital. And some left Nottingham for the Wood."

"The wood?" asked Anna.

"The Shire Wood and royal hunting forests, many places to hide there. If the bailiffs cannot find ye, they cannot tax ye," John leaned in close and lowered his voice, "though I heard tales of where some hide."

"Good!" said a man in a fine cloak flanked by soldiers. "Ye can lead us to them."

"Gisborne!" said Little John.

"Sir Gisborne, to ye." He nodded to his men-at-arms. "Seize them."

The Shire Wood

The Shire Wood, or Sherwood Forest, Nottinghamshire, 1214

It was a long hike. There had been cattle grazing and crop fields beside the first stretch of the York Road leading north out of Nottingham. This gave way to scrub and heathland, which in turn became overgrown by a mix of birch, beech, and chestnuts. Ancient oak trees soared above and spread their canopies, gradually conspiring to close in on the muddy pathway, elbowing the sky aside. The deeper they were marched into the forest the denser the foliage, now thronged with stands of pines competing for the remaining patches of blue sky.

Anna was exhausted. "Of course, the soldiers ride horses while we walk," she muttered, so their captors could not hear.

"Of course," answered Little John, quietly.

"How much further?"

"That depends."

"On what? I thought you knew where this hiding place was?"

"I do, but I will not take them there."

"Then where the hell are we going?" hissed Anna, at the end of her endurance and starting to feel as frightened of the dense forest as she was the soldiers.

"As far as it takes for those hidden to find us."

Anna cast a sideways look at Little John, trying to work out if he was serious. Unfortunately, he looked most earnest. "What if he catches on?" she gestured to the fine cloaked man on the lead horse, flanked by a dozen mounted men-at-arms in red and yellow tunics.

"Gisborne? He be full of himself, and I will lead him in circles before he knows."

Anna bit her lip; she was so tired she dragged her boots along the dirt track and fought to stay upright. She recognised the name Gisborne from folktales, but couldn't remember how he was supposed to fit in. Sir Guy of Gisborne? They had come to search of folktales, and they should have been more wary of finding them.

Rob trudged beside her. He had hardly uttered a word since they started out at dawn. The night in the castle cell had been hard on all three of them and Little John had sat brooding while a scrawny grey rat chewed at the scraps of straw scattered over the stone floor. On reflection, Anna thought John had seemed the most oppressed by their arrest. By contrast he now looked as if he were out on a stroll in the woods, not a captive of the Bailiff's deputy and righthand man. She had considered fleeing into the forest but realised how easy it would have been for the mounted men to run her down. That must be why they hadn't bothered binding them.

At mid-day the soldiers dismounted and made a fire, scooping armfuls of twigs and slender branches from the undergrowth and laying them in a neat cone. One drew a tinder box from a pouch on their belt and struck a shower of sparks that caught and smouldered. The fire was for their benefit, not their prisoners. Of course.

Anna sat heavily on a mound of moss and looked around her. She had never really considered her relationship to town and country before. Her walks across the heath into Greenwich Park with her mother had been bright and uplifting. A pleasant tonic to dusty streets. But these were urban parks where nature was contained and controlled. The trees of the Shire Wood closed around them like a shroud, stifling her. Their wild proliferation mocked her. Threatened her. Dared her to tread deeper.

She was hauled to her feet again by a soldier and given a rough shove. Despite the cart tracks and hoof prints, Anna wondered whether Little John was leading them along the York Road or some lesser known byway. There had been few passing them in the other direction and none in the last couple of hours. The only sound other than the suck of mud on hoof was birdsong. Blackbirds, wood pigeons and Robins. The deeper they penetrated the forest, the louder the song became to the point where it overwhelmed. She felt she were intruding on a domain that was forbidden to humankind. Only the rutted track reminded her that people trod here too. It was hard to reconcile this ancient forest path with the future motorway that would link north to south.

A cry like a child shrieking made her start. It took a moment for her to recall the sound of a fox bark and supposed it to be one. It reminded her that it was not just birds that roamed medieval forests. This was no fairy-tale of merry men in The Greenwood, this was where people hunted stags and wild boars. And if you were hunting in the wrong place then the king's rangers would hunt you.

Another shriek, this time much nearer. Little John whispered to Anna and Rob, "Be ready to run on my word."

The track wound slowly towards a wooden bridge that spanned a forest stream. Anna scanned the trees, searching for some reason for John's warning. The birds sang out loud, but the fox was silent, if that's what it was. The rush of running water joined the noises of the Shire Wood, splashing over stones beneath the oak planks of the bridge. They had barely reached the far side when John stooped to pick a fallen branch off the ground then pushed Anna off the track.

"*Run!*" he urged.

A whipping whistling sound. A shout, a cry of pain. A horse bolted, rider-less past Anna. Rob grabbed her hand and pulled her to a laurel bush. Another whistling whoosh, another cry. Someone shouted orders, Gisborne? Hooves clattered and slid. Shadows slipped in and out of sight. Spirits of the forest.

A crack of wood on wood. Little John wielded the branch, driving a man-at-arms from his horse. A fox shrieked. The trunks appeared to split and move. Forest sprites? No, men in dark green running, throwing knives, leaping logs, hurling themselves at riders who fell like sacks of grain into the mud.

Rob and Anna cowered in the laurel, watching, eyes wide. Gisborne attempted to rally his men, calling them to him. Blade bared, he swung a wide arc warding the green men back. A pair of men-at-arms held their swords high and charged. Little John coiled back then jabbed his branch forward like a spear, throwing one rider. The other turned but was caught and pulled down from behind. The rest of Gisborne's men ran.

He was alone. Surrounded by the green men, stalking him as prey. He circled slowly, sword out, dagger in the other hand. He made sudden swipes, slicing the air perilously close to Little John, trying to catch him off guard.

But Little John seemed to know his distance, stepping just out of reach. He swung his branch, knocking the sword from Gisborne's grip. Backed by the green men, Little John advanced. He stopped in front of Gisborne who faltered at the edge of the oak planks. Little John raised his branch. Gisborne shuffled again and found he had run out of bridge. He swayed, grasping at empty space then tumbled into the stream. He resurfaced, coughing water, and waving his dagger wildly, scrambling for the bank in front of Rob and Anna.

"Come, Gisborne," called Little John. "Face your end like a man."

Anna could see Gisborne shaking yet spitting defiance. Little John had been handed a woodman's axe by one of the green men and stepped forward to finish the job.

"NO!" shouted Rob. Anna realised he had left her side and was striding towards Gisborne and the others. Little John stopped short, a mix of surprise and amusement on his face.

"Would ye stop our sport?" he asked.

"Killing en't sport," said Rob. "I were professional once."

Little John regarded Rob as if reassessing him. "Aye, 'tis no sport. And Gisborne would not play fair if it were. But he must pay for the lives he has ruined. The folk who could not afford to pay when he came taking taxes."

"Take his purse," said Rob. Gisborne looked genuinely shocked as if Rob had ordered they take his breeches down. "Take his money an' pay them people back."

Little John held Rob's eye, then turned to the green men standing beside him. A couple of them nodded. One muttered something to John who relayed their concern. "He will only carry on his extortion if we release him."

"If you kill him then Bailiff will replace him," argued Rob. "If we let Gisborne live, he'll have this day to think on."

"Aye, fair point," agreed Little John. The green man who had cautioned him conceded reluctantly.

Gisborne looked at Rob, shame, hate and relief all jumbled on his face.

"Give us y' purse," said Rob.

Gisborne took a leather pouch from under his cloak and threw it reluctantly at Rob's feet. "I doubt those coins will ever see the poor ye speak so nobly of," he sneered.

"I'll make it my business they do," said Rob.

"I will help," said Little John.

Rob plucked up the pouch as Anna emerged from under the laurel, feeling foolish. He handed it to her, and she was a little shocked by the weight of the coins inside. "Maid Marian here is most honest one I know," he said with a twinkle in his eye. "She'll make sure we're all good as our word."

"No honour among ye, I'll warrant," muttered Gisborne. "Give me a horse so I may leave ye to your thieving."

"Ye will walk," said Little John, "as ye made us walk here. Go straight back to castle. Do not try to seek our retreat. Ye will be stopped and Robin may not be there to plead your life again."

Gisborne pulled his muddy cloak around him and stalked south with as much dignity as a damp defeated deputy would ever manage. Little John nodded to a pair of the green men who slipped away into the foliage beside the path, no doubt to make sure Gisborne made no attempt to track them.

"Well, Master Loxley and Maid Marian," Little John placed his huge fists on his hips and smiled. "It seems we must offer ye the hospitality of Shire Wood." Anna was overcome by a wave of tiredness and nausea, sinking slowly to her knees. Shock, relief, and exhaustion all played their part. Little John stooped and lifted her up, so she clung to his great chest like a child. "My turn," he smiled gently.

Anna guessed she must have faded in and out of consciousness a few times on the journey to their hideaway. She hated showing weakness but was so fatigued she was grateful to be carried. She was aware of Little John and Rob chatting easily, more easily than she had heard him talk to anyone else before, which puzzled her yet made her happy for Rob. Quiet, awkward, difficult Rob. They seemed so different. One large and brawny, one wiry; one fair haired with a generous smile, one dark and broody; one optimistic and one wary of all the world. However, she saw how Rob's sly charm complimented John's easy manner, and there was more.

"... and I understand your wisdom there, Robin," John was saying. "De Ferrer would have another hunting dog in his place, and he would have made sure that dog had sharper teeth and worse bark than Gisborne. This way we have some small hold on him. A little mercy may be more powerful than revenge."

"Tried revenge," said Rob, looking away into the forest. "Didn't make aught right. Made me worse."

Little John gave Rob an understanding look and changed the subject. "Today we feed ye, take ale. Tomorrow we go to Brother Tuck."

"Tuck? He still 'round?" asked Rob.

"Much rounder, I'd say." One of the green men chuckled and John rubbed his belly with a free hand. "Likes a little food and ale himself."

"Good man," nodded Rob. "Be good to see him an' all. But why tomorrow?"

"The folk who lost most to the tax collectors are at his hospital, taking alms to keep thisens alive. Best place to take Gisborne's purse."

The hideaway was not at all what Anna expected. The films she had watched had treehouses and log platforms all connected by rope bridges. What she found was a regular village with timber houses, thatched roofs, and stables. The difference was that it had been hidden in a hollow, surrounded by deep forest, and screened by thick bushes. The thatch was interwoven with leafy bowers to help with the camouflage. For the last couple of miles, they had scrambled through thickets and moss coated mounds without a path in sight. You had to know where you were going to get near, let alone find it.

The trees loomed over her while the brambles scraped at her arms. They were so deep within the forest that nature left no room for visitors. She felt uneasy and would have felt fear if it were not for Little John's confident embrace and the presence of his green men. No. Not all men. Now she looked carefully a few faces beneath the green hoods looked feminine. Their bodies more slender and graceful. All the warriors in green moved quietly through the undergrowth, parting bowers with the gentlest touch. Yet one of the women made this an art. She ranged ahead of the troop who spread themselves out among the foliage, pausing to look around them like a herd of deer.

Anna was also relieved to find as many women as men in the hidden village, she had been worried it might be a predominantly male encampment. She didn't see herself as a great civilising influence but acknowledged that a balance of men and women tended to be healthier. She was nervous of being surrounded only by men. An image of the man in the jacket following her down the lamplit street and the young lads came back to her. Being pressed into the doorway. His face invading her space. His breath.

She shivered.

"Ye cold?" asked Little John. "Let me get ye to our fireside."

It was almost dark, so the villagers were lighting hearth fires without the worry of smoke being spotted from afar. John took them to one of the thatched huts. The woman who had scouted silently ahead of the green men appeared without word beside the door and entered with them. There she pulled her hood back and Little John introduced them to the fair-haired young woman called Ruth. She smiled warmly and waved them to a heap of furs beside their hearth. While Little John lit the fire, she took a pot and heated it over the flame. It smelled good. The pain of emptiness returned to Anna's stomach as she realised she had not eaten for over a day. Was it a day? It was so hard to tell where one started in the twenty-first century and the next finished in the thirteenth. Ruth heaped cuts of stewed boar into bowls for them.

Anna had that odd feeling she recognised Ruth, the same feeling she had when she met Beatrice's mum and the serving woman in the cave of columns. Little John noticed Anna staring at Ruth. "Ruth, this be the woman who pulled ye and your sister out of the bakery when ye were small."

Ruth stood frozen as if ransacking the fragments of memory from her three-year old self. Then her eyes widened, and she stepped forward and to hug Anna. "Thank ye," she whispered.

Anna didn't know what to say. She clung to Ruth as hard as Ruth clung to her. It felt strange yet right. A moment of belonging. Anna had no idea why her heart filled with such emotions. Why hugging this stranger felt so natural.

Rob and Anna ate as if they hadn't seen a proper meal for a month, which wasn't far from the truth. Once their bowls were empty Ruth filled them again and passed a large skin pouch full of ale for everyone to take a swig. This small corner of the world seemed good, a refuge indeed. Though Anna noticed again that Rob only touched the pouch to his lips out of politeness and passed it on swiftly.

Anna smiled. Then sniggered.

"What?" asked Rob.

"Today you robbed the rich," she said. "Tomorrow you give to the poor."

Rob snorted and grinned. John and Ruth looked puzzled. "That be a dangerous and, some might say noble thing," said Ruth, "not to be laughed at."

"You're right," said Anna, suppressing another snigger. "It just seems..."

"The stuff of folklore?" suggested Little John.

"Guess that's what we came for," said Rob, still grinning.

Hidden Village, Shire Wood, Nottinghamshire, 1214

Anna peered from the tiny window at the morning mist gathered in the natural bowl cradling the village. Little John had explained the place was given no name. If there was no name it could be passed off as myth, much harder to betray it unaware. The scene at the window looked as if the village might come and go with the mist, a mythic place indeed. Each house seemed to float in a sea of white. Wisps of vapour curled under eaves and through windows like the spirits of long-lost woodland dwellers. A bird called. Another answered and before long the dawn chatter filled her ears. A thin shaft of sunlight filtered through the dark speckled foliage at the edge of the clearing and the ghosts of the village materialised from their doorways.

This was new. Anna realised she had slept and woken in medieval Nottinghamshire. Before she would have roused in the twenty-first century, but this was the first time she, and Rob, had both arisen in the time they had sought. She wondered why. What had changed?

Rob rubbed his eyes and yawned, leaning forward, and pulling the fur cover around his thin shoulders. They seemed to hang naturally, rather than hunched as she had seen him sit before. He looked refreshed. Relaxed. She realised that she too felt more relaxed than she had in a long time. Maybe they both felt safe enough to wake here, now, rather than in modern Nottingham?

Ruth took small loaves of hard baked bread from a waxed wrapper and passed them around. Breakfast. Washed down with fresh water. Simple yet welcome. Anna would have been grateful for a mug of coffee but knew better than to ask. Her caffeine fixes had dwindled since she started her life on the streets. An infrequent luxury. She looked around at the spartan interior of Ruth and Little John's hut and understood that luxuries were hard to come by. Yet it still felt comfortable. A bright red cloth here, a carefully polished copper jug there. A home, not a hovel.

"Time for practice," said Little John. "Have ye any skill?" He pointed to the smooth yew bow in his hand. It looked modest against his big frame, yet Anna judged it was almost as tall as her.

"I haven't, but Rob has," she answered.

"Come," said Little John, "Rob can practise, and I can show ye. We all need some skill with a bow to survive here."

Anna assumed Little John meant that they had to protect themselves from Gisborne's soldiers. But as they emerged from the hut she saw a green-clad hunter returning from the forest carrying a bow over their shoulder and clutching the hind feet of a rabbit in their free hand. Their bow was their access to food. Without it they would starve.

The mist was evaporating as John led them to the edge of the clearing where targets had been painted on tree trunks. There were already two men in green taking shots at them. "This be Will," John introduced a young red-haired man who smiled and shook their hands. "And Alan." A dark-haired man with a short-cropped beard bowed formally to them then handed each a bow and a quiver full of arrows. Anna tugged at the bowstring experimentally and was surprised by how much force it took to move it. Will and Alan had turned their attention back to their targets, nocked arrows and pulled with a fluid motion, releasing without appearing to apply any special effort. Rob took his bow and stood naturally, legs apart, fitting an arrow to the string and holding the fletches between his fingers, just like Will and Alan. Just like Will and Alan he pulled with an easy motion and released after a minimal hold and aim. Unlike Will and Alan his arrow struck the bullseye first time. So did the second.

"Blow me down!" said Little John, under his breath. The other two had stopped to watch Rob who nocked a third arrow and placed it in the bullseye again, touching the other two. "Where did ye learn to do that?" he asked, his admiration undisguised.

"Spare time," said Rob, "Got a bit of that."

"That be unnatural skill, Robin. Come and compete at Fair."

"Done it before," said Rob, "won mesen the odd prize."

Anna remembered the fair and smiled. "Yeah, he was pretty generous with his prizes too."

Little John and the others looked stupefied. "Ye shared a gold arrow and a purse full of gold coin?" he asked.

"It were just stuffed bears last time I did it," said Rob, scratching his head.

John looked at Alan and Will, "We could be giving more than Gisborne's purse to the poor at Hospital of Saint John today."

"Is fair on today?" asked Rob.

"Aye, and ye must enter."

"What if Gisborne sees me?"

John rubbed his chin then took Rob back to his house. "Ruth?"

"Yes, my lover?"

"Would ye fetch a hood for Robin here?"

Anna's shoulders started bobbing up and down, her hand over her mouth as if she were having convulsions.

"Y' alright?" asked Rob.

"Robin bloody Hood!" she managed through tears of laughter that rolled down her cheeks.

The Golden Arrow

The Hospital of St John the Baptist, Nottingham, 1214

Tuck was delighted to see Rob and Anna again and, just as Little John had said, compared to their last visit he was far wider. He was also far more puzzled by their youth than Little John. He had been in his twenties when he first met them, so perhaps they had appeared a similar age to him then. Now in his forties, he likely had a better measure of the passing of time than John who was only a child before. Anna evaded his immediate questions by placing the heavy purse in his hands and asked him to share it out to those worst affected by the war taxes. Tuck emptied the coins out onto the table in front of him and gasped. "There must be enough here to feed everyone in our hospital for a year!"

"Good," said Anna. "Tell them that the Hood," she glanced at Rob, "and the people of the forest are looking out for them." They were all wearing the hooded cloaks to avoid easy identification by Gisborne's men. She had been offered a frock but insisted on a cloak like them. Tuck followed them to the marketplace and reminded them to pull their hoods up over their heads. It was buzzing.

Many in the crowd had hoods, hats, and wraps that kept the frosty air from their faces. Anna sensed their excitement in the happy chatter and eager barter for fancy sweetmeats and trinkets. It was so far from the night of the siege when Nottingham had burned, and Saxon and Norman alike had fled for their lives. She was amazed by the variety on offer: one stall sold Lincolnshire sausage, one had pies from Melton Mowbray, another had eels fresh from the River Trent. A carpenter had a bench laden with hand carved bowls next to a farmer who'd placed a low wicker fence around a gaggle of geese, reminding her of those taken to Goose Fair. A woman in a burka wandered between the stalls selling handfuls of fine silks.

Anna was mildly surprised to see more people originating from Arabia in medieval Nottingham, but when she considered what the men in the tavern had said about the aftermath of the crusades, it seemed logical. Once you stopped making war the only sensible thing to do with your neighbours across the sea was trade with them, and the River Trent allowed small sea-going ships to reach Nottingham. Likely the trade carried on anyway, war or peace: what do ordinary people care about the power struggles of royalty? So long as they don't come and burn the city down.

A long thin space was cleared at one side of the marketplace. One end had a straight line of sand poured across it with amazing precision. Fifty paces away stood a dozen target boards made from woven straw with dyed linen pinned across them, each showing concentric rings. Beside the space was a platform built from crates and boards and on it were a row of folding canvas stools. On the opposite side stood a pair of men in the red and yellow tunics that Gisborne's men had been wearing and one of them was calling for competitors.

"Come," beckoned Little John. "Ye must place your name on the list."

"What name?" asked Rob.

"Gisborne only knows ye as Robin," said Little John, "He were too stupid and arrogant to ask more. Make up a name, he will not recognise ye with the hood."

Rob rubbed his chin, clearly uncomfortable.

"Perhaps you could give your father's name?" suggested Anna.

"Mamsūh Ahmed?" said Rob. "Not very Nott'n'm, not now anyhow."

"I wouldn't be so sure," said Anna.

"A Saracen," smiled Tuck. "I had wondered about the darker hue of your skin. The accent confused me but now I understand. It will be good to make your father proud."

"And it will upset Gisborne even more when ye win!" laughed Little John. "He hates Saracens!"

Rob approached the pair of men in Gisborne's colours and gave his father's name for the contest. There was already a score of other names on their list and others queued behind him to add theirs. "They come from all over the shire, and those neighbouring," explained John. "Surely ye know this contest be the greatest in all England." Rob nodded to cover his ignorance. "Today will sort real archers from competent bowmen. Tomorrow will be far harder."

Rob and Anna found out there were two rounds to whittle down the number of competitors. Rob would be sent to shoot a quiver of arrows with eleven others and so long as he was in the top three, he would be invited back the next day. Little John suggested Rob might want to send the odd shot a little wide to avoid drawing too much attention to himself on the first day. "Don't worry," said Rob, "nerves 'll do that anyhow."

The wait to be called only seemed to make Rob more nervous, so Anna asked him to teach her, following Little John's help in the morning. It was too crowded to shoot but they found a space to go through the motions, without using arrows.

"Show me how y' stand," he asked. Anna stood upright, heels together. "No, show me how you stand to shoot." She placed her feet apart like John had said and stuck her left arm out rigid holding the bow, the other arm mimed a nocked arrow between her fingers. He took the bow from her, "Relax," he said, "are y' comfy?"

"Not really," admitted Anna.

"Get comfy," said Rob, "or you'll be fretting on that rather than where arrow goes."

Anna pulled her feet a little nearer without closing them, then shook her arms out and relaxed her shoulders. Rob gave her back the bow and asked her to mime placing an arrow and pull. She pulled slowly, grimacing with the force needed to take the string back to her chin, then her arms began to wobble and she loosed the string which whipped across the inside of her arm, making it burn.

Rob didn't laugh, nor did he get impatient. He held the bow while she rubbed her arm then suggested a better way of doing it. "Pull a bit faster. Not too fast, but not slow. Slow 's hard. I'd shake too if I pulled slow."

She pulled a little quicker, smoother and steadier than before, but started wobbling again as she held it to aim. "Loose now," said Rob and she let go of the string, relieved to stop fighting against its pressure. "Good. Again, but don't hold it so long."

"But it feels like I rushed my aim," complained Anna.

"Practise," said Rob. "You might miss to start, but if you watch where each goes, you'll know to nudge it back right way."

"Easy for you to say," said Anna.

"Yeah, but only 'cause I've practised."

Anna tried again and found that loosing the string earlier helped avoid the shakes. She vowed to find some arrows and a target to practise with later.

"Robin," interrupted Little John, "they be calling ye to shoot!"

"Hope they're calling Mamsūh Ahmed, not Robin," said Rob, and followed John back to the competition. Anna came too, wondering why she felt a little annoyed that her lesson had been cut short.

She stood between John and Tuck, craning her neck to watch from the crowd that had formed behind the rope marking the edge of the shooting range. She saw Rob, third from the end on her right and the targets on her left. Opposite were the canvas stools on the platform, most of which were empty apart from a couple of men in expensive looking robes. Naturally, there was a gap in the crowd behind the targets, but a few idiots or optimists had crept in beside them.

Rob's first shot went wide, just catching the outer edge of his target circles. Anna could see he looked nervous, but he stopped, shook his arms out, breathed deep and stood naturally with his feet about as wide as his shoulders, side-on to the target. He gave a tug on his hood to keep it up, took the second arrow slowly and rested it along the top of his right thumb. It was only then she saw he was left-handed: leading with his right and pulling with his left. She hadn't noticed at Goose Fair; she had probably been too high on the fun. At morning practise, she had goggled at the arrows in the bullseye, not at how he stood. Rob pulled the bowstring, not fast, not slow, but steady in one fluid motion. He held for a heartbeat then loosed. Her head and the heads either side of her whipped from right to left, like sitting in the front row at Wimbledon, yet too quick for the eye to follow. His arrow had pierced the edge of the bullseye. Anna blew out a silent sigh of relief, having held it for longer than she realised.

Rob's third and fourth crept nearer the centre. The fifth was dead on. Only then, with his sixth and final arrow in hand, did Rob seem to pause and look at the other competitor's targets. Most people had hit them with most of their arrows, but there was only one other where all had hit the bullseye, shot by a tall man with broad shoulders, a bald head, and a black strapping across his left eye. None had anything like the grouping around the bull that he or Rob had shot. Anna knew what Rob would do next and sure enough the sixth arrow hit a point almost exactly halfway between the bullseye and the outer circle. The bald one-eyed man shot his final arrow which hit the centre ring, just as his other five had. The official declared Master Stutely the winner of the heat, with Mamsūh taking second place. As the other bowmen turned to leave, Master Stutely smiled and made a theatrical bow to the crowd who cheered. Many took up a chant: "Blinder! Blinder! Blinder!"

Rob slipped through the crowd and stood silently until his friends turned and saw a coy smile on his lips. He was pleased with himself. "Played that one well," exclaimed John, giving Rob a hearty slap on the back. "Had us all thinking ye were too nervous with first, then made us think ye were over-confident with last."

"Aye, well, not far from truth," admitted Rob.

"Hah! Go on, it were planned," said Little John.

Anna suspected Rob might not have planned any such thing but was delighted by his success. "You're in the finals tomorrow Rob, well done."

"Come," said Tuck, "I'll get ale for ye at The Bell." He led them through the crowd to a tavern standing in a row of houses on the south-west corner of the marketplace. They had to walk one at a time down a narrow passage, like a little indoor street, between tiny bars and into a larger room at the back. It all felt weirdly like she had been in the place before. When Tuck leaned across the bar to order four tankards the penny dropped: she had. The Bell was another contender for oldest pub in twenty-first century Nottingham, alongside The Road to Arabia, even if she couldn't judge their right to be oldest in the country.

"Mamsūh Ahmed!" toasted Tuck, "Soon to be finest archer in the shires."

"Mamsūh Ahmed!" they echoed. Only Anna noticed Rob cuffing a proud tear away.

Tuck invited them back to the hospital, offering a simple straw bed for the night and a bowl of soup for breakfast. For the second time Anna slept soundly and woke again in medieval Nottingham, feeling rested and safe. Rob sat beside her, mopping the bowl with a heel of bread. He looked as relaxed as she had ever seen him and wondered if he even remembered his life in the twenty-first century.

"... and when ye win," Little John was saying, as much to himself as Rob or anyone else, "ye take the purse and the golden arrow. Remember it be tradition to give the golden arrow to the fairest woman in the crowd, but it also be tradition to give it to the bailiff's daughter should she be there, and I know she will."

"Why?" asked Rob, who seemed to have surfaced from a daydream.

"Why? Because bailiff will take offence if ye does not. Do not anger him, Rob!"

"He could make life hard for ye," said Tuck.

"And we don't want ye drawing any more attention to y'usen in front of Gisborne," added Little John.

"Winning might draw attention," said Rob, thoughtfully.

"Aye, but attention will be on Mamsūh Ahmed and the bailiff's daughter, not on Robin of Loxley," argued Tuck. "Or usens."

Christmastide Fair, Market Square, Nottingham 1214

If possible, the marketplace felt even more crowded than the day before. Anna guessed people had come from all over the county to be there, as well as from other counties nearby. She noted the wall down the length of the market square was still there and the archery range stood on the Norman side of it. It was evident from the pageantry of flags and shields that the contest was run by the Norman descendants, and everyone was expected to follow their rules. She also suspected they would want the winner to be Norman. She began to understand why Little John had said a Saracen winner would upset Gisborne so much and she started to feel nervous of Rob winning.

Anna, Tuck and Little John pushed their way gently forward, near the front of the crowd so they could see and cheer on their man. There would be three more rounds: two to pick the best from yesterday's winners and a final with just six archers to decide it. Rob was in the first round. The competition was much stiffer than before, but he held his nerve and grouped all six of his shots in or just outside the bullseye. Only one other person bettered him, and he wore the red and yellow tunic of the Gisborne family. Anna could see Gisborne, sitting on the elevated platform opposite.

"Who's that sitting next to Gisborne?" she asked.

"De Ferrer, Bailiff of all Nottinghamshire and Derbyshire," answered Tuck. "And the young woman beside him be Annabel, his daughter."

"The one who's expecting to be given a gold arrow?"

"The very one." Anna was unsure how to put her thought politely, but Tuck saved her the bother, "Not the most cheerful soul in the shire," he added.

Annabel was dressed in a fine lace-embroidered white dress with a velvet over-cloak and a white fur collar. She had beautiful blond hair platted and looped back onto her head and delicate pale cheeks that blushed in the cold winter air. She obviously did not lack for anything, except perhaps a happy thought in her pretty pampered head. It wasn't so much she looked like she had tasted a bitter lemon as swallowed it whole and tried to wash it down with a cup of cat pee.

"Good job Rob only has to give her an arrow," muttered Anna.

The second round saw Blinder give another perfect performance with all six of his arrows in the bull. He bowed again and the crowd applauded loudly.

"Blinder seems popular," said Anna.

"Aye," smiled Little John, "because he does not belong to Gisborne."

"Why don't they react to Rob?" she asked.

"He hath been careful to come second in each round so far. They do not think of him as a contender. Not yet." She was surprised by Little John's faith in someone he had known for such a short time.

Yet thinking on it she realised he had known of Rob, albeit from one visit, for most of his life. Rob must have made a strong impression on the little boy.

A pair of men ran out to remove half the targets and moved the remaining ones back by ten paces. The finalists were heralded and stepped up one by one. Master Stutely got a big cheer. Gisborne's man was introduced as the Head Forrester Fitzooth, who received a cheer from the platform and a muted clap from the crowd. Three other foresters also in Gisborne's colours had diminishing responses. Mamsūh Ahmed stepped up last in silence, apart from Anna who stopped her solo clap as quick as she started. She could see Rob's face harden, like an invisible suit of armour had been drawn around to protect him from the world. It reminded her of the day they had met at Hope House.

The finalists were allowed three shots each. Fitzooth, Blinder and Rob hit the bullseye with all three of their arrows. The other three had varying success, all missing the bull at least once at the greater distance. They were invited to step away. All targets were removed except one and that was pulled back another ten paces.

Fitzooth shot first and hit the bullseye, just a shade to the left of centre. Those seated at the platform clapped. Anna sensed an inward drawing of breath from the people around her. Blinder shot next and hit the bull just to the right of centre. The crowd cheered loudly. Rob's face was a picture of concentration as he tugged his hood forward, nocked his arrow and lifted the bow to shoot. She wondered if he held his aim a fraction too long but could see no sign of a tremor. She appreciated just how much strength he must be exerting to do that. He let fly.

The arrow looked precisely the same distance to the centre of the bull as the other two. There was a moment of dumb silence and then the crowd erupted, shouting for their newfound hero: "Ahmed!

Ahmed! Ahmed!" It took a moment for Anna to realise she was yelling along with them all. It took a few more for her to realise it wasn't over yet.

The target was pulled back another ten paces. Each finalist drew another arrow from their quivers. Fitzooth eyed Rob, perhaps realising he had greater challenge than expected. He shot again and hit dead centre of the bullseye which drew a loud cheer from the platform and a hushed silence from the crowd. As Fitzooth stepped away he looked at Blinder and Rob as if to say, 'beat that!'

Blinder made a courteous nod to both of his competitors and nocked his arrow, taking a little longer to aim. Perhaps it was too long, wondered Anna. She wondered if she detected a slight tremble in his arms. His arrow hit the bull, but an inch or so high of Fitzooth's in the centre. The crowd applauded but there were a few groans. Anna could tell they were disappointed for him.

When Rob stepped up, they resumed their chant for Ahmed. She wondered what was going through his mind, but his face gave nothing away. He had the same invisible armour on as before.

Rob took his time. He checked his stance, shook his arms to loosen them then placed the arrow over his right thumb and gripped the fletches firmly in the middle fingers of his left hand. A little wind blew the edge of his hood across his face. He stopped, lowered the bow and pulled the hood back so his head was free. Anna stifled a gasp. She could see Gisborne leaning forward, squinting. Rob started his preparation again from the start and took a steady pull on the bowstring. Anna thought he held his aim even longer than before but again there was no sign of trembling. He loosed. There was a metallic click. One arrow stood dead centre forcing the other over at a wild angle. There was a roar from the crowd which quickly fell into chatter and speculation. What had happened?

An official examined the two arrows in the bullseye then walked slowly up the length of the range towards Rob and Fitzooth. He took each of their quivers and examined the feathered ends.

"Checking colour of fletches to see which arrow holds bullseye," explained Tuck.

Little John was too busy peering between target and official to say anything. Anna found herself holding her breath again.

After an eternity in a minute, the official took Rob's hand and raised it, victorious, in the air. The crowd erupted and shouted "AHMED! AHMED!"

Little John yelled with joy and grabbed both Tuck and Anna in a bear hug, dancing them up and down. When they put Anna down again, she could see Rob shaking hands with Blinder and Fitzooth. He was led to the platform, applause still ringing around the marketplace. She slipped to the very front of the crowd so she could see.

If de Ferrer's daughter looked like she had swallowed a lemon, then de Ferrer and Gisborne looked as if she had brought it back up again. They looked at Rob as if he were a particularly unpleasant posset, regurgitated in front of them by cruel fate. Fate smiled, or rather Rob did. A particularly cocky smile, thought Anna, starting to cringe. 'Put your hood back up you idiot!' she thought. But it was clear from Gisborne's disgusted stare that he had already recognised Rob. Anna saw Rob wink at him. She covered her face with her hands, then dared to look again to see de Ferrer handing Rob the purse of winnings with as much reluctance as a miser prised from his hoard. Then Gisborne handed Rob the golden arrow with a look that clearly said, 'be careful who you give this too, it may be the last thing you do.'

Rob held the arrow over his head for the crowd to see. They cheered their new hero as if he were a knight in shining armour. He smiled then turned to de Ferrer's daughter, Annabel, who was not smiling and looked as if the whole concept of smiling were some new and divisive idea. To Anna's horror he blew Annabel a mocking kiss then walked in the opposite direction, across the range. Towards her.

'NO,' she mouthed to Rob, trying to stop him, 'NO' and shook her head. But there was nothing she could do. Rob stopped right in front of Anna. He took her hand, kissed it, and placed the gold arrow into her fingers. She met his eyes. He seemed like a small boy wanting approval. She looked past him at the platform opposite, where de Ferrer was talking to Gisborne and Gisborne was staring straight back at her. If looks could kill, then his would have hung drawn and quartered the pair of them.

Tuck gripped Anna's shoulder, "Time we leave."

Outlaws

The Archangel, Hounds Gate, Nottingham, 1214

Anna ran. Tuck weaved down a dozen alleyways. The claustrophobia of shadowed jettied streets closed in on her while panic propelled her after him. Snatches of urban life flickered past: a carpenter sawing, the smell of wood shavings, a washing line hung low between windows, the glint of a butcher's blade dripping with blood. She glimpsed castle battlements before being bundled through a backdoor, down rough steps into darkness.

"Stay hidden! I shall return," called Tuck before he closed the door, and all was black.

She sat in shock. She was celebrating Rob's victory only moments ago, now she was in a cellar close to the castle. Was she in danger? Where was Rob? Little John had fled with him, but she had no idea where. No phones. No communication but for word of mouth or notes. Alone in the dark, again. Anna bit her lip.

She felt around. Her hands touched something smooth, round, and wooden. A barrel? An ale cellar? At least she wouldn't go thirsty. She ran her hands across the tops of several barrels until she found a short waxy stump: likely a candle. Next, she touched something metallic on a scrap of oily cloth. She thought they were junk and left them, then it occurred to her there was no such thing as matches in medieval Nottingham. She remembered the tinder box the soldier had used in the Shire Wood. Perhaps you struck the metallic thing against another hard surface and used the oily rag to catch the sparks? After much blundering, dropping, searching, and cursing she assembled them: the candle, the rag, the metal bar, and a flint she only found by stabbing her hand on it. She put them on the floor, crossed her legs and struck the flint against the bar.

Ten minutes later all Anna had achieved was a couple of fleeting sparks and sore fingers. She was feeling claustrophobic and close to panic when the door opened and a silhouette stood, ringed by stinging daylight. "Ye alright down there my dear?" A woman's voice in a French accent, friendly and concerned. Anna let out a long and ragged breath.

"Where am I? Where's Rob?"

The woman started down the stairs. "Your friends be fine, don't ye worry. Ye be in The Archangel Gabriel Salutes the Virgin Mary. And I'm Mary, no virgin I'm afraid." Anna didn't know quite how to answer that last statement. "I see ye found the tinder and candle," Mary pointed to the assorted pieces on the floor. "Here, let me help." She struck the flint hard against the metal bar with a flick of her wrist and a big spark jumped onto the oily rag which started to smoulder. A small flame took, and she held it against the candle wick in cupped hands. In moments the cellar had a warm glow. Now Anna could see Mary's long dark hair tied in a practical plait and her cream white apron.

"Look here, there be bench to sit on and a fur. I'll fetch ye soup."

"Thank you, Mary," managed Anna, a slight tremor in her voice.

"Poor waif, ye must be terrified," said Mary. "Tuck told me a little of the tournament. He will come for ye tomorrow, but till then ye must hide."

"But this place, The Arch..."

"The Archangel Gabriel Salutes the Virgin Mary," filled in Mary smoothly. "Could do with a shorter name and that be no lie. Perhaps someone may shorten it to 'The Archangel' or 'Gabriel's Salutation'".

"The Salutation..." Anna remembered another familiar local pub name before returning to her worries. "Isn't this place near the castle? Won't Gisborne's men be looking here?"

"Here? Not for a day or two. They be searching all over Saxon Burgh, high and low," Mary pointed to the street above and the cellar below to make her point. "No chance of them looking on their own doorstep 'til they have the rest of the city searched."

That made some sense, thought Anna. "I'm..."

"Marian, aye, Tuck told me. Good to meet ye. So sorry I cannot entertain ye upstairs, but I will fetch that soup for ye now." Mary bustled up the stairs, shutting the door on the candlelit cellar.

Anna sighed. No point trying to set people straight on her name now, she had become Marian. And it was likely she had landed on the wrong side of Norman law. Fitting, and uncomfortably familiar.

Mary carried in a tray laden with hunks of fresh bread, a jug of water and a large bowl of soup which steamed enticingly. She set it down on the hand-carved bench beside Anna and pointed to a corner of the cellar which harboured a pot. "I will empty it in the morning, dear."

It dawned on Anna that was her pot to piss in. At least she now had one, "Thanks." She felt better cared for here than on the streets of twenty-first century Nottingham.

Mary climbed the steps again and waved to 'Marian'. Anna guessed Mary might be the keeper of a safe house, and Anna did indeed feel much safer. She also made a mental note to speak to the twenty-first century landlords of The Salutation, The Bell and The Road to tell them they could all confidently paint 'Since 1214' on their walls, though 'Established in' may need a few more research trips for her and Rob. Preferably paid for in steak sandwiches.

Rob. She hoped he and Little John had made it into hiding. She would have to wait for Tuck to find out. She tried to lie down but something hard pushed against her leg. Searching through the folds of her cloak she found the arrow Rob had given her. It was beautiful.

A polished copper shaft, half normal length, bright yellow feathered fletches and a tip of solid gold. "Silly sod," she said softly, lying down again and held it to her chest.

Darkness, all but black. Weightlessness. Her mind was floating up and away from her body. Peering upwards through the gloom she saw a distant shimmer, like sunlight playing on the surface of the ocean. Pale shafts penetrated the first few fathoms only to fade, overcome by the depths.

A part of her wanted to float up towards that sunlit surface. Enticing her. Entrancing her with rhythmic laps and ripples. It seemed brighter, clearer. Familiar.

Another part of her warned her away from that light. It wanted to stay. The darkness lay around her, brooding, brimming with hidden threat. Yet there was also something warm and familiar there.

Her mind spun slowly, revolving, suspended in space. Which way was up? Which way should she go? Did the sunlit surface promise safety or the stark reality of loneliness? Were the depths veiled in darkness to conceal her enemies, or herself from them?

Gradually she grew aware of something grasped in her hand. The cool smooth touch of metal. A handle? Or a fisherman's rod? The hint of a line threaded sinuously through the void, drifting away from her. The line unravelled. Pulled taut. She felt a gentle tug on the rod in her hand. Instead of struggling or letting go, she allowed herself to be pulled. It seemed important to hold on. Safer.

The line drew her down into the velvet blackness below, where the depths were murmuring to her. Calling her. Beckoning her back.

Voices woke her. Confused, Anna didn't know if she was in the Castle Rock, the ale cellar or another of the many places she had woken recently. The door opened and daylight flowed down the stone steps. A wide figure blocked the doorway.

"Marian? Are ye safe?" Tuck's voice.

Another behind him called, "I have breakfast for ye dear." Mary. Anna was still in medieval Nottingham, still on the run, still protected by friends.

"Hello," she called back, sitting forward and hugging her knees. "Yes, I'm alright, thanks."

Tuck and Mary came down to set bread, ham, water and an oil lamp on the tray beside her. Mary discreetly removed the full pot, leaving Tuck with her to sit and talk.

"Rob and Little John are in a hermitage, to the west of here," he began. "They be safe for now, but ye all need to be moved." Anna breathed out; they were okay. "Last night the whole of the Saxon Burgh was turned inside out by Gisborne. His men came to the hospital in the small hours," he paused, looking at the stone floor, "they found Gisborne's purse and took it."

"No! Did they suspect you?"

"I am a man of God," he smiled. "I said I did not know who gifted the purse to us and they believed me. For now."

"They didn't see you with us yesterday at the contest?"

"Brothers do not attract attention. The Saracen who wins a golden arrow and the young woman he gifts it to do. Especially when Sir Guy of Gisborne recognises both from his recent humiliation."

"I guess that makes us outlaws."

"Aye, along with anyone caught helping ye."

"Sorry."

"I have not been caught yet. Neither has Little John, though Gisborne will be searching for him. That be why I must move ye. Having ransacked Saxon Burgh, he will send men back to the castle, then north into the Shire Wood."

"Where will you take us?"

"South, across the Trent."

The Hermitage on the River Leen, Nottingham, 1214

Anna was given a change of clothes. She was irritated to find they were the pinafore and bonnet for a milk maid. Anna didn't do girly, but bit her tongue, understanding that to protect her and Tuck she had to be disguised. She was even given a pail of fresh milk. She almost curdled it with her disgusted stare.

They followed a small river upstream, which gurgled around the southern edge of the Castle Rock. Little John called it the Leen. Anna wondered if it had any connection to the student district called Lenton. She couldn't remember a river there in twenty-first century Nottingham but knew of a canal nearby. She guessed that one had been diverted and turned into the other. They walked the riverbank, as if on a morning stroll, at least that was what they hoped it would seem to the men-at-arms who guarded the castle walls high above. She started at something large and furry with a weird flat tail that scurried down the bank into the water.

"What's that?" she pointed.

"Only a beaver," said Tuck.

"But..." she trailed off. This was the thirteenth century, so yes, there were plenty of beavers in England.

Sandstone cliffs rose along the northern bank stretching upstream, and pocked with open cave mouths, just like the one she and Rob had climbed into before entering this medieval world. At the foot of the cliff several wooden houses leaned against the stone as if seeking support. Most looked as if they would fall over without it.

"Who lives there?" asked Anna, pointing at the shaky shelters.

"Hermits," said Tuck, "like the one we are to visit. I shall bless him, and ye shall bring him milk," he nodded to her pail.

Hermits. Hermitage Court. Anna realised with a start that she was walking along the bottom of the escarpment that she saw from her aunt's old home in The Park.

They stopped about a mile along the riverbank, beside a particularly ramshackle pile with a few planks of wood bound together at one end. Tuck knocked against the planks and waited politely. Eventually the planks were lifted to one side by a scrawny looking man, possibly in his fifties, with a beard so long it dangled around his ankles. He smiled to Tuck but seemed flustered when he saw Anna and ducked back into the gloom.

"Good morning Brother Walter," said Tuck, "This be Marian."

Brother Walter bobbed up and down, looking nervous. He pointed into the shadows.

"Thank ye," said Tuck and stepped in. Anna followed.

The bare cave walls had been etched with crosses and alcoves excavated for candles. One held a simple wooden crucifix. There was no furniture. No wall hangings or rugs. Nothing to mitigate the winter weather except the wooden barricade they had come through. The hermit subsisted with less than many Anna had seen sleeping rough on the modern streets of Nottingham. There is always someone with less than you, thought Anna.

Brother Walter took the pale of milk from Anna and bowed to her in thanks. He poured a little into a wooden bowl and Anna watched in bemusement as he started lapping it like a cat.

"Tuck! Marian!" came a familiar voice. Anna's eyes started to adjust, and she realised there was a deeper cavern beyond. The random pile of wood was just a shield against the wind, Brother Walter's hermitage was the cave.

"Little John!" said Tuck. "Where be our prize-winning archer?"

Rob stepped out of the gloom looking coy. "Hi," he said quietly. He looked at Anna who wondered whether to hug him, slap him or both. Again. He cracked a grin. She was definitely going to slap him.

"See y' put the maid in Maid Marian," he said, looking at her pinafore and bonnet.

"See you're still alive," said Anna sourly, "More than I expected after your cocky stunt."

"Still got arrow?" he asked.

"Only so I can beat you with it."

"Time to go," said Tuck diplomatically. "Brother Walter has taken a vow of silence. I doubt he wishes to listen to a lover's tiff."

Anna's face was thunder, but Tuck guided her gently back out through the gap in the logs. Little John followed and Rob came after, using John as shelter from Anna's gathering storm.

The Rivers Leen and Trent, Nottingham, 1214

Tuck led them where the river fanned out and slipped between rocks in rivulets. They hopped from stone to stone across the cascades or scrambled through ankle deep water. On the far side they poured mud out of their boots and dried their feet on a fistful of leaves. They followed him again, threading between pools of black water and rushes, to reach a much wider river, the Trent. Its silver waters flickered in the pale winter sun. Anna saw many row boats and a few with sails. Few passed their stretch of river because most stopped in the pools at the foot of the city walls where they moored and offloaded their wares. It occurred to Anna that medieval rivers were as busy as modern roads and served as well to connect towns to each other. Even other lands.

Tuck searched the bank until he found a pile of branches that he lifted away. Underneath was a crude little paddle boat made of animal skins stretched over wooden spars. He dragged it down the bank and slid it in where it bobbed around on the water like a cork. "Get in," he waved.

They looked at it doubtfully. It barely looked capable of carrying one person, let alone four. "I think I may take my chances at the bridge," said Little John who could have filled it all himself.

"Gisborne has men on the bridge," said Tuck. "They be looking for ye. Get in or swim."

"Ye know I cannot swim," said Little John, testily.

"Then get in," said Tuck. Little John frowned and stepped awkwardly into the tiny boat which rocked madly. "Sit down in the middle and stop rocking it," said Tuck.

"The boat rocks, not me!" complained Little John.

"Ye rock it. Place your weight in the middle. Good, see? Now it hath stopped." His passenger clung to the edges and gritted his teeth. "I will paddle ye across and come back for Robin and Marian. They be smaller and make less fuss."

Little John would have complained again but gripped the boat, knuckles white, while Tuck climbed in. The brother was surprisingly nimble and sure footed for a man of girth. Rob and Anna watched as the two of them paddled for the far bank, Little John muttering thinly veiled threats under his breath and Tuck telling him to stop whining.

"Just like an old couple having a tiff," smirked Rob.

Anna gave Rob a look that was calibrated to burn the smirk off his lips. "You have nothing to laugh at. If you're found, Gisborne will hang you."

"If," said Rob.

"And likely he'll hang Little John and me for helping you."

Rob stopped smirking. "Sorry."

"What the hell were you thinking? This isn't some folktale, Rob. There are real soldiers with real swords trying to find us and kill us!"

Rob turned away; his shoulders hunched forward in that defensive stance he took when the world was against him. Anna's own shoulders slumped. She did not want to fight with Rob and she hated seeing him cower. Yet he had been incredibly stupid. It didn't help that she was dressed as a maid, she almost felt like hitting someone just to vent her frustration.

She could see Tuck returning in his boat out the corner of her eye. He weaved expertly between a pair of low slung barges being poled by their boaters.

"Your turn," Tuck's smile faded as he sensed the tension on the riverbank. "It be done and cannot be changed. Robin wanted ye to have the arrow, Marian, and ye deserve it far more than Annabel de Ferrer. Now get in."

Anna muttered an apology and lowered herself carefully into the boat opposite Tuck. Rob looked sideways as if wondering whether he should get in too.

"I'm not sorry," he said. "One time in my life I achieved something. Just one time. I weren't going to give it to someone mardy an' stuck up like her."

"I know," said Tuck, surprising both Rob and Anna with his understanding. "I should have foreseen it, but I did not. Now get in so I can hide ye." He cast his eyes around, watching for soldiers.

Rob slipped in beside Anna without looking at her. The two spent the crossing pretending the other one wasn't there. Anna felt sorry for Tuck who silently paddled his troublesome passengers to safety. At the far bank he helped them ashore but stayed in the boat. "Little John knows the way from here," said Tuck. "I am needed at the hospital."

"Take this," said Rob who held out the prize purse to Tuck. "Gi' it to them that needs it."

"Thank ye," smiled Tuck. "Ye have a good heart, Robin Hood. And Maid Marian has a good head on her shoulders. Between ye, ye may yet survive." He looked about for soldiers and pushed away.

The Village of Gotham, Nottinghamshire, 1214

Little John led them along dirt tracks, between empty fields and a scattering of farm cottages. A cold wind whipped across the open ground and Anna pulled her maid's shawl tight. They spent half an hour climbing a gentle incline, another half an hour on the far side descending, and all the while they watched for pursuers.

The land rose to their right, into a wooded hill. They caught the smell of woodsmoke before they saw the village. The houses were tiny, the eaves so low that Anna could touch the thatch without reaching past her head. In the centre was an open patch of dirt with a shabby chapel dedicated to Saint Lawrence, a mud wall around a well, a tiny timber tavern and a fenced in hawthorn bush. A blackbird came to perch on the fence then flew away as they approached.

Anna jumped at movement, but it was only an old man limping out of the tavern. He saw the three of them and bowed deeply.

"Welcome to Gotham," he said. "What be ourn be yorn, and half of nothing be nothing." He tapped the side of his nose in a conspiratorial way. Without waiting for a reply, he hobbled to the well half dragging his right leg. He pulled on a rope to raise a pitcher of water and poured the contents on the ground. Then he picked up a walking staff leaning against the mud wall, placed it under his arm beside his good leg, and half hopped, half stumbled down the lane.

Rob shook his head.

"Did he..." started Anna. "Shouldn't he have... Is he drunk?"

"No," said Little John.

The man hopped to a cottage, fifty paces down the lane, stopped and put the staff by his bad leg. He pushed the door open and walked in far more comfortably than he had reached it.

"He be one of them wise men," said John.

"What's wise about throwing water on the ground and using a walking stick for the wrong leg?" asked Anna reasonably.

"Ye will see," said Little John who took them to a little house beyond the chapel. A middle-aged woman with brown hair in a bun and a stained apron opened the door, looked up and down the lane as if to check if anyone had followed, then beckoned them in.

"I be Edith, I were told to expect ye. My husband, Edwin be mending the harrow but will return for supper at sunset. Sit y'usen down and I will fetch a little bread and ale."

"Edith seems normal," whispered Anna quietly to Little John.

"Edith is not normal," he replied. "Like most in Gotham, she be uncommonly clever."

They spent the rest of the afternoon chatting to Edith who asked all about the archery contest, had guessed Rob was the winner and that the three of them were on the run from Gisborne's men. She was particularly interested in Rob.

"I met folk from Arabia at market," she said. "Some o' them settled here with little 'uns. Good to have a few Nottingham folk who make other travellers feel welcome." She carried on talking about the crusades and what a waste of people's lives they had been.

Later Edith explained she knew Ruth and was aware that Anna had been the one who saved Ruth from the fire. "One good turn deserves another," she said as she scrubbed and chopped a table full of parsnips, turnips, and leeks to put into a stew.

Edwin arrived, tired from his repairs in the barn. He smiled warmly and shook their hands. He seemed happy to let his wife continue leading the conversation and sat back on an old wooden chair, watching them. The vegetable stew was simple, tasty, and filling. The candle on the parlour table burned low and one by one they found a corner of the kitchen to put their heads down and wrap a fur across themselves for the night.

The same strange dream revisited Anna. The sensation of floating, looking up to the light and back down into the depths. Only this time the depths did not seem so dark. An indigo glow suffused the space between the shadows which shifted around her. Some shadows seemed familiar, some threatening, many more unknown. Again she found a rod in her hand and allowed the sinuous line to reel her in like a willing catch. Again it made no sense.

At dawn they woke to the sound of hooves clattering on frost hardened ground. Anna sat up with a start, had they been discovered by Gisborne?

"Stay here," Edith said and put on a tattered brown cloak and wooden clogs to go out. John, Rob and Anna peered through the cracks in the shutters at the riders. Half a dozen knights wore plate armour and carried a variety of brightly coloured shields slung over their backs. Anna shivered; had they been betrayed?

Edith curtseyed, twirled herself around like a drunken dancer then swayed as if her head was still spinning. "Ye be welcome to Gotham, good sirs," she faltered in an uncertain voice. "And indeed, ye all be welcome to it, such as it be." She waved an arm towards the random huddle of cottages and the decaying chapel.

The first knight eyed her as if it were not just her body that was unbalanced. "I am de Blondeville, these are my knights," he gestured to the other five. "We seek suitable accommodation for when our lord and king travels north, later this year." Anna felt the knot of fear unwind a notch, they weren't here on Gisborne's business, yet they were still a threat.

"King Richard? *Here*?" answered Edith getting flustered.

"King John. His elder brother Richard be dead these last fifteen years."

"Dead? The king be dead? Oh, sweet Lord protect us," and she capered in circles like a dog chasing its tail.

"Calm yourself, woman. The king be John and most definitely alive."

At this point Edwin blundered out in his bare feet to join the pantomime. "Dead? The King be dead?"

"The king be dead, and he looks for food and lodging," answered Edith.

"Sweet lord," exclaimed Edwin, "we have no place fit for dead kings here," and started to pull at his hair.

"Stop!" called de Blondeville. "Just show me to the inn."

Edwin held Edith to stop her swaying, their understanding seemed like a reluctant candle catching light. They wandered in the direction of the tavern then paused, beckoning the knights follow, as if only just remembering them. Anna risked pushing the shutters out a little so she could watch.

She couldn't hear, but the innkeeper looked utterly bewildered by the visitors. She saw Edith wave her arms again and guessed she was telling him about dead kings. The innkeeper threw his hands up then bolted back inside, leaving the knights outside. De Blondeville turned to his companions for an exchange which involved much shaking of heads and shrugging of shoulders. The knights evidently decided not to waste any more time in Gotham and left.

Edwin held Edith's hand as she wobbled, and her arms moved around her head like fronds of seaweed caught by the ebb and flow of the tides. After a couple of minutes her hands dropped to her sides. She knocked on the tavern door, talked to the innkeeper then hurried back to the cottage with Edwin.

"That hath seen them off," said Edith.

"No need to tell them of the cuckoo fence," said Edwin.

"What's a cuckoo fence?" asked Anna, suspecting she would regret it.

"If unwelcome guests be slow to get the message, we tell them of the fence we put around the hawthorn bush," explained Edith, while she stooped over the fireplace to clear it. "We tell how the cuckoo comes when summer starts and how sensible we are to put a fence around the bush to stop it from leaving. That way we get to enjoy summer all year round." She looked at Rob and Anna's blank faces. Little John was trying not to laugh. "Course it never works. Little bugger flies over the fence."

Anna now realised the people of Gotham were not only wise, but gifted clowns who put on a show every time some official turned up looking to drain their meagre resources in the name of the king. She wondered how many everyday folks played their lords and masters for fools and smiled.

"Course, ye better not be here when the king comes this way," said Edith as she lit the kindling with a deft flick of flint on flint. "If ye takes that long to catch on ye will give our game away."

Wills

Shire Wood, Nottinghamshire, 1214

Crows cawed. Sun speckled a drift of dry grey leaves. Anna's breath froze, hanging in the air in front of her mouth. The boughs of the pine trees drooped low over her head, crowding the sky and closing her in once more. Her first encounter with the great Shire Wood had been in fear, yet she ended up taking shelter there. They now sought that same shelter again and the forest no longer threatened Anna in the same way. Yet she was still afraid. She still found the gloom under the feral foliage disturbing. But she was beginning to understand that it was a refuge as well as wilderness.

They had followed Little John north from the country lanes that skirted the city into ever smaller tracks that became engulfed by bowers. Now they walked further and further from manmade paths, deep into the forest. Ever since they re-entered the Shire Wood she had started at every fox bark, flinched at every pigeon that took sudden flight. Distant screeches from hidden prey made her shudder. She tried to copy the way Little John carefully placed each step to diminish the sound, but it tired her, watching between shadows and her feet.

A branch cracked noisily, and she recoiled, eyes darting among the tree trunks. Little John froze and motioned for them to stand still while he listened. Nothing but the crows. He led on again, weaving between pines, steering them onto their muffling carpet of needles. Anna was just finding her stride again, when she noticed Little John had stopped abruptly in front of her. Looking beyond, she saw a tall, well-built man leaning against a fir tree, a bow slung over his shoulder. She gasped. Rob crouched, snatching an arrow to his bow.

"Blinder!" exclaimed Little John. Anna saw his eye patch and recognised him from the archery contest.

"Afternoon!" said Master Stutely quietly, still inclined against the trunk.

"Come to challenge Mamsūh to another contest?" asked Little John.

"Mamsūh won fair and square," said Blinder, talking so quietly they were obliged to draw nearer. "Never seen shooting like it and never will I forget it." He nodded behind them, "Neither will Fitzooth." Anna and the others tensed at the mention of Gisborne's Head Forester and looked about. "I suggest ye walk with me to yonder thicket," he gestured with a tilt of his bald head. "And redirect your bow, if ye will."

Rob lowered his bow but kept the arrow ready. They followed Stutely into the thicket of dense holly and crouched, looking back the way they had come. "Wait," whispered Stutely. "He be near."

"Fitzooth?" asked Anna.

"Aye, and his foresters," murmured Stutely. "Four in all."

"There," hissed Rob. Anna strained to see what he was pointing at. "And there," he swung his hand across left.

"Where?" Anna could only see trees. It was not the first time she had struggled to see what he did.

Stutely strung his bow and Little John hefted a long branch to wield.

"Take the two on the right," Stutely whispered to Rob, "I will take the pair to the left." Rob looked worried. "I saw ye shoot, Mamsūh, yet ye fret?"

"Yeah but... I don't want to kill them," he muttered.

"Noble," answered Stutely. "They have no such worry about killing ye."

"Don't like killing."

"With such an aim, ye need not kill."

Understanding dawned on Rob's face, who raised his bow at the pair on the right. Anna could just see them now, creeping from the trees. A whip of the bowstring and a rush of air followed by a yelp of pain from one of the men who clutched his leg. Three more arrows sang out in succession, Blinder and Rob found their marks each time. Three more cries followed. There was cawing of crows and low groans.

"They will live," said Stutely, standing.

"If a boar does not find them," said Little John.

"At least they have a chance," muttered Rob, as if to excuse himself.

"And so will we, if we move quicker than they hobble," said Blinder.

"Suppose ye better follow us," said Little John.

"Suppose I had," smiled Blinder.

They pushed their way through the far side of the holly, spiked leaves scratching at their arms and faces. Anna cursed the wretched milk maid's clothing she wore as it snagged on every branch. They picked up a gentle jog through the dense woodland beyond, trusting to Little John's sense of direction.

"Will Stutely at your service," he offered a hand to Rob who shook it firmly.

"Rob. And this is Marian," he said nodding at Anna, who rolled her eyes and offered her hand to Will.

"Mamsūh is not your real name?"

"My father's."

"Ah, that makes sense. Fitzooth and his men have been following ye from the forest edge. It be fortunate I were watching, or ye would have led them to the village."

"You know of it?"

"I am a regular guest."

"And a welcome one," added Little John. "He be one of ours, Will keeps an eye out for us all."

"But only the one," smiled Will.

"What happened to the other?" asked Anna.

"A forester's arrow." Anna winced. Will shrugged. "He did not kill me. And the foresters still do not know who tracks them."

"Which is why you could compete without being recognised," realised Anna.

"I can see well enough through one eye, maybe better as I have less distraction."

Anna reflected again that Rob must have exceptional eyesight. She considered hers to be good, but she hadn't seen the foresters until well after Rob had spotted them. It was no accident he could shoot so well.

Hidden Village, Shire Wood, Nottinghamshire, 1214

A flood of relief washed through Anna crossing the threshold of Little John's cottage again. Ruth welcomed them and sat them down with a steaming bowl of rabbit stew each. The wood fire drove away the shivers, so Anna loosened her shawl. This was as near to home as she had felt for years and clearly Rob felt the same way. His shoulders no longer hunched, and he smiled easily, listening as John told Ruth of the contest, their flight to the hermitage and on to Gotham. Will Stutely told how he had tracked the foresters and of Rob' merciful shooting.

Ruth regarded Rob, and Anna saw respect in her eyes. She also found herself nagged again by Ruth's familiarity. She had dismissed it when she learned Ruth was one of the children she saved from the fire, but that did not explain what Anna felt now. It was as if she had seen Ruth's face before, the same feeling she experienced with Beatrice's mother and the lace makers' serving girl. Anna had roamed so many ages that it was a challenge to picture the faces, but she felt sure she had seen Ruth's before (or later). It was infuriating. A fragment of knowledge that hovered on the edge of knowing. Normally people would talk about 'déja vu', but Anna's difficulty was working out whether she had seen before or after. Time did not flow in a straight line for Anna, it was strewn about in a chaos of loose pages.

"... isn't that right, Marian? Marian?" Little John repeated. Anna was slow to recognise her medieval name.

"Sorry, I was miles away." Miles or years?

"Robin's shot that won the contest. It pushed Fitzooth's arrow from the bull. I swear if it were a fraction further over it would have split his arrow in half!"

"Gisborne wasn't happy," remembered Anna.

Little John roared with laughter, "Happy! First time I seen him look unhappier than de Ferrer's daughter!"

Anna turned to glare at Rob whose smirk wilted.

"Oh, come on, Marian," cajoled Little John, "It were funny".

"We are hunted now," she said.

"Not since Will and Robin's shooting today."

"That won't stop them sending others."

"Let them come. They been looking for this village for years and not found it."

"Because Will stood guard and headed them away."

"Yes, Will and others who take their turn and right grateful we are too," he patted Will Stutely on the back.

"It can't last," said Anna, feeling bad for dismissing small victories.

"Nothing lasts," said Ruth. "So we enjoy it as we can."

"Well said my love," agreed Little John.

"Take some ale," said Ruth to Anna. "Hits you hard first time: finding y'usen outside law. But we muddle through."

'Muddle through', mused Anna. Who else did she know who would say that? She wracked her memory for people who might look or sound like Ruth. She took a long swig from the skin that Ruth gave her and passed it on to Rob. "Here, drink this and don't start another muddle." He barely pressed the skin to his lips and passed it straight on. Anna frowned at Rob, "You okay?"

He gave a curt nod and looked away.

Anna was relieved to wake and look out again on the misty hidden village. The other Will, the one they met on the morning before the contest, approached their door and knocked. He was young and red-haired with an open freckled face.

"Morning Master Gamely," said Ruth. "Your turn today?"

"Aye," he answered. "Thought I might ask Little John and Blinder about yesterday afore I go."

Ruth invited Will Gamely inside where he sat down with Will Stutely and John. Blinder explained where he had found the foresters and how long he had tracked them before catching up with the others. "Young Marian be right, of course," Blinder looked at Anna then back to Will Gamely. "Gisborne will send more. Ye should search the southern edge of the Wood for them."

"Can I come?" asked Rob.

"Dangerous," said Little John. "Ye be Nottinghamshire's most wanted man."

"Makes a change," shrugged Rob.

"That's not a good thing," said Anna.

"I can shoot," he said.

"No one will argue that!" said Blinder. "Perhaps he could come? Perhaps a few more well-placed shots may make the huntsmen cautious. Give us space to breathe."

Little John seemed to weigh both arguments then nodded. "Robin needs no target practise today, except the kind Gisborne's men will offer him."

"Come then," said Will Gamely. "Fetch bow and follow me."

"Hey! What about me?" asked Anna.

"Come too," suggested Rob.

"No," said Little John firmly. Anna was about to argue but Ruth cut in.

"Perhaps Marian may practise the bow today, ready for another time."

Anna was less offended by this compromise. Little John agreed to spend a few hours teaching her in the morning. Ruth took over in the afternoon and she proved to be a very capable archer in her own right. More patient than John. After many shots which hit the ground short of the target, Anna started to understand how an arrow would fall over distance. The further the target the higher she needed to aim to compensate. She also began to understand how a breeze would carry an arrow downwind. She wanted to wait for the air to still, but Ruth insisted she learn to compensate for that as well.

By the end of the day Anna could hit the target consistently with every arrow in her quiver and felt rightly proud. Her goal for the next day would be to place all shots in one of the inner rings. Little John came to watch and said he was impressed.

"Ruth's a good teacher," said Anna.

"I am not?" he feigned injury.

"You're a fearsome fighter," she tried diplomatically.

"Ye have yet to see Ruth fight," laughed John. Anna suspected there was truth spoken in jest. "Come, it be supper time. Robin and Will Gamely will be gone a few days, so there be time for ye to impress them when they return."

For almost a week Anna worked hard on her archery skills. She went from hitting tree trunks to rabbits and Ruth showed her how to skin and cook them. She learned to cut firewood, make a fire using a flint and search for edible mushrooms. Anna was also grateful for the chance to know her host better. As they sat by the hearth one morning, Anna asked Ruth how she came to be living hidden deep within the Shire Wood.

She sat still, staring at the flames for a while before answering. "My aunt. My mother's sister, Edith, died in de Ferrer's castle. She were flogged to death."

Anna baulked, "What had she done?"

"Gisborne's soldiers came to collect her taxes. It had been a poor harvest and a long winter, so she had little to give. They shouted at her. Pushed her. She pushed back…"

Anna had no idea what to say. Instead she put her hand on Ruth's until she was able to say more.

"De Ferrer told Gisborne to make an example of her. He didn't want the people of Nottingham to think they could question his authority. I wanted to kill him. But John held me till I stopped crying. Said he were lucky, that he'd been held in the castle and lived to tell the tale. Warned me keep away from it and told me there was more 'n one way to fight back. Then he took me here, to the hidden village. Taught me to hunt with a bow."

"But you still go into the city?"

"Yes. No one knows I live here. Except my mother, and she don't know where 'here' is."

"You still see her?"

"Yes, I visit. I bring her game we've hunted in the forest. Helps her make ends meet. We do it for as many as we can without getting caught by Fitzooth and the other huntsmen. It helps keep Tuck's kitchen going at the hospital."

Anna was beginning to understand what a precarious balance life in medieval Nottingham was. "I expect your mother misses Edith."

"Both do. I were fond of her. I used to tell her she were my favourite aunt. Truth was, she were my only aunt."

"I have a favourite and only aunt. Or at least I did."

Ruth looked at her, "What do ye mean, 'did?'"

"I've been hunting for her for months. I can't find her."

"Hope she isn't in De Ferrer's castle."

"I doubt that."

Anna was wondering whether she would ever see her aunt Jane again when Will Gamely returned, looking as if he had been dragged through a holly bush, panic in his eyes.

"Where's Rob?" asked Anna, heart in mouth.

Will stood before her, mute, on the edge of tears.

"Sit down, tell us what happened," said Ruth calmly, taking his hand.

Little John appeared in the doorway behind Will, frowning.

"It were going so well," explained Will. "I were teaching him woodcraft. How to hide, how to track..." Ruth waited patiently. Anna wanted to shake it from him but held back. "We saw pair of young 'uns in chains, led by one of Gisborne's men. Thought we could help. It were trap."

"A trap? There were others?" asked Ruth.

Will nodded. Shame and frustration written across his face. "Rob put an arrow in soldier's leg. He went ahead of me to free the children... Dozens more came from all 'round. They seized Rob. They're heading for castle."

Chase

Shire Wood, Nottinghamshire, 1214

Little John's easy manner fled. His eyes narrowed as he and Ruth questioned Will Gamely, working out where the trap had been sprung. Will said it was due east of the hidden village on the York Road. It had taken him about an hour to find his way back. If they left quickly, with enough people they might intercept the soldiers before they reached the castle.

"The castle," repeated Little John darkly. Ruth looked sideways at him and placed her hand on his as if to soothe an old wound. He scowled just as he had when he was held there overnight with Anna and Rob.

Will explained that Rob had been chained to a cart, so they would only be able to travel as fast as they could pull it. He had seen no horses. Anna fervently hoped they could catch them. Once inside the castle there would be little hope of a rescue, the expression on their faces told her that, even if she hadn't been an unwilling guest herself.

Little John organised two parties of a dozen each to leave immediately, one led by Blinder and one by him. Each would follow a different route to the point where the York Road emerged from the southern edge of the Shire Wood. The plan was to converge on Gisborne's men from two sides, just before they left the cover of the forest. John was too busy giving orders to notice that Ruth and Anna had picked up bows and were following Blinder's party.

"Hope ye will not put me in trouble with Little John," asked Will Stutely when he saw them jogging along at the edge of his group.

"Never mind us," said Ruth. "We be here to make sure John avoids trouble."

Blinder chuckled and led them on. He set a blistering pace which Anna would not have managed a week before. After days of wood cutting and gathering in the forest, she felt a good deal fitter. Though she cursed at the low branches which whipped across her shins and face and learned to keep a healthy gap between her and the person in front. Was she fitter, Anna wondered? Had she a physical body here in the thirteenth century that was building strength?

Anna had been wondering how her strange ability worked. The mechanics were important to her. She did not believe in magic even though she had lived with a talent that seemed magical almost every day of her life. She wanted some rational, scientific explanation for it. While she had only observed the past she had wondered if she possessed an insight into some shared human memory. Her body went nowhere, while perhaps her mind floated freely, surfing the recollections of others. But now she was taking part in the past she must look for a new explanation. It was no longer easy to say it was all in her mind when she was carrying coins back from the past. Did her body exist in two different times at once, or did it disappear from the twentieth century and re-emerge in the thirteenth? Was it possible to for her body to shift in time or had she taken on some other phantom form? Anna had no easy answers, but what kept her sane was knowing that someone else could do it too. She would not let Rob be taken from her.

They kept the pace for miles, pausing only for the briefest of moments to draw breath and check their whereabouts. Anna felt torn between her desires to rest and keep chasing. Daylight was fading, and she guessed it must be mid-afternoon, given the November sun set so early. Now she had a new worry that Gisborne's men would slip past them in the dark.

Anna was struggling now, despite her new fitness. Blinder stopped them with a signal from his upheld hand, and Anna slumped forward, hands on knees, grateful for a chance to rest. She noticed the others fanning out either side of her.

"We have reached the road," whispered Ruth. "Stay with me."

Anna nodded, drawing deep breaths. She could see no sign of the road. She would have to rely on Ruth and Will Stutely's better knowledge of the woods. All was silent apart from the birdsong. Not a sound from the dozen hunters who had faded into the foliage like forest sprites. The only person she could see was Ruth who crouched beside a clump of ferns. Anna crouched too. Where was Little John and his party, she wondered? Were they first to arrive? Had Gisborne's men already passed taking Rob to the castle?

She felt guilty for bringing Rob here. It was naïve of her to think they could just muddle along in this dangerous medieval world. Sure, the hidden village might be safe, but the woods were stalked by Gisborne's hunters, gamekeepers, and soldiers. She should have told Rob not to go with Will. She should never have brought him here.

A fox barked. Or was it a fox? Was it the signal that Little John's men had used when they came to the rescue before, by the little wooden bridge? Another bark, this time close by. Had Blinder answered?

The minutes passed, or so Anna guessed. She had no watch, no phone, no means of measuring time. What use would a watch be when her journeys spanned centuries? What awkward questions would a phone raise? It had never occurred to her, until the episode with the coins, that she could attempt to carry objects with her from the twenty-first century. They had carried a sandwich to Little John and his family in their moment of need. Why not something else? Something that would give them a clear advantage over the more dangerous people of medieval Nottinghamshire. It grieved Anna that her first thought was a gun, though given her current need it did not surprise her. She hated herself for thinking it. Besides the obvious question of how to find one, what kind of mess might that cause if she brought one to this time? No. No guns. But what?

A fox call, then another. What was happening? Voices, some way off. Could it be Gisborne's men? Were they in time to save Rob? The voices grew louder, nearer. Another fox-call. "Get ready," whispered Ruth. Anna fumbled for the slung bow and nocked an arrow. Her hands shook. Ruth rose slowly, silently, bow held ready. Anna rose too, breath coming in short rasps. Movement only thirty yards away. Oh god, would she have to shoot someone? Kill them? She didn't have Rob's choices; she didn't have his aim.

A flicker at the corner of her eye. A twang from Ruth's bow, echoed by others. The air pierced by arrows. Cries of pain. Shock; hers and theirs. A horn-blast. Shouts, clattering shields, swords slid from scabbards. Another flight of arrows. More cries. Anna hadn't even drawn her bowstring. Soldiers drew back, formed a circle of shields. Where was Rob? More arrows, more shouts.

"Come," beckoned Ruth. Anna ran after her, stumbling over bracken. Roots grabbed at her. Yells, sharp clashes of steel on steel. Green hooded figures emerged all around, some leaping at the soldiers. Swords swung, daggers flashed, a long wood staff swiped down. Little John. The circle of shields broke into a confusion of struggles. There! Rob, chained to a cart, tugging at his shackles. Anna ran.

A huge man in chain mail stepped before her, raising a six-foot sword. Any other would have used two hands, not him. Anna skidded to a halt, bow raised and loosed before thinking. A grunt of pain. An arrow shaft pierced the man's right forearm, forcing him to drop the massive sword. Anna dodged around him and leaped onto the cart.

"Here!" shouted Ruth tossing her a small wood cutters axe, then plunged her dagger into the big man's thigh, bringing him to his knees.

"Put your hands out!" Anna yelled.

Rob looked confused. She pulled his chain to the side of the cart and swung the axe before he had time to flinch. A sharp ring and sparks. Rob fell back, the chain cut. A week cutting firewood, thought Anna, now this. She grabbed Rob's arm and jumped from the cart.

"Down!" yelled Ruth. They dropped to their knees; a whoosh of air crossed their heads. Anna looked around, another soldier with a sword took a backswing. Rob thrust his wrists up and caught the blow on the manacles. He cried out in pain.

The soldier pulled back for another swing. Anna dragged Rob up to run. Little John barged into the soldier, so the swing went wide, then tackled him to the ground. Anna and Rob ran. And ran. And ran.

It was fully dark when they stopped on a rocky outcrop, at the edge of a stream. Panting, shaking with fear and exhaustion. They had no idea where they were and could not hear anything other than the hoot of an owl. Anna glimpsed the half disc of the Moon through the lattice of dark branches overhead.

Rob's hands were still shackled together, the cut end of the chain dangled from them. There was blood around his wrists. Anna tore off a strip of cloth from the edge of her cloak, soaked it in the stream and dabbed the blood away before wrapping it tightly over the wound. After scooping some water with her hands, she lay down next to Rob. Her breathing started to slow. Rob leaned in and rested his head against her chest. She cradled him, resting her back against a tree trunk. Where were they? They had run too far, too deep into the forest, into the darkness. Lost.

Something gave a long tortured howl in the distance. A wolf? Someone suffering? Anna was both scared and drained. Her instinct told her to be ready to flee, yet her body would not obey. She felt her head droop and her eyes flutter. She knew they should be seeking help, but she couldn't focus anymore.

Between Times

The Arboretum, Nottingham, November 2019

Darkness. Anna woke freezing, damp, and hungry, with every muscle in her body rebelling. Rob still rested his head on her chest, murmuring softly. He seemed to hover between sleeping and waking. A noise nagged her ears, distracting yet familiar. Traffic.

When she tried to get up, she found the ground rocky and uneven. She slipped and there was a splosh as her foot disappeared into water. Dim light filtered through trees from the street about fifty yards away and she could see a shimmer of reflections on water all around them. Where the hell were they? On a rock in a pool?

It was night and car engines grumbled from the road beyond. How long had they been there? Rob muttered again. She looked down and saw his wrists bound by iron shackles, a strip of green cloth and dripping blood. How long had he been lying there bleeding? She panicked, staggered to her feet, braced against the rock, and yelled for help. She shouted and shouted but no one replied.

Rob curled up on the stones, shivering. Anna knelt to cradle him, hugging him to her for warmth.

"Help! Please *help*!"

She could just see distant figures walking the pavement beyond, but no one stopped. No one seemed to hear her. The sharp chill of an idea froze her: had they become ghosts? Had they slipped from the twenty-first century as life slips from a cadaver?

"HELP! HELP ME!" she screamed, wiping her face with her cuff. Her green cloak cuff that Ruth had given her. Rob was still in his, so were they in medieval Sherwood looking at modern Nottingham? Had they fallen into some hidden place between times? Why could no one hear her?

"HELP!"

Would she have to swim and pull Rob through the water? She could swim but was afraid that Rob might sink. What if she left him to fetch help? Would they even see her? Would he bleed to death before she got back? If she got back.

Oh god, oh god, what had they done? Would Rob die? Would they both die here? Were they dead already?

"Hey? Are you okay?" a voice shouted from the edge of the pool. Thank you, thank you.

"Please, help! We're stuck. My friend is bleeding."

"Stay there," a young guy and his mate. "We'll calling for help," he was already dialling. "Erm, ambulance... Couple stuck in the middle of the pool at the Arboretum off Waverley Street, so Fire Brigade as well, I guess. One of them 's hurt... Don't know. Screw it, send the police as well, send the lot!"

Queens Medical Centre, Nottingham, November 2019

"Back again?"

"Huh?" Anna rubbed her eyes and tried to sit. The room swam and she slumped.

"Take it easy dear, you're still dehydrated."

A familiar smiling black face, "It's you."

"Yes, me, your own personal nurse, Christine Lamwaka. Your knight in shiny plastic apron."

"Where's Rob?"

"Your friend is in the next ward. Treated him just in time, close to hypothermia, he was. He'll be fine. Tougher than he looks that one."

"Thank you."

"No problem. Just don't do it again, whatever it was you were doing and it's no business of mine but... damn, what were you both doing on a rock in the Arboretum pool? And why did he have chains on his wrists?"

"It's not, you know..."

"Don't worry, I've seen it all sweetheart. Handcuffs, hamsters, hoover attachments stuck where the sun don't shine. Nothing embarrasses me."

"No, it really isn't, I mean..." oh god, where should she start?

"It's the rock in the middle of the pool bit that fascinates me. Have you any idea how many firemen it took to get you both off? And policemen? And paramedics?"

"We were looking for shelter."

"Couldn't have found anywhere more exposed! Enough for your friend to get close to hypothermia."

"We had nowhere else to go," not quite true and she could tell that Christine wasn't buying it.

"Good job I phoned Hope House for you. They tell me you don't need to go swimming or rock climbing; they have dry beds on the first floor."

"Thank you, you..."

"Shouldn't have, yes I know, but I can't help myself. I wouldn't mind if you told me how he got that cut on his wrist though. I'm no expert, but I doubt he cut it on the chains."

Anna was at a loss so tried the truth, "Sword cut from a knight who wasn't as shiny as you?"

"Nice one, dear. I'll add it to my list. Drink this water and get some more rest. I'm off soon but my friend, Sasha will take care of you until I get back tomorrow. Then we'll get one of the consultants to check you over and see if you're ready to go."

Christine walked off shaking her head, as well she might, thought Anna. Her knight in shining armour: that's who Christine was.

Despite Christine's order to rest, Anna slipped out of her bed and went to look for Rob. She needed to see him. Check he was okay. Check he still existed at the same time and place as her.

So Anna was distressed to find his bed empty.

The tag beside the bed read Rob Ahmed. Either he had left or someone had the tags mixed up. She wandered the men's wards looking for him. Most people ignored her, as if she were a ghost wandering the corridors in a parallel dimension. A few glanced absently at her then returned their vacant stares to the ceiling. There was no sign of Rob.

Anna returned to the bed with his name tag and sat in the visitors' chair beside it. Perhaps he had gone to the toilet. She described Rob to a passing nurse to check this was the right bed. He nodded when she mentioned his wiry frame and Middle Eastern features. But he shrugged his shoulders when she asked where he'd gone and told her to go back to her own bed. She pretended to leave then did a U-turn as he moved on to the next ward.

It was late. The usual chaos had subsided a little while some patients tried to sleep. Anna slumped back in the chair and closed her eyes against the electric lights. She realised she had become accustomed to the gentle glow of candles and camp fires. Artificial light jarred by comparison.

She had not expected to fall asleep but when she woke it was still dark outside. Perhaps an hour or so had passed. She looked to her side and found Rob asleep on the bed, on top of the sheets. Anna breathed a long sigh of relief. He looked slight and vulnerable, curled up on his side like he had been on the rock in the pool. If she hadn't been in the hospital, she would have slipped in beside him and held him. Instead she pulled the edge of the sheets over to cover his shoulder then left to find her own bed.

She felt much stronger the following day and went to look for Rob again. The nurses weren't keen on their patients going walkabout to other wards, but she wasn't in a mood to ask permission. She found Rob still asleep in more or less the same position she'd left him. She wanted to hug him but felt embarrassed by onlookers. Instead, she sat on the edge of his bed and took his hand. She sat there a long time. Plenty of time to think.

Anna thought about the people they had met. Little John, Ruth, Tuck, the Will's Stutely and Gamely, Edith and Edwin, Mary at the Salutation and Brother Walter in his hermitage. Perhaps they were the work of her imagination, sparked by folktales. But they had all seemed real to her, and Rob. They had become friends. She could still picture Little John's smile and hear Ruth's soothing voice. They were everyday people to Anna, not legends nor ghosts, but genuine and fallible. The memories of real people from long ago.

She considered the length of time they had spent in medieval Nottingham against the time that passed in the present. The present was a tricky thing for Anna, it was whenever she was, so she decided she would call the twenty-first century 'modern day', not 'the present'. She had worked out that two November days had passed in the modern day, while she was sure they had spent well over two weeks in medieval Nottingham. What did that mean? Was their adventure there a dream where you imagined the passing of weeks or months in a night? If so, then how could she explain the chains on Rob's wrists? Or the hooded green cloaks they brought back with them. Hers was carefully folded in a plastic NHS bag in the locker by her bed. She opened the cabinet door beside Rob's bed and found his cloak in another bag. She had never brought souvenirs back while using her ability in London and, as far as she was aware, she hadn't sleepwalked into a fancy-dress store.

A hallucination? Caused by what? She had been sober for every trip back in time. She hadn't been high and neither had she seen Rob take anything. In fact, she suspected Rob was teetotal and might have a similar attitude to drugs. Had anyone given them something dodgy without them knowing? Not unless Jamaal slipped uppers in among their chips and that seemed even more unlikely. But what about all the recent times she had talked to and touched people from the past? She had never done that before. She had looked, but she hadn't touched. Not until she came to Nottingham. Not until after she met Rob.

She looked at Rob, sleeping, hunched into that defensive curled up ball like a hedgehog. She had only known him a month. She had only begun to understand him in medieval Nottingham, over the past two weeks (days?) He infuriated her and endeared her in equal measure. She remembered his face when he brought her the golden arrow, so proud yet so desperate to be acknowledged. She realised how much he seemed to need her praise and yet she had scorned him for his stupidity and recklessness. She squeezed his hand and he murmured something. She leaned in closer and heard him whisper her name. Something inside her fell away. Some great rampart she had tirelessly constructed to protect herself had been remade with a little door that swung open. Did she care about him? Obviously. Did she love him? She wasn't sure because she had never really fallen in love before.

She drew up a chair and sat with her head resting on the pillow beside Rob's, holding his hand. She considered how well he fitted life in medieval Sherwood Forest. She wondered whether she wanted to return to the hidden village or whether she was glad to be back in the modern day. She found herself wrestling with the question as she slipped into a fitful sleep where mist flowed through open windows, sunlight dappled dry grey leaves and ferns swayed with woodland sprites. Gisborne glared at her, accusing, vengeful. Men on horses chased her, swinging swords. Hooves on hard ground. Footsteps on a pavement. A pool of yellow lamplight in front of her, just out of reach. The footsteps grew louder, nearer. A hand on her shoulder...

"Easy! Easy, sorry I made you jump, I had to wake you."

Anna looked around; the whole ward was looking at her. She was aware she had cried out and felt embarrassed. It was Nurse Christine, come to take her back to her ward.

"Come on dear, he'll be fine, we'll look after him. Consultant wants to see you now."

The consultant looked at Anna's notes and examined her, then Christine took him aside talking quietly. When he returned, he smiled and said Anna was well enough to go but should call the number on the sheet he handed her. It was a counselling service. "We think you may have experienced something that troubles you," he explained. "Nurse Lamwaka tells me you were here before and that you may have been attacked." Anna nodded. "Call them. They can help."

Anna doubted anyone could give counselling that covered time travel trauma. She had to admit that she was still shaken by the man in the jacket. She realised she hadn't talked to anyone about what happened, had tried to bury her memories of him each time they surfaced. She was avoiding the fact he had almost raped her. Perhaps she should talk, but should she talk to a stranger or a friend?

"What about Rob?" she asked.

"We'll want to keep him in for another day or so," said Christine. "You can visit."

Anna thanked them and started to take her clothes out of the bedside locker while Christine drew the curtain around her bed. Inside the NHS bag were her old boots and her new green hooded cloak. Or were they new boots and an old cloak? The age of things had become even more confused in her mind. Fortunately, they had provided some fresh underwear for her too. When she went to pull the cloak on, she felt something hard and sharp in its folds. She drew the golden arrow out and turned it over in her hands.

"You alright in there?" called Christine.

"Yes," said Anna, stuffing the arrow behind her back. "Yes I am."

Hard Truths

Loxley House, Nottingham, November 2019

The woman on the other side of the desk peered at her laptop, searching through a database. Anna had been going from one counter to another, one form filling session to another, feeling more depressed and frustrated each time. She couldn't claim benefit until she started searching for work. She couldn't find work because her address was unconfirmed. She couldn't confirm that she was homeless until she had confirmed whether Jane might take her in. Now she was trying to find out what had happened to Jane.

"Name?" asked the woman.

It was on the tip of her tongue to say Marian after learning to respond to it for the last couple of weeks (days? She still wasn't sure which). "Mary Ann Partington... but my father's name is Fitzwalter," she added reluctantly, realising it could help.

"And the name of the person you're trying to trace is Jane Fitzwalter?"

"I think so. It was her maiden name, but I don't know if she kept it or took another."

The woman continued to peer at the screen. Anna wondered if they could be doing this over the phone, except she no longer had a working one. She could have borrowed one, the duration of eye contact would have been about the same.

"Last address 14a Hermitage Court, The Park?"

Hermitage Court. She remembered the hermitage at the foot of the escarpment, just beyond Jane's old house. Brother Walter's hermitage: the one she and Rob had been in. She pulled her mind back to the modern day, "That's right."

There was a pause. The woman continued to examine the screen but after a minute or so Anna could tell she had stopped reading it. Her mood seemed to shift from professional detachment to unease.

"This record says there was a Ms Jane Trudy Arnold living at The Park address you gave until July last year and it gives a Mr Harvey Warren Fitzwalter as next of kin. For some reason she was listed under another surname altogether until after she... after arrangements were completed. Is this the person you are trying to trace?"

Anna was confused. She recognised Trudy, taken from her grandmother's name. But not Arnold. She guessed it must have been the ex-husband's name. "I think so. The next of kin is my father, so it must be."

"Ah." Anna could feel her heart sinking. The woman coughed uncomfortably and went on. "It says she died from pancreatic cancer on the third of July last year. The next of kin, your father, was contacted on the same day. Were you not informed that she had passed on?"

Ann said nothing for a while. Part of her had suspected her aunt was dead. Part of her just wanted the woman opposite to make eye contact. Anna knew she would want to grieve but just then she felt nothing. Only emptiness. "No," she replied.

"Your father didn't tell you?"

"No."

"No?" said with a mix of surprise and indignation.

"We haven't spoken for well over a year. When my mother died."

"I see." The woman resumed her typing, no doubt updating notes so a colleague wouldn't fall into the same bear trap at a later date. The fact that Jane had died seventeen months ago, and her father had never tried to contact her, was unsurprising and upsetting in equal measure. The two emotions seemed to cancel each other out, for now. At least it explained why Jane hadn't been at her mum's funeral, she had been too ill.

"Does it say where she was buried?" Anna asked.

More typing. More searching. "Church Cemetery, Forest Road East. Plot 468334."

"The Rock Cemetery?"

"Yes, I believe some call it that. There's one more thing you should know." Anna braced herself. "I can see why the name Jane Fitzwalter hadn't shown up in other searches: the name on her burial plaque is Jane Trudy Baker."

Rock Cemetery, Forest Fields, Nottingham, November 2019

Anna brushed the leaves away from the small black plaque over Jane's grave. It was right at the back of the cemetery, near the wall that ran along its northern boundary and under a stand of stark denuded trees. Not far from where Rob had helped her over the wall after Goose Fair. She would have walked within a few yards of the grave.

Anna could now confirm she had no home. On the one hand it added to her feeling of emptiness. On the other it allowed Hope House to loan her a small sum of money to tide her over until the benefits might start, in January if she was lucky. Perhaps not. She had bought a pair of white lilies and placed them in a jar of water beside the plaque. Then she wiped the dirt out of the letters so she could read them more clearly. 'Jane Trudy Baker. 8th May 1959 – 3rd July 2018. Rest in peace.'

Baker turned out to be her grandmother's maiden name. The mother of Jane and her father. Only when she stared at the black letters raised off the metal surface of the plaque did it dawn on Anna that Jane had shunned her father's name and taken her mother's. Just like Anna.

She felt a new bond to her aunt. Something she could say they shared. Anna was clear why she had chosen her mother's maiden name, because she wanted nothing to do with her father. Anna's grandfather had died before she met him, so she had no idea what kind of person he had been. Now she wondered.

Anna was not ready to search for Jane's ghost yet, any more than she was her mother's. Let them rest, she thought. And yet she was curious. Could Jane tell Anna anything if she went back to when she was still alive? Could she console Anna, pass on any words of solace or advice? Or perhaps explain why she used her mother's surname. Anna tried to picture Jane's face. She found it harder than she expected, though she remembered her warm smile and intelligent grey-blue eyes. She tried to picture that smile now, but there was nothing she could pin her memories to, they were clouded and confused.

After some time, Anna stood, stretched her back and walked slowly between the rows of plaques and gravestones, hugging herself tightly, still unable to cry. She made a promise to herself that one day, when she was ready, she would come and find the ghost of her aunt. And her mum.

Nottingham Central Library, Angel Row, November 2019
Anna peered at the list of fictional characters that had appeared in all iterations of the legend over time. The distinction between fact and fiction had blurred for Anna and she remembered what Rob had said about folk tales and their origins. Will Stutely, Will Gamely and Guy of Gisborne were mentioned in most versions of the folktale, though there was no mention of Ruth or of Robin's ethnicity in any. She was not surprised. Though she was surprised to discover that the

wise men and women of Gotham had their own tales. After an hour or so she realised that visiting time at the hospital was due to start so she got up to go.

A small brightly coloured children's book caught her eye as she descended the stairs. A wry smile creased her lips when she saw the merry neat-bearded man with noble features in a pointy green hat. He stood, hands on hips, with his bow slung casually over his shoulder. He looked more like an aristocrat playing panto than an outlaw. She flicked through the pages and stopped at the picture of the beautiful blonde heroine in spotless silk dresses and a veil. Anna pulled at the cuff of her oversize overcoat and scrubbed pointlessly at an unidentified stain before she noticed several others and gave up. She was about to put the book back on the shelf when a mischievous mood caught her, and she stuffed it in an oversize pocket.

On her way to the Queen's Medical Centre, she stopped at Boots the Chemist, took a few coins from her precious stash, and went inside. Next door was a bakery and she entered that too.

Rob was up when she arrived. He looked less pale, but he seemed strangely awkward and out of place, hunched forward in a light blue hospital gown on the edge of the bed. Out of time, as much as out of place. He perked up when Anna arrived.

"Sticky bun?" she offered him the bag from the bakery. He took it eagerly and allowed himself a thin smile.

"Didn't know if you'd come," he said quietly.

"Well, it's not as if I know many people in Nottingham."

"You do. Just not now."

"True."

"I want to go back."

"To medieval Nottingham?" He nodded. Anna rolled her eyes. "They want to kill you."

"They want me. Don't care what for."

"We don't belong there, Rob. This is when we come from, now, twenty-nineteen."

"I don't. Family's dead. Army friends don't want me. No home. No job. Nobody wants me here."

"I want you." There, the words were out of her mouth.

Rob looked at her, as if searching her face for any hint of sarcasm. "I keep pissing you off."

"Yes, you do. And you keep doing things that surprise me."

"What?"

"How did you learn to pick locks? How did you get to be such an incredible shot with a bow? How do you do such dumb things when you're so clever. And how is it you're so generous to people when life's been so shitty to you?"

Rob scratched his stubbly chin and looked at the hospital gown as if he were surprised to find he was wearing it. "Dunno."

Anna regarded him, trying to work out the enigma that was Rob Ahmed. A scrawny young man you wouldn't look twice at if you passed him on the street. Ordinary. Unremarkable. Or was he Robin of Loxley? A wiry, golden arrow-winning sharpshooter with a cocky smirk and a big-hearted sense of social justice. At that moment he looked neither, just lost.

"Where did you go that first evening we arrived here, in hospital?"

Rob frowned, "Nowhere. I were out of it for a full day and a half."

"But you got up for the loo in the night, because you were gone for a long time when I came looking for you."

"Was I?" Rob looked even more confused.

"Well where else could you have gone?"

"I tell y', I don't remember getting up. I were out cold. Didn't wake till following day, and only for a few minutes then."

"Well you must have gone somewhere. I was here, at your bed and you'd disappeared."

Rob shook his head, mouth open, "No. Can't remember. I had strange dream though. Like I were back out in cold and dark. There were wild creatures calling to each other while trees were creaking..." he trailed off, staring at his hands on the stiff white bed sheets. "Like I say, strange dream."

Anna considered him. She still contended with strange and unsettling dreams of her own. Usually nightmares that started with being followed and ended in running down lamplit streets. She knew why. Rob's dream also seemed straightforward to explain, "Sounds like you dreamed you were back in the forest after our escape from Gisborne's men. Neither of us will forget that in a hurry." It still scared her, and she wasn't the one who'd been captured and chained. "Doesn't explain where you went though."

Rob watched an elderly patient being wheeled out of the ward on his bed and pointed, "Maybe that's where I went. Taken for examination by orderlies."

Anna shrugged. That seemed the most rational explanation, but she remembered his bed was still there. The sheets looked as if he had just been sleeping under them. When she woke up he was lying on top of them. Perhaps the orderlies could have lifted Rob into a wheelchair or another bed, but surely they would have tucked him in again? She was still emotionally drained from her visit to Jane's grave, so she didn't have the energy to push Rob on something he didn't understand. Another question had been lurking in the back of her mind and there was a chance Rob might answer it. "When Little John asked you about letting Gisborne go, you said you'd had enough of killing," said Anna. "Do you feel you can tell me about that, Rob?"

Rob stared out the window, took his time before answering. Anna had time; she would wait.

"I were sniper, in army" he started. "Me and my mate, Raj. It were our job to take out them with guns before they took one of us."

"Must have been hard."

"Not at time. Training. Do what you're told, when you're told. Pull trigger, someone falls over, long way away. Don't even look like person. A target. Hit targets all time at target range."

"But what about your skill with a bow?"

"Rifle, bow, same difference. Practised with both, one for work, one for fun."

"What changed?"

Rob stared out the window for a while before resuming. "Raj stepped on IED. A mine." He paused again. Anna held his hand – this much she had heard before, though the friend's name was new. "I wanted revenge. I wanted to kill them who did it. Course I didn't know who, so any of 'em would do. Next day we got tip off. Found out where they were making IEDs. Might have been same people who hid the one that did Raj. Might not, didn't care. I were told to cover squaddies that were about to go in. But I could see through window. I could see pile of ammo boxes. Thought I'd save squaddies the bother. Thought I'd pay back for Raj... so I took the shot."

Anna waited again, holding his hand. She didn't want to judge, she just wanted to listen.

"Hell of a bang. Then fire started. Whole house were in flames. I could see them inside, they were burning. One were thrashing around, I could see him through window. See him in my sights. He were like a man all made of fire, staggering, waving his arms. And there were this noise." Rob winced and covered his ears, as if hearing it again.

"What kind of noise?" asked Anna softly.

"I'd heard it before, when I were kid. He were wailing. Screaming like he couldn't stop, not ever. I wanted him to stop 'cause I could remember screaming just like that." Anna remembered him saying how his father and brother had died when he was a small kid, burning to death in their home. He probably heard them scream too.

"He jumped out window, two floors up. You don't do that in your right mind, but he were out of his mind in pain, wailing... wailing. Then it stopped."

Rob hung his head. Some parts of the Rob Ahmed jigsaw slotted into place in her head. His fear of fire. Politely sipping at alcohol and pushing it away. The repeated declaration that he was no hero, despite all he had done. Rob was likely suffering from shock: post traumatic shock disorder, PTSD. Likely he had taken to drink to drown his memories at some point then sworn himself off the stuff. No wonder he was on the streets like her. The wonder was that he functioned at all given what he had been through in his short life. It made Anna feel guilty that she was on the streets as well, with nowhere near the same traumas to deal with. Even so, Rob had comforted her saying it didn't matter how you ended up there. That was all part of the puzzle: this traumatised young man could still rise above his own struggles and be generous to others.

"I know what I did were wrong. I were discharged. Said I'd exceeded my orders, said I were unfit for duty. Sent me back to Nott'n'm. But I were no use to anyone. No home, no job, no bloody use."

Anna hugged him tight.

They sat, in silence, holding hands, until a consultant came to discharge him. Again.

Loxley House, Nottingham, December 2019

Anna sat on the steps outside Loxley House, huddled against a concrete column to keep out of the wind. Like waking up under the colonnade at the Council House a couple of months ago, she remembered. Since then, she had gone everywhen and nowhere.

She had finally phoned that number for counselling. The woman had been pleasant, patient, eager to empathise, and bloody useless. No, that wasn't fair. Anna realised it would take a lot more than one session to start unravelling the fear she felt, let alone face it and deal with it. But how could the woman begin to understand what Anna had gone through?

She had told the counsellor about the man in the jacket who tried to rape her, who had pushed her into a doorway and pressed himself against her. Anna told her that she had kneed him in the groin to get away. The woman had asked her how she felt about that, which seemed an odd question. She said she hadn't thought about it. Now she thought again, and she realised it was the only part of that nightmare that gave her any sense of control. It was an odd thought, but it seemed important to Anna. She did not like it when she could not control what was happening to her. Her slide into homelessness had been out of her control. Her lurches into the past had suddenly gone wildly beyond her control, immediately after that man had attacked her. Only now was she starting to feel she could travel back in time under her own volition. It was travelling forwards to the modern day that she did not yet fully understand and that still scared her a little. Though not as much as being followed. And raped.

She flinched involuntarily as she remembered the man lunging at her and falling over something, some dark shape on the ground. What had he fallen over? Whatever it was had allowed her to escape, into the pit, into Beatrice's Nottingham. Somehow the shape on the ground seemed familiar.

Rob emerged and she could tell by the look on his face that his own attempts hadn't gone any better than her own. When you needed benefits, you had to show you were looking for work, but if you were applying for benefits it was less likely anyone would employ you. His shoulders were hunched forward, and his hoodie was pulled up over his head, so he didn't have to meet her eye.

"No luck?" Anna already knew the answer.

"No. No use to anyone here."

"Don't say that."

"'s true," said Rob, starting to shamble back up to the city centre. Anna followed.

"We're all useful somehow," she said.

"You can say that. You got education. You've even got an accent."

Anna grabbed Rob's elbow and stopped him, angry. "What do you mean by that?"

"You got chances; you'll get job eventually. Not me. People like me don't get chances."

"If you keep telling yourself that it'll come true."

"*Is* true. I wouldn't give me a chance, don't deserve it."

"*Stop it*! Stop talking shit Rob Ahmed, I know what you can do, I've seen it," and Anna pulled the golden arrow from inside her second-hand overcoat and waved it in his face.

He staggered back staring dumbly at the arrow, "You kept it."

"Of course, I kept it, you idiot. How many golden arrows does a girl get given in her life?"

Rob scratched his chin, "Annabel what's-her-miserable-face prob'ly got a few."

"She didn't deserve one of them, especially not from you." Why did she always end up wondering whether to hug him or slap him? This time neither happened. Rob leaned forward and kissed her, tenderly.

"Will you take me back there again?" he asked. She knew when he meant. She knew it would be a mistake but...

Ghost Town

York Road, Nottinghamshire, December 1215

The ground was bleached white by frost. Furrows in the fields glistened under the low winter sunshine and bare trees drew long skeletal shadows. Ice sparkled on the spiders' webs that festooned the bracken and gorse bushes either side of the road. Anna wound an old scarf around her neck and turned up the collar of her overcoat. She could see her breath hanging in the air in front of her. Rob pulled the hood of his jacket up over his head and put an arm around her, perhaps as much to keep himself warm as her. It felt good, thought Anna.

Her lips still tingled with warmth where Rob had kissed her. Despite the crystalline cold, that warmth seemed to spread all the way through her. Anna had enjoyed a couple of fleeting relationships with lads before but they had been cut short. The first time because she needed to spend so much time visiting her mother in hospital. The second time because she had been forced to move on from the friend's flat where she was couch surfing. She had not been that sorry. There had been far more pressing problems for her to face. Perhaps if things had been different then she may still be with one of them. Perhaps if they had cared more about each other then she may still be seeing one of them. But this felt different.

When Rob ran, after their first journey into the past together, he had fled from his experience of the sand mine and the shock of time travel. But he had not run from her. They had taken two more journeys to medieval Nottingham and he had stayed by her side, despite all the traumas they had faced together. He shared her exotic ability which meant he understood her, even if he found it hard to understand what he himself was doing. His arm around her shoulder gave her strength. She slipped her arm around his waist and hoped he could feel the same strength returned. Redoubled.

A little way down the unmade road they saw a couple past their middle-age coming the other way. They lead a shire horse that pulled a cart piled with sacks, rolls of cloth, a pair of matching oak chairs and assorted cooking pots. They wore cloaks that may once have been fine and colourful but looked faded and threadbare now, like an old tapestry exposed to the sun. The man had a strip of pale cloth wound over the top of his head and under his chin, as if binding his jaw tight for some ailment. Both had battered leather boots that flapped as they walked. The woman's head drooped, staring at ruts frozen into the hard mud. The man eyed Rob and Anna suspiciously.

"Hello," said Anna.

The man stopped. The horse and cart trundled to a halt beside him, but the woman carried on, never lifting her head. "Most are leaving," the man said, his French accent was muffled by the wrap around his chin.

"Leaving, why?" asked Anna.

"Be it not the same where ye come from? This time last year we had a house and a thriving trade in fine cloth, but more taxes and levies from de Ferrer have ruined us."

"What is he raising taxes for?"

"Have ye not heard? The king comes. He declared war on all northern barons who oppose him. De Ferrer and Gisborne raise wickedly high taxes to pay for the war against our king and those who cannot pay are set to work on the castle walls and ditches. We leave with all we have left," he thumbed at the cart behind him. "I do not know where we will go, but we do not wish to be here when King John arrives."

Anna and Rob looked at each other, remembering the siege that King Richard had laid on Nottingham and the burning of the townhouses. They were confused by this new twist. "Didn't John's people try to defend Nottingham before?"

The man looked at Anna, as if trying to work out what she was saying. "Surely ye be too young to remember when John was a rebellious young prince, and his elder brother came to beat him?"

Anna remembered rescuing Ruth and her sister from the burning bakery when they were small. "We were only children, but we remember the fires."

"Then ye will remember enough to turn thisens around now. I doubt King John will show more mercy for his subjects than his brother did." Anna remembered the tales of good King Richard and evil Prince John, now king in his turn. But Richard had not returned to save his people like the tales, he had come for bloody revenge on anyone who was unlucky enough to stand in his way. She had seen no evidence of a crusading man of God. Heaven only knew what his brother might do.

The man tugged the horse's bit which strained into its harness. The cart lurched forward, out of the rut it had settled in, then rumbled on. The man, the horse and the cart trundled after the woman, who was already a hundred yards down the road to nowhere.

"No change," said Rob sourly. "Them at top go to war and everyday people suffer. Everyday ghosts when they die."

"Sounds like those two had more to lose than some," said Anna.

"Had," said Rob. He looked at Anna thoughtfully, "Bit like you I suppose."

"I had a good home. Mum had a decent university job, and she always put food on our table. I had an education and a future. But I had to look after her when she got cancer, and everything unravelled. It wasn't war or fire; I didn't suffer like you did. I was just... unlucky."

"Like I said, don't make any difference how you get there," Rob reassured her, watching the couple with the cart make their way slowly up the road. They turned away and walked on towards Nottingham, holding hands. "Tell me 'bout your mam," asked Rob, surprising her.

Anna hesitated. She realised that Rob's mum had died before he could remember her. Perhaps he wanted someone else's memory to console him? "Small, dark brown hair, quietly spoken. And a smile that made me feel like the world was a good place."

Rob looked at Anna and gave her hand a squeeze. "Reckon she passed that on then."

She faltered. No one had said that before, and Rob didn't seem given to exaggeration. "She seemed happiest when she was studying. It was like she drew strength from her books and papers."

"Passed that on an' all."

"The chemo made her too tired to read. It was like a part of her had already died. It broke my heart."

"Did she know about your time travelling?"

"No," she paused. "Well, at least I don't think so. She always changed the subject when I told her about people I could see as a small kid, so I stopped trying to tell her. I think you're the only one who knows."

"Maybe."

"What do you mean by that?"

"Big thing to hide. If your mum were so clever, she might have known."

Anna stopped. It seemed obvious when Rob put it like that. "You think she knew and chose not to say?"

"Perhaps," Rob shrugged. "Perhaps she thought it were for best. Perhaps she thought she were protecting you?"

"Oh god! I wish I'd asked her."

"Guess you can if you want."

Anna had often thought about returning to her living mum but shied away. The idea seemed unnatural: deliberately seeking someone you loved who had died. And yet she had never said she wouldn't, just not yet. Now she had a compelling reason to return to her. "Yes, I can."

"You're lucky," whispered Rob.

Anna frowned, "But you could too, couldn't you?"

"I just tag along with y'. Can't control my time travel. Not like you. You're a natural, I reckon. Figuring it out for y'self."

Anna opened her mouth to answer but wasn't sure what to say.

Rob placed his lips to hers to save her the bother.

Further on, they found a stark post and gallows bracket standing empty at the top of a rise. Anna shivered involuntarily. She remembered the hanging they saw on the hill beyond the Rock Cemetery and she realised that was exactly the route they were walking. Had this been a hanging site for centuries, she wondered? As they passed the grim structure, she wondered how recently it had been used, who the victim might have been and what heinous crime could have sealed this fate. She remembered the nineteenth century poacher who had been hung by the baron for stealing something to eat and wondered how little you could be hanged for six-hundred years earlier. She pulled her gaze away from the gallows towards the city, trying hard not to follow such thoughts. She felt Rob tense at the sight of the noose and put her arm around his waist to hug him close.

Rob reacted strongly to injustice. She suspected it was why he had taken the shot at the bomb makers in Afghanistan whom he suspected of killing his friend. Yet it his vengeance had only brought him misery. She also wondered what injustices the Afghan bombers may themselves have suffered. A thought that would be difficult, yet perhaps not impossible to raise with Rob. Anna had learned not to underestimate him.

Anna had been expecting to see Tuck's hospital first, just outside the city defences. Instead, there was a sprawl of huts, tents and make-shift cabins littering the field to the east of the York Road. Some had dug into the soft sandstone and ringed the shallow pit with rough blocks of what they cut out, covering it with branches and hessian. Primitive cave houses, little better than holes in the ground. They could smell woodsmoke drifting from one cave house near the road and a woman clambered out clutching a tatty rag to her. She didn't seem aware of Rob and Anna passing by, she didn't seem aware of much. Anna was reminded of the same hopeless stare she had seen on the young mum with the chocolates outside the Vicky Centre. A few chickens wandered aimlessly between the detritus of habitation and a scrawny goat stood tied to a post, bleating. Anna suspected its days were numbered.

A man crouched beneath a white painted wooden cross at the side of the road. His left leg was missing below the knee, the stump swollen and discoloured in a way that Anna had never seen before. As they drew near, he stretched out a hand, palm up, in a universal gesture. Anna searched her pockets for change and placed a pile of odd silver and coppers into his hand. He seemed grateful if puzzled by the strange symbols on the coins. Twenty-first century sterling was just as much out of place here as her civil war coins, though she hoped the metal itself could be traded.

How long had they been away? It was a relief to see the familiar log chapel with its silvery wood shingle roof that shone in the weak sunshine. But Tuck's hospital had grown from a few tents into a permanent structure with rough red brick walls around an open courtyard and a simple half-timbered refectory hall. On the opposite side of the road there was a long line of crosses over fresh dug graves which, like the shanty town, had not been there before. Anna saw Tuck emerging from the refectory and she waved, calling to him.

"Praise the heavens, ye live!" he cried and rushed over to embrace them. "Where have ye hidden so long?"

Anna realised that Little John and Ruth may have seen them many weeks ago, running deep into the Shire Wood, away from the soldiers. "We got lost in the forest."

"For a *year*?" he asked, incredulous. "I be impressed by your woodcraft!"

Anna and Rob looked at each other. They had tried to find the exact same moment to return to. They had no machine to tell them the date, only their gut feel. She supposed it was a miracle they had arrived only a year away as they had no control other than searching for memories.

"We laid low," said Rob, glancing at Anna. "Safer for y' as well as usens."

Tuck stepped back to look at them, holding the sides of his belly, noticeably less wide than the last time they had seen him. "Well, that be true enough. Gisborne hath been so busy wringing taxes from us that he may have forgotten ye."

"What's going on here?" asked Anna, pointing at the mess of humanity behind them.

"People call it Whiston," said Tuck, "after the Whiston gallows and Whiston Lings where they gather bracken further up yonder road. The taxes for living inside the city defences are so high that the poor live outside, along with the beggars and the lepers. We do our best to feed them," he nodded at the hospital refectory. "Sometimes our best is not enough," and his eyes fell on the row of crosses at the other side of the road. His face looked as if it had aged twelve years in the last twelve months.

"We didn't know," said Anna, feeling deeply guilty that they had fled and left their friends to such bitter times. She thought of the beggar's deformed stump and wondered if he suffered from leprosy.

"Where are my manners? Please come in and take food with me." Tuck led them into the refectory.

"Can you spare it?" asked Rob, doubtfully.

"Always. Without the funds ye won for us last year we would have had no hope. Little John and the others bring us a share of their hunts, but that be harder each day with Gisborne's foresters out to catch them. Those they catch are hung at Whiston gallows. No trial, no last rites. A hanging almost every day this past two months."

Anna's hunch about the gallows had been right. Death came fast to those who were unlucky enough to be caught stealing to feed themselves, assuming they didn't starve before.

Tuck sat them down on benches at the end of a long table and went to fetch a pair of bowls. Anna took a sip. A few desultory slices of leek and parsnip floated in hot water. She smiled and took another sip. Rob lifted his bowl, knocked it back, wiped his mouth with his sleeve and said thanks. He looked as if he had just been fed a rare feast. Perhaps a few years on tour in the army taught you not to be fussy. A few years more living on the streets would teach you to be grateful for whatever you could get, thought Anna.

When she looked back at Tuck he was staring into space. "What's the matter, Tuck?"

He didn't answer. A tear ran down his cheek and his shoulders started to shake with silent sobs. Seeing this strong man of God cry was all wrong. It shook her. She placed a hand on his shoulder.

Tuck drew a long breath and wiped snot from his nose. Anna dug in her oversize pockets and found a handkerchief for him that was almost clean. "Thank ye," he said. "Sorry. They look to me, ye see. They look to me when I help bury their father, their mother...

their children. And they ask me to tell them that life will get better, that God has a plan for them." The tears cascaded down his face then, rivers of torment and despair. "And I do not know. I do not see it."

Anna saw the great weight that lay on Tuck's heart. How could the helper help when there was no one to help him? Rob and Anna moved as one, sitting either side of the big man on the bench and hugging him tight.

Tuck seemed to draw new power from them like a battery re-charging. He calmed himself, wiped away the tears and drew long calming breaths. "I am glad ye came back."

"We passed a couple who were leaving," said Anna.

"Nottingham is half empty. Those that can have been leaving for weeks. They know the king seeks revenge on de Ferrer."

Anna remembered the knights in Gotham. They must have been scouting the way ahead for the king's campaign. "The couple we met said King John wants to punish the northern barons," said Anna.

"Aye," frowned Tuck. "Ordinary people will die again, whether they support the barons or not. King John returned from Normandy in September. He made his presence known in the south and now he marches north. He took St Albans a few days past and I hear he be set to take Northampton. We expect him here soon. Some say he will arrive by the feast of St Nicholas."

Rob looked blank. "Christmas," explained Anna quietly.

"Rubbish present for Nottingham," he muttered.

"I think it best we get ye to Little John in the forest," said Tuck. "We will soon be under siege by a vengeful king... again."

Shire Wood, Nottinghamshire, December 1215

Little sunshine reached the forest floor. All Anna could see was a flicker of blue against the dark green boughs of pine above her. She guessed it must have been between three and four in the afternoon from the failing mid-winter light, late enough that she was glad to hear Tuck say they were nearing the hidden village at last. It had been a long cold walk, giving Anna plenty of time to think about the poor and wretched of Whiston. She was lucky. She had somewhere warm to go and the promise of food.

Anna waited until Tuck was a little way ahead of them before asking Rob a question that had been forming in her mind. "I thought I knew Nottingham pretty well for a visitor, but I never heard of Whiston. Have you?"

"Kind of," said Rob, with annoying brevity.

"Either you have, or you haven't. You can't just rub a place off the map, can you? Or is it a made-up place?" she asked, finally voicing the thought that called everything they were doing into question, a question of her and Rob's sanity. Were they really walking through a thirteenth century forest or was this a walk through some shared imagination?

"I heard people mention it, older folk at Hope House and at the queue for Tina's. They said it were roughly where Vicky Centre is now, reaching up along Mansfield Road. Gone now."

"Gone? How can a district be gone, like it's some... ghost town?"

"Dunno. Heard rumours it died after Plague. Others said name were still used by Victorians but made part of other places long back."

"But it did exist?"

"Seems so."

"Hope so, otherwise I'm going mad."

"No more 'n me," grinned Rob.

Anna took Rob's hand again. If this was madness, then she was glad to share it with him. The lower layers of hawthorn and holly closed in around them and the undergrowth clawed at their shins. She saw mounds of moss the size of boulders, and lichen dripped from the damp boughs of gnarled beeches. It reminded her of photos she had seen of rainforests and it occurred to her that medieval Sherwood may have harboured remnants of the great forests that cloaked the old world. Was such detail too real to be imagined?

The ground rose gently, and she suspected they were on the lip of the dell where the village lay. Another kind of ghost town, hiding away of its own choosing. After pushing back the umpteenth spray of clawing foliage she saw a clutch of thatched rooftops and knew they had arrived. She breathed and felt the muscles in her back and shoulders unclenching. Sanctuary?

Half Measures

Hidden Village, Shire Wood, Nottinghamshire, December 1215

Little John clasped them both, stepped back and laughed. "I knew it! Ye were hiding. Didn't I tell ye, Ruth? Robin and Marian, they be too clever to get caught by Gisborne and he would have been crowing over their dead bodies if he had."

Ruth didn't answer. Her eyes glistened as she wrapped her arms around the pair of them and held them tight to her.

"I'm sorry," said Anna, mistrustful of her own voice. "We should have..."

"Never mind," cut in Little John, "ye be living, ye be here, and by our God, ye be needed."

Once Ruth had been gently persuaded to let go of her two lost souls, she sat them down and brought bread and water. The bread was a little stale, yet Anna understood, even if Rob was wolfing it down without a care. Tuck, John, and Ruth were eating slowly, savouring each mouthful. She suspected this was the best they could muster right now, and more than many would enjoy for a while yet. She gave Rob a subtle nudge with her knee under the table and gestured with a look for him to slow down. He looked at her blankly for a moment as she exaggerated her slow chewing, then nodded and took his time.

"The people of Nottingham are under siege and the king has not even arrived," said Little John. "De Ferrer and Gisborne squeeze them all for more taxes to pay for war, until they leave or starve."

"I buried another this morning," murmured Tuck, a look of desolation returning to his eyes. "She were barely five winters."

Anna quietly put a supportive hand on Tuck's back. "We spoke to a couple who were leaving," she murmured. "They said there was nothing here for them."

"There be too many of Gisborne's men to confront," said John, "If they leave that castle they travel in packs like hungry wolves, ever since we jumped them to free Robin. They hunt us and they hang us with few questions asked. We have to do something to feed others but hunting and poaching be more dangerous every day."

"What about King John?" asked Anna, "I still don't really understand why he's coming to attack Nottingham."

Little John looked at Anna and rubbed his chin. "I suppose much hath changed in the time you were hiding. De Ferrer is one of the northern barons who band together to defy King John. They did not care to send men and coin to support his claims in Normandy. Instead, they would have the taxes for thisens. Now King John be returned from across the Channel, and he seeks to put the barons in their place. To us ordinary folk it matters not where the wars be fought, we still end up paying. But when King John brings war to de Ferrer we will pay with our lives."

"If we all hide until the king comes then he might defeat Gisborne, de Ferrer and their men. They might put an end to the high taxes," suggested Anna, though she realised how naïve her words were even as she spoke.

"And after the killing, what then?" asked John. "Another man steps into Gisborne's boots, King John's man. Remember how John were when he had the castle? It will not change. The new man will take and take, just as now. Rob woke us all to that."

Anna hung her head. They were right: different bailiff, same task. They'd still be taking money for the next siege further north, and the next, and the one after that.

"The York Road," said Rob, "there's money on that. I seen it." Anna wondered what he was saying when Tuck latched on.

"Aye, some wealthy folk travel that road, and it passes through many dark corners of the Shire Wood. I hope ye do not suggest dark work, Robin?"

"A tax," he said simply.

"People do not want more taxes," frowned John.

"Ordinary people don't. What about the rich? Do they get taxed?"

"Strictly speaking it be the rich who are taxed, not the poor," said Tuck. "But they take money and food from the poor in their estates and cities to pay the barons... or the king."

"So they e'nt paying any themselves?"

"Not exactly."

"Time they did," said Rob, a sly look on his face. "Time there were tax for travelling through our wood."

"Robin Ahmed of Loxley," said Anna, fists to hips, "I do believe you're about to suggest we rob the rich to give to the poor."

"No. A tax. Half of whatever they have," he looked a little defensive for a moment then added, "that's fair, e'nt it?" The corner of his lips were just beginning to curl into a half smile.

Little John slapped Rob on the back and roared with laughter. Anna and Rob shared a knowing look.

York Road, Shire Wood, Nottinghamshire, December 1215

Snowflakes glided gently through the bare outstretched fingers of the oak trees, drifted across the hardened dirt road, and settled against the base of their trunks. A fine white cloak was enveloping the Shire Wood and it sparkled in the hint of sunshine that nudged at the edge of the clouds. The trees were hushed. Birds were silent, breath hung on the air and words between the watchers and waiters were whispered. Three parties had already passed by, utterly unaware that their passage had been observed. The first was a pair of wood cutters, axes hanging from their belts and bundles of firewood tucked under their arms. The second was an elderly couple riding a cart, pulled by an equally aged shire horse. The third party was a trio of nuns, likely on a holy pilgrimage to the abbey at York.

Rob slunk through the holly after the nuns had passed, leaned back against the snowy trunk of a fir tree, and pulled his hood down over his face as if ready for a snooze. Anna sat beneath a pine, beside Ruth.

"I'm sorry," whispered Anna, "that we didn't tell you where we were, that we were okay." Anne felt guilty. Ruth deserved the truth about where they had gone and for how long, yet it seemed far too difficult to explain.

"Ye did right," said Ruth, quietly. "No one knew, so no one could give ye away."

"I know you and Little John would never have given us away."

"Not willingly, but if they had caught us then they would have made us. De Ferrer were in a fury after the archery competition and Gisborne were an evil hound at his heel."

"I'm sorry they took it out on the people of Nottingham."

"Oh, they did not do all that on account of ye. De Ferrer knew King John would return, and he wrung every coin from the people of Nottingham to make good his defence. They would have suffered any which way."

"It seems they will suffer even more when the king arrives."

"That they will, no matter who wins."

Anna was thinking hard, trying to remember her history. She knew of a peasants revolt yet had little idea when it had occurred, let alone whether it had been successful. "Could they ever be driven to... rise up? Rebel against the barons and the king?"

Ruth looked at Anna, studying her face carefully. "That way lies pain and death, Marian. The barons and the king can call on many men-at-arms and levies who they pay well to put rebellion down. Brutally. Do not go putting such ideas into hot heads. We are already acting on the very edge of provocation."

Anna felt chastened. Ruth was right and she should not even ask such a question, let alone turn it into a suggestion. And yet the thought smouldered, lit by the burning injustices that she had witnessed in Whiston and Nottingham. She was starting to understand the power of ideas: the idea of rebellion and the idea of taking back from the barons what they had unfairly seized from their citizens.

When she looked back Ruth was clenching her teeth, scrutinising the empty road in front of them. Something of her profile, the set of her jaw, conjured that illusive sense of familiarity again. The answer felt on the edge of Anna's mind, like grasping for a name that she felt she should know. An answer that seemed even closer now for some reason. The muffled clopping of hooves on hardened mud and the grumble of cartwheels distracted her. Another party of travellers approached.

Anna leaned forward, taking an arrow from her quiver, and nocked it to her bow. Ruth's bow was already aimed at the two riders walking their horses into view from the south, followed by a fine carriage drawn by a pair of white mares. Little John stepped out from behind a fir tree holding his staff up as a sign for the riders to stop. Rob, Will Gamely, and Blinder stood behind, bows raised.

"Halt!" called Little John in a firm yet relaxed voice. "Welcome to the Shire Wood toll," and he winked at Rob over his shoulder. The riders wore leather jerkins and shields slung across their backs. Their hands were reaching for swords in scabbards that hung from their belts, but Little John warned them off. "Easy, folks, my friends here may be offended by drawn swords." The men stopped and looked at each other. There was a call from inside the carriage, covered by an embroidered purple awning, a call from someone who sounded as if they were used to being obeyed.

"Why do ye stop?" called the voice. "Who seeks to delay us?"

"Thieves, Your Worship," replied the first rider.

"Show them your sword, man," His Worship replied.

"They have bows, Your Worship."

Anna could hear grumbling from inside the carriage. It swayed violently as if something large was shifting its weight around inside, then a huge white pointy hat stuck out the side of the awning with a disgruntled red face underneath it. "How dare ye!" His Worship accused. "How dare ye threaten a man of God and his attendants!"

There was a whoosh of air and the pointy topped hat was separated from the paunchy beetroot head and pinned to the back of the carriage by an arrow. "Like that," answered Rob, casually.

Shock and outrage vied for supremacy on His Worship's face. Outrage won. "YOUNG MAN!" he pointed a chubby finger at Rob as if a divine thunderbolt would jump from it. "DO YE HAVE ANY IDEA WHO I AM?"

"Tubby and lary?" asked Rob, obviously starting to enjoy himself. Anna suppressed a snigger. So did the second rider, she noticed.

"I AM THE BISHOP OF HEREFORDSHIRE!" A little righteous spittle sprayed from the corner of His Worship's mouth.

"Good for you," said Rob.

"And good for the people of Nottingham who will thank ye kindly for your generous offering," added Little John.

"Offering?" asked His Worship. Clearly the Bishop of Herefordshire was baffled by the idea of making one rather than receiving it.

"Aye, road tax," said Rob, gesturing at the rutted muddy track that claimed the grand title of York Road, or even Great North Road when the sun shone on it at a flattering angle. "And well, look at the state of it. Needs every offering it can get."

His Worship's eyebrows worked their way up his forehead before realising there was no longer a large pointy hat to disappear under. "Tax?" he asked incredulously. Again, the implication seemed to be that he was unfamiliar with the concept of paying it.

"Yeah, it's easy. All you need is some money," explained Rob, reasonably.

His Worship eyed Rob and Little John, as if judging how little he could get away with paying. "How much do ye wasters threaten to steal?"

"How much y' got?" asked Rob.

His Worship frowned, a ferrety shrewdness on his rounded face. "I travel light," he waved a hand at his purple embroidered carriage as if to imply that many took half their household with them, which was probably true for a privileged few, "so I only have a small pouch of coppers for my expenses."

"Doubt that's true," said Rob.

"WHAT? Ye doubt the word of a man of *God*?"

"I doubt *your* word," said Rob, emphasising 'your' to make clear there were some men of God he trusted. "Bet you got more 'n that."

"We had better take a look," said Little John and the pair of them sauntered over to His Worship's carriage. As they walked past the riders, the first one made a subtle move for his sword. A whoosh and twang from Ruth's bowstring followed instantly by an arrow that shuddered in the ground at the feet of the rider's horse, made it rear up and unseat him.

Little John and Rob turned to look at the man sprawled on the ground. "There be many more of us watching," said Little John, "please stay put and no harm will be done."

The fallen rider sat up, looking at the arrow's shaft which still waggled. Rob reached the carriage and drew the cloth to one side. Two men wearing gowns cowered at the far side of the carriage seat opposite His Worship. On the other end of the seat was a wooden chest about the size of a holiday suitcase.

"Bit bigger 'n a pouch," said Rob, nodding at the chest.

"Keep your thieving hands off," snarled His Worship. "It carries holy relics which we are entrusted to carry to the abbey at York."

"Holy relics?" asked Rob, who sounded genuinely fascinated.

"Saint Oswald's finger bones," said His Worship, his voice dropping theatrically to hushed awe.

"Better take a look so," said Rob. "Never seen saint's fingers."

His Worship flung his body across the chest as if he protected the life of the saint himself. The carriage lurched nastily with the shift of weight.

"Found the money," called Rob over his shoulder to Little John. John stepped up and lifted His Worship off the chest while Rob slid it out onto the snowy road.

"THIEVES!" shouted His Worship. "May God and Saint Oswald forgive ye."

"Aw, thanks guv," said Rob, opening the chest. "Reckon we all need a little forgiveness." His eyes widened. "Looks like you got loads." He gave a nod to the Wills who trotted up carrying sacks.

They stood alongside Rob. Blinder gave a long low whistle. "Never knew Saint Os carried so much coin about him," said Stutely, rubbing his bald head in surprise.

"We'll have a job finding his finger bones in there," said Gamely.

"Remember," warned Rob, "Only half."

"Half?" His Worship spluttered.

"Yeah, only half. It's tax, not robbery."

"Which half?" asked Gamely peering into the chest.

"Shinier half, 'course," said Rob.

"This *is* robbery!" wailed His Worship.

"Well, that's the thing about tax," said Rob, leaning back against the carriage, while Little John continued to pin the bishop down and keep the other holy men at bay with a threatening glare. "It often feels like robbery, but it can't be 'cause it don't take everything..."

Hidden Village, Shire Wood, Nottinghamshire, December 1215

Tuck's eyes were big as collection plates as he gawked at the sacks full of coin. Sensibly, he had kept away from the 'tax collection duties' so he could remain plausibly innocent of any connection to it. His task would be to distribute it among the needy of Nottingham, a task which the others trusted to him without question. The hardest part of that task would be to do it in a way which avoided suspicion.

"Should have been there, Tuck," said Little John. "'This *is* robbery', says the bishop. 'That's the thing about tax', says Robin, 'it often feels like robbery!'" and he roared with laughter along with everyone gathered around the haul. "'But it can't be robbery 'cause it don't take everything!'" Tears were running down his cheeks he was laughing so hard. "'Just most of everything!'"

Brother Tuck was as helpless as Little John. They'd been starved of laughter and this was a feast. "I should be warning ye of the seriousness of stealing from the church," said Tuck when he caught his breath. "But if this be only half of what he carried..."

"The shinier half," corrected Will Gamely.

"... then the church can probably manage," finished Tuck.

"Reckon he'll manage," said Rob. "Even if he has the dull half!"

"I shall need help," said Tuck, still shaking his head at the enormity of their first tax collection. "I cannot even carry this by myself, let alone share it out to everyone."

"I'll go with you," Anna said. She had been moved by what she saw in Whiston and, despite Ruth's reassurances, she still felt a little guilt.

"Too dangerous," warned Ruth.

"They will recognise and take ye," said Little John.

"Everyone was looking at Rob after the archery competition," argued Anna. "They only glimpsed me, and I had my hood on... unlike Rob," she gave him a meaningful look. "I can dress as a nun, that way it won't seem strange me handing out coins to the poor."

"I'd like t' see that," grinned Rob.

Anna gave Rob a stare that could melt coins.

The arguments continued but Anna was resolute, she was coming with Tuck to help.

Finding, Giving, Taking

Ruth came too. That was the compromise: two women dressed as nuns taking alms to the poor. Nuns rarely made lone missions, argued Tuck and it made sense that the two should look after each other. Anna had to admit she was glad of Ruth's company. Not just because Ruth was handy with a bow, but because she felt relaxed with her. They could walk in silence as easily as talk, a measure of their mutual trust and understanding. Anna realised that she had missed that. It was a quality few of her friends or family had shared.

"We should offer a prayer," said Ruth, as they stood by the white wood cross on the edge of Whiston. "It be as nuns would do."

Anna rarely prayed. She felt foolish praying to someone or something she didn't believe in, though she had often wished for someone to confide in. She looked around the scruffy tents and cave houses, and the remains of humanity that scratched about them, then she knelt alongside Ruth and put her palms together.

"Dear Lord, we thank ye that we have gifts to give to your people in need," began Ruth, quietly so only Anna could hear. "We pray ye protect your people from war and hunger, from pestilence and death. And we thank ye for protecting Robin and Marian, for bringing them safely back to us. Thank ye for all they do to help us. Please bless them both. Amen."

Anna looked at Ruth out of the corner of her eye. No one had ever prayed for her like that before. She felt humbled and strengthened all at once. Maybe she didn't have to believe in God for a prayer to move her.

They stood and walked to the edge of the nearest cave house. House was too grand a name, it was a hole in the ground with a manky sheepskin stretched across it to keep the worst of the sleet off. Ruth lifted a flap and called to see if anyone would answer. A pair of eyes blinked at them from the gloom. As her own eyes adjusted, Anna thought she saw more pairs looking back. Four? Five? Maybe six people all huddled inside. Her heart surged as she remembered her own fight with destitution, and yet here she was, with Ruth, offering them some hope of survival. It felt good. It drove away some of the feelings of helplessness she had endured on the streets of modern-day Nottingham.

"With the grace of Saint Mary, take this and find food to eat," said Ruth taking a few coins from a pouch and handing them down into the darkness. A dirty scabbed hand reached out to receive them. A woman's hand.

"Thank ye kindly, sisters," said the woman. "God bless ye both."

That was the second time Anna had been blessed. She was feeling uncomfortable and unworthy. Yet it was not the last time that day.

Some blessed them. Some smiled. Some stood open mouthed staring at the coins in their hand, bewildered by the unexpected gift. Anna wished she could have given a whole pouch to each of them though she understood why Ruth did not. Openly waving large sums of money around would draw excess notice, maybe even a riot. It would only take one waif to approach the market with a bulging pouch of coins for Gisborne's men to be alerted and come looking for a pair of generous nuns. A little here, a little there, that way their work passed largely unnoticed.

The work was light enough physically and yet Anna felt drained by the end of the day. It was the children. Hard enough to see grown men and women on the verge of starvation but the tiny skeletal bodies and the dark hollows where bright eyes should have been haunted her. How could this happen? She wanted to say the future would be better, but poverty simply moves out of sight of many. It moves behind closed bedsit doors and onto friends' couches; it moves into remote places where life is cheap and lives a daily struggle.

Hopelessness threatened to overwhelm her again, but Ruth squeezed her hand, seeming to sense a little of Anna's thoughts. "The ones we gave to will eat today. And we will come back to find more tomorrow."

Hospital of St John the Baptist, Nottingham, December 1215

The aroma from the servery made Anna's stomach complain out loud. Tuck had used some of the coins to fetch food from the market, so they found him stirring an enormous caldron of stew, abundant with fresh vegetables and cuts of beef. The trestle tables were full of people and a long queue had formed that snaked back out into the courtyard. Tuck beckoned Ruth and Anna over and pointed to a couple of bowls and hunks of fresh bread on a tray behind him. "Take that and find thisens a space to sit in the back of the kitchen," he said as he ladled another bowl for an eager customer.

The stew was wonderful: rich, tangy, and satisfying. Anna remembered the watery gruel she had been given on their arrival and wondered how long Tuck and his flock had been forced to subsist. The buzz of happy conversation coming from the servery beyond told her that this was a rarity, a banquet.

If Anna had been nursing any doubts about taking 'taxes', then they evaporated in the steam that wreathed around the cauldron of Tuck's stew.

"See this," said Ruth. "Robin and ye hath done this."

"We all..."

"No, this came from your thoughts, your sense o' justice," she insisted.

"It was Robin who said there was money on the road," said Anna.

"And ye who said we must take from the rich to give back to the poor. The pair of ye saw it so clear, as if ye had seen it before."

Anna wanted to say she had, and that only begged the question which had come first: the story or the people who started the story? Again, she thought of all the characters in their tale as just ordinary people, doing their best each day to stay alive. They were not superhuman. They were not pure of motive or thought. It was their efforts to feed more than themselves that became worthy of telling and the telling became a worthy legend.

Anna felt moved to be a part of such a legend, and desperately unworthy.

St John's Bar to Market Square, Nottingham, December 1215

The sleet had eased, and a weak ray of sunlight escaped from the grey ceiling of winter cloud. Anna and Ruth crossed the bare dirt-track bar that spanned the defensive ditch along the north edge of the city. They wore heavy wool cloaks instead of habits as today they would be ordinary citizens of Nottingham on their way to the square. Tuck had taken over distribution of coins in Whiston and the two of them would seek out the beggars in and around the market. The plan was to make it seem as if donations were being made by many people in different places to avoid suspicion.

As they walked Ruth turned to Anna, "May we stop at my parents' bakery?"

"Of course," said Anna, though she felt nervous to meet them again after such a long time, from their perspective. Would they notice how little she had changed? Would they ask awkward questions?

The bakery had been rebuilt with a new clay tiled roof which appeared a little luxurious for thirteenth century Nottingham. Below were bright, white-washed walls and a hand painted sign hanging from a wooden bracket that showed a smiling couple carrying trays of freshly baked loaves. Anna's mouth watered as she smelled the real thing. Inside there were a pile of round brown cobs heaped in a wicker basket on a table in the middle of the room. The oven door was open and a grey-haired man in his fifties stooped to place a dozen balls of dough into it with a long paddle. Ruth waited until he had shut the oven door before going over to give him a hug.

"Ruth! My goodness! Come here, Jane," he called, "Ruth be home, and she hath brought a friend." He beamed and threw his arms around his daughter. Anna heard footsteps coming up the stone stair from the basement and a moment later she had to grasp the table to stop herself from stumbling with the shock.

A thin faced woman with neatly trimmed brown and grey flecked hair arrived at the top of the steps and beat the flour off her apron in white clouds. She was small, barely five-feet two, with high cheek bones and intelligent grey-blue eyes that flicked around the room, sizing up everyone and everything in an instant.

"Ruth! What a lovely surprise," and with a shrewd glance at Anna, "And here be the wonderful young woman who saved ye and Rachel from the fires all them years ago."

"My goodness, Jane, so she be," said Ruth's father. "And she hath not aged a day!"

Anna gripped the table in the centre of the bakery.

Jane, the baker. And if she had a pair of metal rimmed glasses with fashionably small lenses then she would look exactly like her late aunt Jane Baker, thought Anna, her head feeling thick and woozy.

"Feeling unwell my dear?" Jane asked and came to hold Anna's hand.

"Déja vu," said Anna, weakly.

"I do not remember ye as Norman," said Jane.

"I'm not, I'm just... never mind." Anna had no clear recollection of Jane from when she had saved Ruth and Rachel in the burning bakery. Her focus had been on the children and where Rob had disappeared to. The revelation was a shock. It was as if her aunt were alive again and standing right in front of her, holding her hand. The reality, if that is what it was, was far stranger. She must be speaking to one of her aunt's ancestors from over eight-hundred years ago. "I'm... I'm Anna..." she realised she had made a slip so she tried to focus and cover it, "but my friends here call me Marian. I'm so glad to see you again," and Anna threw her arms around Jane's shoulders and began to sob like a small lost girl. The grief of losing her aunt Jane finally hit her like the wash of hot air from the oven. Only now did she understand how much she had been holding onto that grief, suppressing it while she had to deal with so much else.

Jane hugged her back, patted her gently and sat Anna down on a chair beside the table. "Fetch some water, dear," she said to her husband over her shoulder.

Ruth came to kneel beside Anna and put her arm around her. She didn't say anything, but Anna noticed she had the same shrewd look on her face as her mother, looking Anna over and putting things together in her mind. The family resemblance to her aunt was now obvious in both. How had she missed it?

Ruth's father returned with an earthenware cup full of cool water and handed it to Anna who drank gratefully.

"We never had chance to thank ye properly," said Jane, watching Anna drink. "Your friend were lost and ye went to find him. Ye are the same young woman who saved our daughters from the fires, are ye not," she stated.

"Yes, I am," confirmed Anna.

"I know my thoughts were elsewhere that day, yet I remember what age ye were then, and it seems the same this day, twenty years later. Either God has blessed ye for the kind deed that day or there be some other explanation I do not understand."

"I'm not sure I understand it all myself," said Anna, truthfully, though she felt she owed Jane and Ruth some attempt at the truth as she perceived it. How do you explain the inexplicable? How do you describe something you grew up with and yet were never able to share with anyone until a few weeks ago? "Rob and I... have been away and come back. We have not aged as we should in that other place."

"I do not hold with witchcraft, so this place must have most unusual qualities," said Jane, evenly.

"I know it sounds as if I'm mad, but I think I can slip between times... like a ghost?" she finished uncertainly.

All three regarded Anna for a while without speaking, watching her with serious and sympathetic faces. At least they were not laughing at her, though she wondered if they might think she were mentally ill. She had often wondered the same. Was this some elaborate delusion constructed in her own mind? But she could smell the bread, hear them breathing, feel the warmth of Jane's hand on hers and Ruth's arm still around her shoulder.

"Ye look and feel alive to me," said Jane, giving Anna's hand a squeeze, "and I do not hold with ghosts any more than witchcraft. Yet I have heard talk of what ye say: of folk who walk between times. I would have dismissed that too, but here ye sit, in our bakery after twenty years and show no sign of age's heavy weight." Jane looked at Ruth. "Surely ye will have remarked on this to Little John and the others?"

Ruth looked away, uncomfortable.

"It's okay," said Anna, "I wouldn't want to say either if I were you. Brother Tuck tried to question us though I didn't give him a chance to ask more."

Ruth looked back to Anna and it seemed obvious now that it was the same intelligent and caring stare that she shared with Anna's aunt. That was the look that had tickled the fraying edges of her mind these past weeks. "John and I have talked," said Ruth carefully. "Though understand that we were young when we first met with ye and Robin. Children find it hard to guess ages much beyond their own. We were so glad to see ye again, we did not want to..."

"...question us," finished Anna. "Don't worry, it's okay."

"There: 'it's okay,'" observed Jane. "I understand what ye say but your speech be unfamiliar. Not French, though ye speak a little. Believe me when I say that many come to Nottingham market from all over this world and I have not heard one person speak like ye. Which time say ye hail from, Marian? Or should I say Anna?"

Sharp as tacks, thought Anna. There was no easy way to say it. "Eight hundred years in your future."

Another silence. Ruth's father drew up a chair and sat down, scratching his head as if someone had presented him with an unusually tricky puzzle. Ruth leaned away from Anna but kept a hand on her shoulder. Jane raised an eyebrow.

"I do not suppose this can be proved?" asked Jane.

"Not easily," said Anna. She wondered if she could give any proof at all, then felt something rectangular and hard under the folds of her cloak. Something she had 'borrowed' from the library before visiting Rob in hospital. She drew out a small children's picture book and placed it into Jane's hand.

Jane lifted it, raising the other eyebrow as she turned it over. "We cannot read," she said simply, and it was Anna who felt foolish.

"It's called 'The Tales of Robin Hood,'" said Anna. "Though it's mostly pictures."

Jane opened the hardback cover and flicked through the pages, each one colourfully illustrated with fantasy pictures of Robin and his Merry Men. "Who be this?" she pointed to the beautiful woman in silk dresses.

"Maid Marian," said Anna.

"Not like ye," said Jane, comparing the illustration with Anna.

"No," said Anna, "She's blonde and I'm mousy brown. She's tall and pretty and I'm... small and plain."

"I think I prefer ye to the woman in the picture," said Jane. "Ye look sharper for a start. I do not recognise this script. I am a baker, not a scholar, yet I have never seen the like of it."

Anna produced a sealed packet of antiseptic wipes she had bought in Boots the Chemist, took one out and showed it to Jane. "This is from my time. You use it to clean dirt out of wounds and stop them going bad. Please take the pack." She felt better that she had brought modern medicine with her rather than her first thought: a gun.

Jane opened one end and gave it a sniff, then recoiled. "Strong cure, indeed!" She passed it on to Ruth who looked at the plastic packaging curiously.

Then Anna felt around and found the last remaining change from Boots. She drew it out and placed a coin in Ruth's palm: a tiny five pence piece. Ruth turned it over in her fingers and peered at the date under Queen Elizabeth's head. "Two-thousand and twelve," she said and passed it to Jane. It seemed Ruth had her numbers though not letters.

Jane peered at the date as well then passed it on to her husband who smiled and shook his head. Anna guessed that he could not read anything at all, which would have been normal for the time. What was unusual was that Ruth and Jane could recognise numbers without an expensive church or gentry education.

"Let us say ye come from year two-thousand and twelve," said Jane. Anna did not want to split hairs and say it was seven years later than the date on the coin. "Why have ye come here, now?"

Another good question, equally hard to answer. Why do we go anywhere? There can be so many reasons, not all of them under our own control. Rob had said he wanted to go far back in time, away from when they were. Anna had found Little John's family toiling along the road to the castle almost by accident, they had sprung out at her like brightly coloured figures in a pop-up book. She wondered why they had been so vivid to her. Then another thought occurred to her. Was it because of the connection with her aunt? "I'm not sure. I can't always control when I go," said Anna. "But I saw Little John's family when he was small. Their presence seemed stronger to me. More alive."

"How did ye find Ruth and Rachel?"

"I don't know. Luck, I guess."

"Luck," repeated Jane. "Maybe. We do not have much experience of luck, but I will be forever thankful that ye did. I can tell ye recognise me, and perhaps not from when we first met."

"I do," admitted Anna. "You look almost exactly, sound almost exactly like my aunt Jane."

"Who lives in two-thousand and twelve."

"She did live in two-thousand and twelve. She died in two-thousand and eighteen. I... missed her funeral. No one told me..." Anna trailed off, choking back an emotion that she had buried and didn't know if she could cope with yet.

Jane reached forward and hugged Anna. Ruth too. "I think ye be here for a reason," said Jane. "I think ye came to find family. And here we be."

Market Square, Nottingham, December 1215

Anna would not have left the bakery, yet Ruth gently reminded her of their mission. It had felt exactly as if Anna had returned to her family home, despite the fact her mother had grown up in a seaside village before moving to London and her father had grown up in his own privileged world. This was as close as she had come to finding home for several years. And by home she meant family, for she could not picture one without the other.

"Would ye prefer I say Anna?" asked Ruth, on their way to the market square.

"I think I like you calling me Marian," said Anna, "Helps me remember when I am."

"Fancy! Here I am, talking to a spirit who slips through time. A spirit who eats stew and cries wet tears," Ruth smiled then frowned. "Will ye stay?"

"I don't know," said Anna. "I have no idea how long I can." She saw a pair of children begging on the corner of Middle Pavement. They must have been the same age as Ruth and Rachel when she carried them from the burning bakery and their plight tugged at her heart, reminding her again why they had come. She drew a few coins from their pouch and slipped them into the nearest little girl's hand. "Take these and buy bread for your sister and your parents," she said, pointing in the direction of Jane's bakery in the side street beyond. The little girl's dirty brown hair flopped over her eyes as she nodded, took her sister's hand, and wandered off in the direction of the bakery.

There was no shortage of beggars of all ages. It was the market stalls that had a shortage of customers. Little by little, as Ruth and Anna worked their way around the edges of the square, the hungry trickled in to buy food. It was slow, difficult to notice the gradual rise in trade unless you were watching carefully. Evidently someone was.

Anna tucked the pouch away under her cloak and turned to find the next soul she could help then bumped her head against a hard metal breast plate. A strong fist gripped her wrist and pulled the pouch back into view.

"I will take that," said a voice she had hoped not to hear again.

"RUN, RUN!" screamed Anna to Ruth. Another armoured man stepped forward to snatch at Ruth, but she bolted down a narrow alleyway, out of reach.

"Your face appears familiar," said the man gripping her wrist. "And ye carry a great deal of coin for someone dressed so plain," he added jingling the pouch, half empty yet still weighing heavily with His Worship's tax payment. He pulled her hood away. "Ah yes, the girl in the crowd who took our young champion archer's attention. We have searched for ye for a long time. It seems we may not have to wait much longer to find the champion archer."

The fine cloak. The shining breastplate. The short clipped dark beard and the supercilious voice. Guy of Gisborne had found Marian. Soon he would take Robin.

Forgetting and Remembering

Inner Ward, Nottingham Castle, December 1215

Anna could hear her breath, drawn in gasps. She could sense her raw blooded hands held inches from her face, even though she could not see them. If she stretched them out, she felt cold rough-cut stone all around. If she shouted, then the only reply was her echo. If she staggered forwards, she collided with a wall in two short steps. She sat down. The floor was just as cold, hard, and sandy as the walls: all one surface cut from the rock on which the castle stood, above her. She leaned her back against one side and found she could just touch her feet on the other.

Anna remembered when her history teacher had taken the class to Warwick Castle where they were shown a claustrophobic stone pit with a metal grating that an over-enthusiastic guide called an oubliette, from the French word oblier: 'to forget'. A bottle dungeon into which the prisoner was dropped and forgotten. Some kids laughed, some made ghoulish faces. Anna had surreptitiously sought traces of the tortured souls left to die from such casually horrific malice yet found no trace. When she asked her mum about it afterwards, she explained that an oubliette was more likely a romantic notion of the Victorians. She said that dungeons were relatively rare in early medieval castles since justice was usually swift and brutal, with little opportunity to languish in a cell. Anna didn't know whether to feel comforted that no immediate brutality had been meted out or unsettled by the suspicion her mum could be wrong. Perhaps the intention was to let her fester in this hole in the ground after all. She fought back a rising panic.

Gisborne's men had dragged her through the castle gatehouse, through the outer ward which was a curious mix of stone and timber palisades, past the tall pitched-roofed keep and into the inner ward. It was a whirlwind tour of a building she had been itching to explore and couldn't help feeling cheated that most of what she saw was metal helmets and the cloak of the soldier in front, flapping in her face. The inner ward was mostly new stonework though she glimpsed one section of old timber rampart being pulled down by labourers and a pile of cut stones ready to replace it. She was manhandled through an archway in one of the clay tiled roof buildings that lined the inside of the walls, on the opposite side to the formidable stone keep, or donjon as the soldiers called it. In the sudden darkness, she had sensed a drop in front of her. There had been some muttering and swearing while half a dozen barrels were hauled out of the ground and she was thrown into it. The fall was not that far but the landing was hard, jarring her hands and knees. She had picked herself up and been about to teach them some wholly new twenty-first century swear words when the hatch was slammed shut and she couldn't see anything.

The fact they had to get the barrels out first suggested the pit wasn't regularly used for prisoners. The fact they knew exactly where to put her without lengthy debate suggested they had done this before. Neither thought comforted. That 'romantic' Victorian notion of the oubliette came back to haunt her; would they leave her here to die or did they have other plans?

Anna tried to calm her breathing. Her hands and knees were raw and bleeding from where she had landed when tossed in like a rotten apple. Anger rose. Her mind worked better when angry. She focussed on the pain and on Gisborne's possible plans. He had said 'we may not have to wait much longer to find the archer' when he seized her. Likely he intended to use her as bait to draw in Rob and kill him. Surely Gisborne should be preparing for King John's arrival, rather than indulging in petty retributions? King John might arrive before Rob, lay siege to the castle and she could end up as one of the casualties of war. Or she could be forgotten completely in the mayhem; dying of starvation while others fought for their lives. Stop! Stop thinking like that, Anna chided herself, it won't help.

Ruth. Ruth saw what happened and got away. She would have told Tuck who would be getting word to Little John and Rob. They would be hatching a plan to break in and rescue her. Except that was exactly what she didn't want them to do. This was a castle. It was built to resist a siege laid down by an army, let alone a bunch of woodland chancers. Besides which Gisborne was expecting them, so any attempt to break in would be twice as dangerous. No. She didn't want them to rescue her. Did she? Well, of course she wanted them to think about it. She didn't want to die in a hole in the ground. Alone. This seemed even worse than dying in a dirty alley. At least her body would be found in an alley, eventually. She didn't want to die here but she didn't want her friends to die rescuing her. Oh hell, thought Anna, her panic rising again.

She tried to re-direct her thoughts. Would her captors bring food and water to keep her alive while Rob attempted to find her? If so, perhaps she could use the opportunity to get out? Her fall had been hard and painful, but it wasn't that far. Maybe less than ten feet? She stood up and stretched her aching arms up to see if she could reach the hatch. No. She wedged her feet against the sides of the pit and tried to walk her way up but kept sliding down again as the sandy surface of the rock crumbled away. She was no good at climbing, as Rob had found when they were clambering up Castle Rock from outside. The sandstone was too soft to grip. Could she dig her way out? What with? Only her boots had a hard surface to scrape with and that would take months or years. There was a good reason why she had been put in here.

Then she remembered the little holes in the wall of the well that Beatrice had used to climb in and out. Could she dig out enough for an escape ladder? She took off a shoe and grubbed at the loose grit beside her. As she worked, she wondered how her captors might bring her food. Would they lower it down with a rope? Could she grab the rope and pull herself out? That would only pull her gaoler in and make him angry. Would they even bring her food, or would they forget about her, let the rats consume what was left of her? She was going around in circles and it wasn't helping.

Anna sat down again and closed her eyes, realising that there was no difference whether they were open or shut. No, not quite. There was a slight difference: with them shut she felt a little calmer. She could imagine she were somewhere else. Some other time... what if she were to use her ability to travel to another time? Could she escape that way? Could she control it like that? All her journeys back in time had been conscious, so could she go back to before there was a castle?

Anna kept her eyes shut and searched her mind for memories. She felt for the echoes of people's thoughts that so often unfurled around her. Nothing. Perhaps she was too stressed out to focus. Perhaps she needed to relax. Not easy in a pit in the ground. Normally she would sense something, but the pit seemed like a blank page. She wondered how old it was. Castles evolved organically over many centuries so perhaps it had only been dug a few years ago. That would explain why she couldn't sense any past lives around her. If there were no echoed memories of the past, then she might not be able to travel back in time. Her only hope may be to travel forwards.

Could she go forwards to the twenty-first century through conscious choice? Before she met Rob, she had never physically stepped out of the present while watching the past, but now they had made several journeys together. Had all their returns to the modern day been accidental and unplanned? Most of the time she had either fallen asleep or been knocked unconscious and woken up to the sound of traffic or the bustle of a hospital ward. Perhaps she needed to sleep? Difficult if she couldn't even lie down straight. Perhaps she would fall asleep anyway, whether she wanted to or not.

Then she remembered that she and Rob had deliberately returned to the modern day after their escape from the collapsing mine. She tried to focus on the moment they had started this last journey, but she barely remembered where they had started. She needed to go forward in time but had nothing to catch hold of to take her there.

She wondered what Rob would do when he heard the news about her capture. Something stupid! But Ruth had a level head; she would try to talk them out of anything rash. Tuck was a clear thinker as well. Perhaps they knew someone in the castle who could get her out? Risky. Perhaps they knew some secret passageway? The Castle Rock was riddled with caves and Anna had the vague memory of a story about someone who had sneaked into the castle through one of them. What if they did sneak in? How would they know where to look for her?

Anna felt anger rising again. Unlike the Maid Marian in the picture-book she showed Jane, Anna was no swooning heroine waiting for her hero to arrive and sweep her off her feet. She wanted to give someone a serious kicking for throwing her into this hole and she certainly didn't want to rely on some well-intentioned yet ultimately doomed rescue attempt. She grasped her shoe and started hacking at the rock again.

As she worked, she thought of Jane, the baker. Jane Baker. She thought again about the uncanny resemblance between the two of them. It seemed more than likely one was a direct descendant of the other. Another face floated into her mind: the serving girl in the cave of columns. Her face had been annoyingly familiar to Anna. Could she have been another ancestor of Jane Baker? The more she thought about it the more similar she seemed: shrewd eyes, no desire to suffer fools. The glimpse of her face had been fleeting and her hair had been covered, but Anna thought she may have seen a family resemblance. And Beatrice's mum: she had that same look. She even had the same light brown hair with flecks of grey. And come to think of it, Beatrice herself had those sparky eyes. Anna had been searching for her aunt, the only surviving relation she had wanted any relationship with. Had she been finding her aunt's ancestors without even realising it? Had she been finding the echoes of her aunt and, in doing so, jumping the time that separated them like placing two pages of a book together?

Perhaps, in her desperate flight from the man attacking her, she had subconsciously latched onto an ancestor of the very person she had been seeking for safety. Beatrice just happened to be walking the same route as her, only two centuries earlier. Anna had found her and tumbled after her, into a cave and into the past. Escape.

Blind panic had been the trigger. Like putting high voltage jump leads to an engine that was reluctant to start, Anna's fear had jump started her physical flight through time. After years of observation from the safety of her own time, she had finally pushed her body through the gap into another century, following what she saw. And she had seen Jane's ancestor, Beatrice.

The thoughts confounded Anna yet were strangely comforting. If she were right then there was some logic to her journeys through time. There were anchors: the people she was related to. And so there may be some measure of control over her travels. Anna needed to feel there was something she could control, because she certainly could do anything about her captivity for now. She unfurled her fingers and the shoe she had been digging with rolled across her lap. It had barely made a dent, despite the softness of the stone. She yawned and slumped down again to lie on her side, curling up in a ball against the cold of the stone floor. Had Anna discovered something important, she wondered? Could she direct her time travelling? She yawned again and curled tighter. Her mind drifted up and away.

A sharp ring of metal on stone. A shovel striking and scooping. Muffled voices above her. The darkness split open and a cascade of stones and dirt slid past. Daylight stung her eyes.

"Found something!" shouted a deep man's voice from above.

"Stonework?" asked another, excited male voice.

"No. Looks like a pit dug out of the rock," said the first.

Anna wanted to shout out, tell them she was there.

"Dozens of those!" answered the second. "Anything in it?"

Yes! *Me*, Anna tried to shout, but no words would come.

"No, just backfill. Probably an old storage pit, forgotten for years."

I'M HERE, Anna screamed in her mind.

"Looks like rain again."

"Better cover it over until we get the rest of the team in. Don't want it filling with water."

"Okay Scott."

I'M HERE! I'M *HERE*!

A few drops of rain spattered on the stones. There was the rustling of a canvas sheet, then darkness enveloped her again.

Anna sat up suddenly. Her head swam, the darkness made her feel giddy and disembodied. Her palms and shins still burned where she had been thrown into the pit and the pain helped to anchor her. Helped her understand where she was. The remaining question was when. She listened hard for the sound of raindrops or voices but heard nothing. Nothing. She had felt as if she were nothing to the diggers. A ghost of the past. All they had seen was a pit full of stones and dirt. Were they archaeologists from her future? Another future? Could she see a different modern day from the one she had left? Would she die here? Would they dig out the dirt only to find her skull and bleached white bones?

Anna shuddered and wrapped her arms around herself. She wanted to believe it was a dream rather than an alternate future. She was finding out all sorts of things about herself and some of them frightened her. What if there were choices to be made when going forward in time? Not just how far forward, but which version of the future. Could she make the wrong choice? Could she get lost among many branches of alternate futures? She may get hopelessly lost and end up in a future where she had already died. Buried in a hole in the ground in medieval Nottingham.

Anna shook her head, that couldn't be right. How could she be dead if she were there watching? No. It must have been a dream. A nightmare.

She thought she heard something, so faint it was almost hidden by her breathing. Footsteps? Probably the men-at-arms walking around the inner ward of the castle above. But it didn't sound as if it was coming from above. It felt like the sound was coming through the stone. How could it? Was there another pit nearby? The second man had said there were dozens of them, but she still wanted that to be a dream. Anna struggled to her feet feeling weak and disorientated. She reached out to steady herself against the stone wall. How could there be footsteps coming from another pit? There was no room to walk anywhere in one. Maybe it was a tunnel?

"HEY! IS ANYONE THERE?" she shouted then coughed and choked. She was hoarse and dry from thirst. She waited for a reply but there was nothing. Even the footsteps had stopped. Anna slumped against the wall of the pit and slid back down to the floor.

Part of her wanted to cry. The other part was too angry and stubborn. Anger helped her focus on what her mind had been doing when she was falling asleep. Her thoughts had been drifting... up. The direction seemed important. Now she remembered when she and Rob were coming back from the past, from the sand-mine, she had felt her mind lifting, as if the mine itself had dropped away beneath her.

Anna closed her eyes and directed her mind's eye upwards. Nothing happened. Then she tried imagining herself floating up, out of the pit. She felt an odd buoyant sensation and an absence of something else...

"Hey, Dad, what's in here?" a child's voice.

"Says 'Pit D' on the sign," a man replied.

"What did they put in it?"

"It says it might have been used for storing barrels of ale."

"Ale?"

"Beer."

"You'd have liked that."

"Who says?"

"Mum says you like your beer."

"Never mind what mum says."

"Why'd they put it in the ground?"

"To keep it cool I suppose."

"Looks deep and dark in there. Did they put pris'ners in it?"

Yes, they have, thought Anna. Get me out.

"Maybe."

"Cool."

Not cool, freezing cold and dark.

"Did they keep them in chains?" asked the child.

Didn't need to, couldn't climb out.

"Perhaps," said dad.

"What's that over there?"

Chains? My rotting remains?

"Says that's the foundations of the keep, or donjon."

"Dungeon? Cool!"

"No, 'donjon'. It's the French word for keep."

"What did they keep?"

Me.

"A keep was the strongest tower in the castle, the last line of defence."

"Were there any fights in there?"

"Probably."

"Cool! Let's go look."

Yes, go look. More interesting than a hole in the ground where I was thrown in and left to die.

Anna shivered and hugged her raw bloody knees. She still didn't want to believe she had seen the future. A new future, rewritten, where she lay dead and buried for eight centuries. She refused to believe she was going to die down here; she was as stubborn as she was scared. But she could not deny she had learned something new. She could choose to travel forward in time as well as back.

The thought scared her almost as much as dying, yet it also excited her. She was no accidental time tourist she was a time traveller. So why couldn't she travel forwards in time, out of this pit? Did she physically exist in two times at once: in the modern-day as well as wherever she chose to travel? Had she been in medieval Nottingham so long she had stopped existing in the modern-day? Was that why she couldn't return now? She remembered her panic when she had woken on the rock in the pool, with Rob bleeding beside her. For a moment she had thought they were already dead and that no one could see them. That they had become ghosts. She still wasn't sure what the truth was.

Rob. Anna realised she felt torn between her new love for Rob and her desire to be back in the twenty-first century. Why? Was it that she wanted to return to her 'real' body? Or was there more? She remembered sitting by Jane's grave and then she remembered another grave: her mother's. Anna was still afraid of looking for her mum's ghost and yet her unique skill would allow her to ask questions that had begun to smoulder at the back of her mind: did her mum know and if so, why not say? One day Anna would ask her, if she lived.

She wanted to live.

And was her skill unique? Rob could see the past, though he needed Anna to take him there. As if he needed a guide. And Jane the Baker had claimed she heard of 'folk who walk between times.' Surely that was just rumour, wasn't it? Or was she and Rob living proof?

Anna made another conscious search for herself in the future that she and Rob had left together. She closed her eyes. First, she looked downwards as she had always done before, yet this time she observed the days themselves, rather than searching for people within them. She beheld a strange vision of days rolling over the pit floor like waves washing a beach, each crest dissipating as the undertow from the previous one pulled from below. Day after day, year after year, each could be seen and yet all lay together, flowing over each other. Gradually she shifted her attention upwards, searching for the days to come. These washed past each other as well, like a diver watching the surface above, yet she sensed those waves parting, as if hitting a boat, throwing ripples out in all directions. Her origin could lay in any direction, along any one of those ripples. How could Anna possibly navigate a course home?

She no longer had any linear sense of time spent in that pit. The hours lay in front and behind her, above, below and spilling out in all directions. She could have been lying there for days, there was no way to tell apart from her hunger and burning thirst.

She strained to hear something: was it those footsteps again? This time the sounds were coming from above. Distant shouts muffled by the stone and the thick oak trapdoor overhead. Had Rob and the others come to get her out? If they had they would die trying. Even if they didn't, they would never find her down here.

More shouting, louder this time. Footsteps from above, maybe people running across the inner ward? Had King John arrived? Would he burn the castle and the city to the ground, like the elder brother had done to John's supporters?

A muffled crunch made the stone she sat on quake, followed by the sound of falling masonry and more shouts. God! What was that? What could shake the foundations of a castle? A trebuchet? Anna remembered seeing models of medieval catapults that were built to hurl great lumps of stone to shatter castle walls. She felt elation: the castle would be taken, and she would be freed.

Another earth-shaking crunch louder and nearer than the first. This time it sounded like an avalanche of masonry that went on for several minutes, punctuated by cries and screams of pain. Now Anna was scared. Was King John's army here for slaughter? What would they care for someone tossed in a pit? The next shot may bury her alive...

Return of the King

Inner Ward, Nottingham Castle, December 1215

The third impact shook sandy grit from the wall of the pit. Anna could hear it scatter across the vibrating floor as it coated her, burying her slowly like sediment over dry bones. She fought her fear. She struggled to her feet and put her hands against the walls as her head pounded and swayed. She even struggled to know which way was up, she had no visual clue.

More shouts and screams, closer this time. The clang of metal, echoes in confined archways, footsteps all around and above her.

"Here!" someone's muted shout overhead. Did she know that voice? "Help me lift this."

Scraping, grunting, swearing then Anna was thrown back by a blinding physical assault.

Light.

It wasn't even direct daylight but reflected from walls and soffits, discoloured by the flares of hand-held torches. Anna recoiled, covered her face and squirmed.

"Anna! Hell, what have they done to you?"

"Rob?" Anna's voice was choked by dehydration, dust, and emotion.

"Stay there, we'll come get you."

"Stay here?" she muttered, cracking one eye open. Anna would have added 'I had such plans today...' but was too drained.

There was a brief exchange of words she didn't catch then she saw Rob's bottom projecting out over the lip of the pit and descending towards her. Not quite the romantic reunion that Maid Marian would have wished for. Anna wasn't picky.

Rob had rigged up a crude abseil and landed on Anna's lap. "I don't think this is the time or place," she croaked. Rob hugged her fiercely and Anna hugged him back with all the strength she could muster. He threw the end of the rope around the pair of them, securing it with a knot.

"Pull us up!" he shouted, and up they rose in jerks and jumps.

At the rim of the pit, they were grabbed from all sides and hauled onto the stone floor where their ropes were freed.

"Take this," said Ruth, placing a water skin in Anna's trembling hands. She took a gulp, coughed, sprayed it over Rob, muttered an apology that he waved away and sucked in more water, trying hard not to repeat. Ruth produced the plastic pack of antiseptic wipes and tried to clean the congealed blood off her knees and elbows. A little late to disinfect the wounds, thought Anna but she appreciated the bizarre out-of-time gesture all the same. Her sore eyes focussed on the back of the packet in Ruth's hand which read 'Made in Nottingham'. She had forgotten Jesse Boot was (would be) a local lad.

"We have to go," urged Little John.

Rob wanted to hold Anna, but she waved him away. Told him to add his bow to Blinder and Will Gamely at the archway. Ruth and Little John supported Anna as she staggered towards the light. Outside Armageddon had arrived.

An ear-splitting crash signalled the impact of another projectile launched by the attackers. Stones the size of her head sprayed across the inner ward and embedded themselves in walls, the dirt floor, and human bodies. Some screamed, some never had the chance. Soldiers were racing up steps to take the place of the fallen or racing down them to flee a hail of burning arrows. A man with a neatly trimmed beard and shining breastplate stood in the middle of the ward, holding a flaming torch and bellowing orders. Their own movement seemed to attract his attention. He turned to look at them and she saw his face: Gisborne.

Fear vied with fury. That man had thrown her in a pit to die. That man had sought to use her as bait to kill Rob and her friends. That man had overseen extorsion, starvation, misery, and execution.

"Give me a bow," she croaked to Ruth.

"Ye be too weak," Ruth started then saw the look on Anna's face.

"Give me a bow," repeated Anna. Ruth unslung a spare from her shoulder and passed it to her free hand. The other still gripped Ruth's arm for balance.

"This way," called Little John. Ruth pulled Anna on after him, stopping her from taking a shot. Rob, Will, and Blinder followed behind, bows raised.

"STOP THEM!" shouted Gisborne, grabbing at two swordsmen and a pair of archers running past him. He pointed at Anna and the others. There was confusion as they turned their attention from siege to intruders, then they raised their bows and swords. Before they could loose a shot, Rob put an arrow in the arm of one archer and in the thigh of the other. Seeing them fall, Gisborne drew his sword and paused to pour a thick black oily substance over it. He held his torch close and flames leapt along the length of the blade. Anna saw Rob's eyes widen as he watched.

Gisborne dropped the torch, hefted his flame wreathed sword, and raised his shield, calling for more men-at-arms. Anna could see dozens of them swarming down from the ramparts. Rob and the others were forced to shoot furiously at the newcomers, distracted from Gisborne and the two swordsmen. There was a shout and the three of them began to charge.

Little John felled one of the swordsmen with a shot that pierced his leg, just below the mail shirt. Ruth clipped the shoulder of the other swordsman and he staggered to one side clutching at the flow of blood. Shots from Will and Blinder grazed Gisborne's shield but he kept coming, his growl rising to a scream. Rob had the bowstring drawn but would not loose the arrow. His hand was starting to tremble on the taught string and Anna thought he had frozen.

"ROB, for God's sake SHOOT!" rasped Anna. She felt Ruth move from beside her, propping Anna awkwardly against a stone pillar while she drew a dagger. Anna fumbled for an arrow.

Rob's hand trembled. Gisborne swung his sword arm back aiming to decapitate Rob in a swathe of flames and as he did so, his shield tilted slightly aside. His shout of rage cut off suddenly, and he crumpled. Rob sidestepped Gisborne's sprawl across the flagstones.

He stood looking at the prostrate man who had dropped the burning sword and pawed at an arrow that protruded from both sides of his neck; air and blood bubbled from the wound. Rob's face was blank, his own arrow was still in his hand.

He looked up and saw Anna's spent bow. She leaned heavily on the pillar, her face unreadable.

Rob kicked the flaming sword away and stared at the man Anna had just shot. Time seemed to have stopped for him, the uproar of battle muted and distanced. Slowly Rob knelt beside the man who would have killed him, putting his hand out, palm down, as if calming a wounded animal. Rob placed his hand on the dying man's chest as the spasms subsided. Gisborne's eyes rolled up towards Rob then his lids fell slowly as if submitting to sleep.

Anna could see the armoured soldiers from the ramparts charging across the ward at them. Blinder grabbed Rob's arm and pulled him away. "Come, Robin, there be more upon us."

Anna stumbled and Ruth caught her, half carrying her away from the onslaught.

The ground shook and a fraction of a second after she heard another peal of thunder. Stones and limbs showered the courtyard, behind their pursuers. There were scores of them now. Perhaps the soldiers thought they were king's men who had found a way in and were charging them to turn back a new assault. They dodged the rain of stones and came on, swords and spears raised.

Little John led the way to a corner of the ward where there was a low doorway and steps. "Down here, now!"

Anna stumbled at the top of a long flight of stone stairs and grabbed Ruth for support. Her head spun.

"Hurry!" called Little John.

Anna looked down into the darkness beyond and a wave of claustrophobic nausea threatened to drown her. Out of one pit and into another. "She won't make it down," said Ruth.

Little John stepped forward and lifted Anna across his back like a fireman then started jogging down the steps as if he were carrying a small child. Anna couldn't bear to look down into the dark, so she looked up at Rob, Ruth, Will, and Blinder firing arrows from the doorway. She was carried, bouncing across John's broad shoulders into the darkness and the three of them receded from her, silhouetted against the bright doorway. One of them turned to look at her. Rob. Was he looking at her or someone else, nearby? The daylight caught the side of his face which gave an odd knowing smile. She stretched out a hand as if to touch him one last time, then they all disappeared from her sight.

The tunnel wound around to the left and downwards. She could sense roughly hewn surfaces, barely lit from below. Below? Were there torches down here? Daylight hit her again with a physical force. John carried her down past a pair of open holes in the side of the tunnel. She caught a glimpse of wide-open horizon, the marsh below and hundreds of dots, like ants, scurrying across the river beyond. She sensed John surging on, faster, breathing harder. It was as if he were in a race to the bottom of the tunnel before the ants crawled through the marshes and cut off their escape.

They took a couple of sharp turns then the tunnel descended in a slow sweep to the right, arriving in a large cavern stacked with barrels. Perhaps they were near the Road to Arabia, at the foot of Castle Rock, wondered Anna. She noticed two young men lying in the corner of the cavern, bound and gagged. One of them seemed unconscious but the other looked petrified when Little John scowled at him. He eased Anna slowly off his shoulders and sat her on a barrel. He was breathing hard, despite his great strength.

"Wait here," he gasped and peered back up the steps of the tunnel. Anna could hear shouts from all around her and had no idea how near or far they might be.

"RUTH! ROB! WILL!" Little John yelled up the tunnel and strained to hear any reply. He went over to a door at the side of the cavern and cracked it open. He cursed under his breath, rushed back to Anna, lifted her onto his shoulders again and carried her to the door, kicking it open with his foot.

Another blast of bright daylight made Anna flinch and screw her eyes up. She heard shouts.

"INFILTRATORS! AFTER THEM!"

Little John put his head down and ran in the direction of the hermitage that Tuck had taken her to when they were last on the run. Anna's world bounced and the horizon see-sawed, filling with more ant-like figures who seethed across the fields. John carried her all the way around the base of Castle Rock, where she could see the scruffy outcrop of the hermitage beyond.

"STOP!"

Little John skidded to a halt, winding Anna with its suddenness. A dozen men-at-arms in bright red tunics spread out across the track in front of them and three aimed bows at them.

"Take them to the camp," ordered the one who seemed to be in charge. He didn't have a breast plate, but his chainmail looked shinier than everyone else's.

King John's Camp, Trent Bridge, Nottingham, December 1215
Out of the frying pan and into the fire, thought Anna as they crossed a long stone bridge with low arches that led towards a field filled with flags, tents, horses and soldiers. Behind her two huge timber frames were tended by scores of men - loading rocks and turning a windlass – the trebuchets that were raining destruction on the castle walls. She barely had time to consider whether she had crossed the original Trent Bridge before they were shoved onto a muddy patch of ground with timber stakes around it, like a high security pigpen. A few of de Ferrer's men were in there already. They either looked dejected or relieved not to be caught up in the fighting anymore. Little John placed Anna gently down on the least muddy patch of ground he could find, stretched his back, and sat beside her.

"Impressive shot back there," he said.

Anna didn't know what to say. She felt numb. The man was a monster, he would have killed Rob, surely he deserved to die, but...

"Are ye in shock?" asked Little John. He rubbed her back gently, "He were evil man, Marian. He would have killed ye and Rob without a second thought. Rob may have taught us all to spare lives when we can, but ye had no choice."

Yet Anna had chosen to. She would have earlier if Ruth had not pulled her away.

"It will be hard," said John. "He were your first."

Anna knew she ought to feel terrible for taking a life, no matter who. No doubt that feeling would come, but the truth was she felt something else that was difficult for her to put into thought. Relief? Not quite. Peace? No, it troubled her and yet perhaps... release?

She remembered being asked how she felt when she kneed the man in the jacket who had tried to rape her. She felt that was the only thing she had been able to control. She remembered that he had fallen over something familiar, allowing her to escape. Was that something her oversize coat? Was it her, from some future day, crouched in the road to trip him up and allow her other self to run away?

"Marian?" prompted Little John.

"I hope Gisborne was my last," she answered, and another weird and deeply unsettling thought crept into Anna's mind: if she could change so much by bringing Rob back in time, what might change by taking someone away? "My last and only," she added firmly.

"Sorry," he said, all energy drained from his voice.

"What for?" asked Anna. "You and the others saved me from that pit."

"But now you be prisoner of the king."

"Rather a pigpen in a field than a pit in the ground. At least I can see the sky from here."

Little John strained a smile. "I wish I knew if the others had escaped."

Anna wanted to say something reassuring but she suspected the chances of them getting away were remote. She ached for them. Especially Rob. She put her hand on John's and looked out across the marshes towards the castle. The walls looked chewed with great ragged gaps where the pair of trebuchets had been hurling their boulders. The roof of one tower was on fire and another had collapsed in on itself. The ant-like soldiers swarmed up the sides of the Castle Rock and in through the gaps in the walls to consume de Ferrer's defenders within.

Anna's eyes drifted east, from the unfolding carnage in the castle to the city. She had expected to see fires raging and smoke hanging in palls across the rooftops, but there was no sign of the King's wrath on the city itself.

"At least the people of Nottingham have been spared. So far," said Anna.

John nodded. "So far."

Anna felt nauseous with hunger and exhaustion. She had lost track of how long they sat there. At some point Little John must have put his cloak around her; they were both shivering in the winter cold. At least it wasn't sleeting or snowing. The distant cries from the castle faded and the tide of soldiers flowed through it, carrying away the trophies of war. De Ferrer had been defeated, Gisborne felled, but who would take their place and what difference would the people of Nottingham see?

Anna remembered how Rob had knelt beside Gisborne while he was dying. For all the man's status and his abuse of it in life, he died like any other: afraid. Rob had looked as if he were trying to bring peace to a frightened man. There had been no hate in Rob's eyes, only grief.

Anna thought she could hear Blinder's voice. "There, I see them in there!" Had he been captured too, or was he about to betray them?

A tall fair-haired man appeared wearing a bright red tunic and, of course, another shiny breastplate over it. He stalked over to the guards at their enclosure. "Those two in the corner," he said, pointing at Anna and John, "bring them to me."

The guards opened the gate and grabbed them by their shoulders, propelling them towards the fair-haired man. Anna stumbled and John caught her before she fell.

"Un-hand them," the fair-haired man told the guards. "They are to be released on order of the king."

John and Anna stood for a moment, bewildered. Will Stutely stepped forward and embraced Little John and Anna then nodded towards the others standing behind him: Ruth, Will Gamely and Rob. What were they doing here? Anna tried to go to Rob, but she only managed one step then the edges of her vision blackened, narrowing rapidly to a tunnel with a tiny pinprick of light at the far end. Then it winked out.

She was aware of being lifted, yet it felt as if it were someone else's body. She was aware of that body being carried and of voices talking urgently around her yet from a distance as if through a thick layer of wool. She was aware of a body being laid down on something soft, of something being wrapped around it and of heat nearby.

Light crept under her lids again, she felt the back of her head cupped in someone's hand and a bowl of something hot pressed gently to her lips. A fire had been lit and the sheets of a tent held some warmth against the December air.

"Drink." It was Ruth's voice, she was kneeling in front of her. Who was cradling her? She edged her head to one side and peered up at Rob's anxious face.

"Go on, drink," he urged. She sipped a little. It was warm and salty. Broth? She didn't care. She sipped a little more. She lifted her hand and found Rob's, gripping it tight. "You..." he started. "I couldn't, but you..."

"Shh," Anna hushed him.

"And at the mouth of tunnel. I saw you. Not you now, but you later..." he was interrupted by a shuffling of feet behind them and a tired voice talking, coming nearer.

"... yes, yes. In a moment. I must see these people first."

The atmosphere in the tent transformed from intimate and peaceful to tense and expectant. She saw Little John and the two Wills go down on one knee. Ruth and Rob were already kneeling, and Anna was in no fit state to do anything other than lie there. There were mutterings of 'majesty' from some of them, hushed silence from the rest. Out the corner of her eye, she saw an average height man with wavy shoulder-length brown hair and a neatly cut beard. The countenance of his face reminded her more of an accountant than a king. It was deeply lined by the cares of office, though she thought she caught a slight twinkle in his eyes that told of suppressed mischief. It was the only distinguishing feature in an otherwise undistinguished middle-aged man. If it wasn't for the deep vermillion velvet that lined his cloak and the deference shown to him, Anna would have thought him most plain.

"Rise," said King John, his tone jaded, yet not unkind. All stood except for Rob, who remained cradling Anna. There was an awkward pause as they looked at him, expecting him to stand up too, but the king waved at him to stay put and then found a folding stool to park the weary royal bottom.

"I come to give ye my thanks, my pardon and my warning," said the king. Little John and Will looked blank. Ruth and Blinder looked wary. Anna couldn't see Rob's expression without squirming and that would have felt improper in the circumstances. One shouldn't squirm in front of royalty, no matter how sick you are. "I thank ye for fighting de Ferrer's men today," King John began. "Though few of ye, they were diverted and that allowed my men access to the inner ward, without the greater loss of life I had braced for. I and the families of the men who fought for me today owe ye a great debt." There was a pause so pregnant Anna could almost feel it kick. "Which is why I am prepared to extend a pardon for a long list of illegal acts such as attacking and injuring Shire Foresters and the theft of church monies on the York Road," he paused to look each of them in the eye. He seemed to hold Rob and Anna's the longest. "I do not know which of ye told His Worship," the honorific was not used with much honour, "The Bishop of Herefordshire, that he was to pay a... 'road tax,'" Anna felt Rob shift slightly behind her. She wanted to laugh and sensed that King John did too, but he appeared good at holding a po-face. "The truth is I do not wish to know. Such an act would normally be punished by death," he let the statement hang for a moment, just in the same way that many others had been hanged for far lesser crimes. "But given the lives that have been saved today, I am inclined to be merciful. I am sure that His Worship," Anna noted the hint of sarcasm in his voice again, "will recover from his trauma. I understand that the 'tax' was used to redress a little of the unjust and over-zealous levies that were enforced by de Ferrer." Anna was starting to understand just how well informed the king was about all sorts of activities in this part of his kingdom.

"De Ferrer and Gisborne were starving the people of Nottingham to death, or hanging them for trying to feed themselves," croaked Anna, remembering the row of crosses and Tuck sobbing helplessly.

The king pinned Anna with a stare that rivalled hers. For a long moment they locked eyes, daring the other to back down, and she sensed breaths held all around them. The king frowned deeper and nodded, appearing to acknowledge the truth she spoke, despite her audacity.

"So here is my warning," he paused to hold the gaze of each of his subjects, lingering longest on Anna. "The pardon is conditional. If I come to hear of any such attacks on my subjects or unlawful redistributions of wealth, that pardon will be revoked, and ye shall be hanged."

"Yes, majesty," said Little John, bowing his head.

"Majesty," echoed Will and Blinder bowing too.

The royal bum was hoisted from the stool with a sigh and King John made to leave the tent. He paused under the open flap and without turning his head, he added, "*If* I come to hear," then swept up his cloak tails and left.

If Anna had had a knife, she could have cut the silence that followed and served it up in slices.

In the Greenwood

Anna was confused. She was in the place she had come to think of as a home, in the hidden village deep in the Shire Wood, yet she did not feel she was home.

Ruth and Little John had taken turns recalling their gamble, sneaking into the castle while de Ferrer's men were under siege. They had reasoned that the cave tunnel connecting the brewer's yard to the inner ward would be lightly defended because de Ferrer would be expecting a siege from across the marshes, not a handful of infiltrators coming from within the city. Lucky for them they were right.

"There were just the pair of them," said Little John, scratching his head. "I could not believe our luck! I expected a dozen at least."

"And they were so young," added Ruth. "It would have broken my heart to kill them, so I told the Wills and John to bind them while I kept my bow on them."

"How did you know of the cave tunnel?" asked Anna.

"The landlord at the Road to Arabia told me," said Little John. "It were cut from Castle Rock to bring supplies direct to the inner ward."

"Supplies of ale and cheese for the soldiers," clarified Ruth.

"An army marches on its stomach," muttered Rob, almost to himself.

"I would like to see how far they march after a belly full of ale," said Ruth.

"But how did you know where to find me?" asked Anna.

Ruth looked at Little John and there was a moment of quiet, all jollity fled. "I were held there myself," he said.

"It were some time ago," explained Ruth. "John were a young lad, not much older than when ye first met him. They caught him stealing bread to feed his family. The bailiff could not hang someone so young in front of the town's folk, it would have started trouble."

"They threw me in pit," said John. "So everyone would forget me. Except Ruth and her mother did not."

"I were working in castle kitchens, helping my mother with the baking. She overheard a pair of guards bragging about a young lad they had thrown into the store pit that morning. She waited until the ward were quiet then lowered me down on a rope."

"Ruth came to me from above like an angel of mercy," said Little John, wistfully.

"More romantic than Rob's bottom," said Anna, giving Rob a sly look. He smiled absently and looked away.

"The point is he came and got ye," said Ruth.

"Yes, he did," said Anna and put her arm around Rob's shoulder. "And what were you all doing in the King's camp?"

"Like ye and Little John, we fled down the cave steps and met the King's men coming up them," said Ruth. "They took us to his camp, but we were met by the very noble who came to call ye. He were charged by King John to find us and take us to his own tent."

"We had no idea if he would reward us or hang us," said Little John. "But the noble did no harm by us. He asked us to wait 'till King came by."

"Ye were lucky the king did not hang ye for speaking out so," Ruth chided Anna.

"Yes," said Anna. "But I needed to tell him, and I think he needed to hear." She was surprised and glad. Surprised that she had found the courage to do so and glad that she had made clear the extent of suffering in Nottingham.

"What do you think the king meant?" asked Rob, "*If* I come to hear'".

"I reckon the king knows more about his kingdom than many would credit," said Ruth. Anna nodded. If he hadn't then she would have been executed for insolence.

"I reckon he wants us to keep an eye on whoever takes over from de Ferrer," said Little John. Ruth looked at him and frowned. "Well, what else do you think he meant?" he asked her.

"We all came this close to death," Ruth held her forefinger and thumb so close you could barely slip a hair between them.

"Many folks died," answered Little John, "and many more would have died if Rob and Marian had not shown us what to do."

Ruth shook her head. Anna sensed there was much to be said but not in front of her and Rob. The talk returned to the details of the rescue while Ruth quietly put bowls of thick stew in front of them.

Anna's palms and shins still burned from being thrown into the pit and she felt desperately tired, yet she needed space to think. After supper Anna grasped the wall for support and made her way gingerly outside to watch the clear night sky, searching for the constellations that her mum had taught her to look for: The Bear, The Plough, Orion...

"I left them to their scheming," said Ruth from behind. "Rob and John are thick as thieves! They'll be plotting the downfall of whoever steps into de Ferrer's shoes."

"Let's hope they don't have to," said Anna, pulling her cloak around her to keep herself warm.

"What do ye think?" asked Ruth.

"I think there will always be people like de Ferrer and Gisborne. People who abuse their power and make ordinary peoples' lives a misery. But there will always be people like Rob and John... and you. And that gives me hope."

"We are just ordinary people too."

"Yet you stood up to Gisborne."

"Ye showed us how."

"We showed each other. It was you who taught me how to shoot a bow."

"Like I said afore, we must all use a bow to survive."

Anna considered that. She remembered her mother say that the bow had been a symbol of strength in medieval England. She wondered if it may also have been a symbol of survival for ordinary people. The nobility used swords and shields, a symbol of their power, yet perhaps they feared the power of the bow? A leveller. An equalizer. Had Anna not taken down a mighty noble with her humble bow?

"And what about ye, Anna Partington?" asked Ruth. "How long will ye be here?"

Anna looked back at the stars. The Milky Way shone like a ghostly ribbon that wrapped the world as a gift. She sensed Ruth could see the torment in Anna's mind. Ruth, John, the Wills, the people of the hidden village all felt like the family she had been longing for. Yet Anna had discovered much about herself in the pit which drew her in another direction. Her ability to walk between times was now a conscious act of will, not some random affliction, and she could use it to ask important questions. Anna wanted to belong here, in the Greenwood, she really did, but at that moment she felt this was just one of many more destinations. And she was not fully convinced that she was really, physically here. Was the real Anna Partington lying in a corner of Nottingham, about to freeze to death if she did not wake up? "I don't know," she answered, eventually.

Ruth put her hand on Anna's shoulder. "We will always be here for ye," she said quietly.

Anna turned and hugged her.

She slept in fits and starts that night. Sometimes she would wake in a panic, thinking she was still in a pit in the ground. Sometimes she wondered what would happen to them here if they had bodies in the modern-day which were dying, or what would happen if they died here in the past. She rolled over and placed a protective arm across Rob's shoulder, and he grumbled contentedly in between soft snores. She drifted back into sleep, in and out of time.

They all woke late the next day, rising one by one as the weak winter sun peered through the tree-tops, making the frost on the thatched roofs sparkle. Anna felt stronger so Ruth agreed she could join Rob and hunt for game to put in the pie that Ruth would bake that evening. Anna doubted she could give Rob much help with a bow but was grateful for the chance to share some time with him without any pressure to talk. A hunter keeps silent if they want to stalk their prey and that suited Anna fine for the moment. It was only after Rob declared that two pheasants, a grouse and a partridge were enough that the unspoken agreement not to speak was lifted.

Rob walked beside her, and his free hand drifted naturally to hers. The pair of pheasants swayed from his belt and his hood was pulled up to keep the fresh December air from his neck. He looked more a part of the Greenwood than ever before. He looked more a part of medieval Nottinghamshire than he ever did the twenty-first century city.

"You mean to stay here, don't you?" said Anna, watching for brambles and roots that might trip her as they walked back to the village.

Rob kept walking for a while before answering. "Yes," he said, finally. "You mean to return." There was a catch in his throat, almost choking on the word return.

"I don't want to..." started Anna.

"... but you don't feel you belong here," he finished.

"You belong here," she said.

"I do," he agreed and smiled an easy smile. The smile of someone who knew when they would eat next and what they needed to do that day. Someone who knew why they were there and felt at ease with it. At long last.

"I don't want to leave you," said Anna.

"Then don't."

"But I've been thinking about what I do. I can walk between times."

"So you can," the corner of his lips twitched in amusement.

"I mean I can control it better now; I think. I want to find out why I do this, and what I should do with it." Rob was silent, so she continued. "I kept wondering what I should take with me from the twenty-first century, or if I should. But now I realise the most important thing I brought was you. You and your ideas."

"Ideas?" Rob looked taken aback. He stopped walking and turned to face Anna. "What ideas? Never had a good one in my life. Except following you, perhaps."

"Fairness. It was your sense of fairness that gave your winnings to the hospital. Your sense of justice to take from those who could spare it and give back to the poor. Can't you see what you've done, Rob?"

"I just helped is all."

"No. It's not all. Think of the tales that people are telling around a fireplace now. Think of the tales they tell for hundreds of years. About what you did!"

"It weren't just me. It were you. It were Little John, Ruth, Tuck, the Wills and…"

"Yes, it was. But it's your name that's famous, Rob. No, not famous, legendary."

"I'm not a…"

"Yes. You are."

"It weren't me that shot Gisborne, it were you. You saved my life. Again."

"And thank god Robin Hood is a legend because he looked after the vulnerable, not because he was a killer."

Rob looked down at his feet, looking confused and lost. Anna wrapped her arms around him and kissed him. For a time that had no measure they clung together. Only when they were ready did they walk on, back through the silence of the oaks, hands held tight.

"You're still going back," said Rob eventually. Resigned.

"I feel... responsible," said Anna.

He looked at her from the corner of his eye as they walked. "Oh aye?"

"I brought you here by accident and luckily it was a good accident; extraordinarily good. But I'm dangerous," she said thinking of her shot that killed Gisborne. "I wonder what other accidents I might cause?"

"Don't take no nuclear physicists back to them Pharaohs. Could be dodgy."

Anna saw his sly grin returning. "I promise to be good. One day I might find mum. Before she died."

"Aye. Thought so. Be weird though."

"Yes, it would. I don't know when I'll be ready. And I don't even know what will happen to our bodies in twenty-first century Nottingham, or if they're even there."

"Mine can stay there if it is, don't care about it anymore."

"I'm worried. I need to go back and see."

"Stay for tomorrow."

"Tomorrow?"

"Christmas Day."

"Is it? God! I haven't got you anything!"

"You got me to here," and he hugged her tight.

Hay barn, southern edges of the Shire Wood, Nottinghamshire, December 1215

Most of the village and several farming families who spared whatever they could to help the villagers in return for hunted game had squished themselves into a hay barn at the edge of the forest. It was a lofty, vaulted space with an improvised open hearth in the middle, dug into a sandstone seam that ran beneath the barn. There were hay bales to sit on and trestle tables down both sides. No more than planks on props. They bowed under the weight of roasted chickens, pies and jugs of ale laid out and constantly topped up as more people squeezed into the barn. They were laughing, joking, and telling tall tales. Tales of kings and outlaws.

Little John was holding court with the Wills and Tuck, waving a skin full of ale around as if he'd had a skin-full: the men were merry, noted Anna with a chuckle.

Anna ate until she felt she might burst then Will Gamely pulled her up onto the table-top to dance, with the rest of the room clapping and singing. They laughed and kicked and sent a pair of bottles flying. She had not enjoyed herself so much since... since the night at Goose Fair. With Rob.

Rob found himself hauled up onto the next table by Ruth who whooped and swung him in an elbow hold. He looked utterly confused and delighted all at once. As if dancing were an idea dreamed up by drunken revellers in another land and he'd never done it until that night. Perhaps both were true, rued Anna.

By late evening many had retreated into huddles or disappeared into nearby cottages. Little John and Ruth had slipped away so Rob and Anna found themselves alone in one corner of the barn, screened by bales. They pulled a fur skin over themselves and watched the flickers in the hearth as the smoke curled and tongues of flame died slowly among the embers.

"When we were hunting yesterday, you already knew I mean to go back," said Anna, "Didn't you?"

"Yeah. I saw you," said Rob.

"You saw me?"

"Like I said to you in King's camp. I saw you in cave tunnel, under castle. It were you, but not here."

"What do you mean?" she started, then slowly understanding dawned. She realised that Rob had seen her back in the modern day, looking at him in the medieval tunnels under the castle. "I'm sorry," she said.

"Don't be," he said. He sounded as if he were trying to be casual, yet she saw the strain on him. The vulnerability. "Just promise to come back... when you're ready."

"I promise," she whispered, and kissed him. Tenderly at first, then with passion.

Anna slid gently into slumber and dreamed. She dreamed she was a wood pigeon perched on a high branch of a great oak tree. She was surrounded by curly edged leaves and shiny acorns in their cups. Sunlight filtered through the leaves and dappled the boughs with splashes of gold. She felt safe. She cooed, the call of a contented pigeon, and was answered by another beside her who cooed his own contentment.

She imagined she might stay in that tree for a long while. But gradually the sunlight faded. She felt a chill breeze ruffle her feathers. She became aware of thoughts unfinished, seeds unfound, and another bird circling high overhead.

She turned to the pigeon beside her and called for him to leave with her, but he clung to the branch, claws sunk into the bark like a ship at anchor. She needed to find another tree, but he would not budge. This is our tree, he cooed to her, but she wondered how it could be. All the time the other bird circled them, calling to them from high above.

And then she dreamed she was that other bird calling with that lonely cry. An eagle soaring on the great currents of air that flowed across the land. She looked down on the forest below and realised she could no longer pick out the oak in which she and the other pigeon had perched. She felt sad. She felt she must find that tree again and yet the winds were carrying her far, far away.

As she soared, she grew aware of another beaked head beside hers, joined to her body. The other head seemed to have the mind of someone else who turned and pecked at her own head, crying to turn around and go back. She became scared. This felt wrong, unnatural. She craned her own neck away to avoid the other beak and found herself falling.

And then she became a magpie. Black and white wings fluttered as she spiralled around and down. Something was clutched between her claws. Something that shone. A great city lay beneath her, buzzing with life. She knew that city. Was it her home? Or was there someone in that city she thought of as her home? She tumbled and fell, the ground rushed towards her, she clutched the thing that shone and fluttered her wings...

Rock Cemetery, Forest Fields, Nottingham, December 2019

Anna prised an eye open, gummy with sleep. Rob lay curled into her, his arms around her waist. She wiped the sleep from both eyes and tried to sit up but was overcome by a wave of nausea and exhaustion. There was a dim light reflected off the sandstone walls as if the morning sun were sneaking into the back of the cave to hide. Cave? Weren't they in the barn at the edge of the forest? She gave Rob a gentle shake, but he was still. Was he still asleep?

"Rob?" she said, stroking his cheek.

He was cold.

She felt his neck for a pulse but could not find one. She put her cheek against his lips to feel for some hint of breath but felt nothing. She started to panic and shook him harder, but his arms and head hung limp. She screamed at him to wake up, but he could not hear her. Then she hugged him to her again and sobbed. Great heaving, gut wrenching sobs that shook her body and his. Her tears soaked his hair and matted it against her cheek.

Eventually silence enveloped the cave again and a calm crept through her thumping heart, steadying the beat. Why had he died? Had she caused him to die? Had they left their 'real' bodies here in the modern day, and had he been away from his body for too long? She remembered how dehydrated and close to hypothermia he had been on their last return. His body was cold in her arms, but she could not tell if that were through the cold of winter or absence of life.

Had he died of shock? Had she taken him on too many journeys through time? She had been dipping in and out of the past all her life, but Rob had barely been aware of his own capability when he met her. Perhaps this had been a journey too far or too many?

Or perhaps he simply wanted to stay. He had found a new life in the past where his existence had purpose, where he felt alive in his own skin. Where he could leave behind the traumas of homelessness, racism, and loss. He had said himself that there was nothing here for him. Maybe his body was here but some other self was still there in the medieval forest. So, for the moment, because all the alternatives were too hard to contemplate, that was what Anna chose to believe.

Rob was home.

In the Greenwood.

After some time, she felt in her pocket and found a Mars bar. She took a few bites and felt the rush of sugar revive her a little. When she felt strong enough, she scouted out the cave and found what she was looking for, a pile of loose stones laying loose at the back of an alcove. She returned to Rob, lifted him, feeling just how slight he had become, and pulled him to the back of the cave where she laid him down so very carefully, with love and care and not a little reverence.

Anna laid the stones over Rob, one by one, covering him as if constructing a small tomb within a tomb. Before she covered his face, she kissed him on the lips and said goodbye, at least for now. Then she searched her bag and found the golden arrow. She placed it on top of the pile of stones, then turned it so the arrowhead pointed north, towards whatever remained of Sherwood Forest.

Anna lay in silence across Rob's grave for a while. It may have been midday when she rose. As she left, she felt a strange presence in a corner of the cave, as if someone were watching her. Not malign, just... there. She dismissed it. Anna was too drained to look.

She closed the gate across the mouth of the cave and went in search of her aunt's grave, outside in the main cemetery grounds. There were other people around, visiting family graves. She noticed that many were dressed up as if for a special occasion. Anna guessed it may be Sunday, a Sunday close to Christmas. Many families would be visiting the graves of loved ones.

Anna found Jane Baker's grave again, on the edge of the cemetery, by the wall, under a stand of stark bare trees. She knelt and placed her hand on the gravestone, staring at the name. "Thank you, Jane," she whispered. "Thank you for sending me to family. Thank you for making sure I wasn't alone."

She was not aware of falling asleep, but she guessed she must have. When she woke again, she was in a strange bed with stiff white sheets and a woman with glasses, dark skin and curly black hair was lying in the bed beside her, looking at her curiously.

Anna sat up suddenly, aware she was in the hospital again. She gripped the sheets tightly, feeling the scars on the palms of her hands. She leaned forward to look at the raw grazes on her shins where she had been thrown into the pit in the castle. Then the reason why she'd been thrown in came to her and she felt sick with despair and loss. She turned back to the woman in the next bed. She seemed to be examining Anna. Not unkindly, but carefully assessing her, trying to understand. There was something of Aunt Jane in that look. Shrewd, yet kind. Anna could not bear to keep her trials to herself any longer. She needed to talk to someone. Anyone who might listen. Perhaps this woman might believe her. Perhaps.

"I buried Robin Hood..."

Epilogue

The Castle, Nottingham, May 2022

I think I made a good decision. Among the perks of being the new manager of Nottingham Castle are choosing my team and taking a few risks. I first met Anna in the hospital ward over three years ago. I took a gamble and invited her to work as a tour guide at the Castle. I was right: she is an excellent storyteller. She still hides inside that tatty oversized coat but put her in front of a bunch of tourists eager to learn some local history and she transforms. A consummate storyteller with uncanny knowledge our local history.

Despite her being an essential part of my team for several years, I felt I had not got to know her properly. I was not the only one who finds her self-contained, private. She would tell us so much and no more. Quite a contrast to the outpouring in the hospital ward when we first met. Every employee has the right to their own privacy, but I was beginning to feel concerned for her well-being. I also admit to being curious about how she came to know so much. She had mentioned in passing that her late mother had been a history researcher, but I could not believe it was all remembered from conversations as a child. Lately she had been asking me a lot of questions that seemed prompted by research into her family history. I wondered whether she has been missing her mother and her aunt. So, I decided to tag along on her mid-morning tour.

Anna waited quietly until the group had gathered then stepped forward to introduce herself. I saw surprise on a few faces. They thought she was waiting with them. She had all the facts at her command, but it was the way she talked, as if she had been there herself, that had them gripped. I still don't know whether to believe half of what she told me in the hospital, but I can't deny the accuracy of her insights. Her entourage followed her across the grounds, some asking questions, some looking around at the restored Ducal Palace and its carefully cropped gardens, but all of them listened when she spoke about its past. I could see Anna enjoyed her work. She shone.

Anna had one eye on the sky and could see that rain was on its way again, so she led her gaggle towards Mortimer's Hole at the southern edge of the grounds.

"Prince Edward was only seventeen, still trying to grow a beard that didn't look like fluff," a boy sniggered at Anna's imaginative description, or perhaps and observation I wondered. "He waited 'til after dark on the nineteenth of October, thirteen-thirty, before he, his loyal friend Sir Montagu and their gang, all heavily armed with swords and daggers, crept up through a tunnel like this," she told her audience.

"Like this?" asked a lad in a puffer jacket that looked far too large. He almost looked like her understudy.

"We think the one they actually took was on the far side of the castle, over there," she pointed north. All heads swivelled to look back across the grounds. "But most of it has disappeared. This here is one of the oldest tunnels in Castle Rock and would have been cut well before Montagu and Edward."

Like me, Anna knew the likely candidate for the drama that had played out so many years ago was Davey Scott's Hole and much of that was probably buried in the grounds of the grand houses at the top edge of The Park. I doubted she would ever earn enough from her tour guide job to afford a house in The Park, but she shares a flat in Lenton now, near enough to walk in. Knowing Anna, she might go searching for that missing tunnel. I just hoped she didn't try sleeping in the cave of columns dug for Thomas Herbert again...

"Imagine a locked door at the top of the steps," she continued, pointing to the top of the tunnel. "The door was unlocked by Montagu's spies. They crept into the castle with swords drawn and caught the guards by surprise. They seized the First Earl of March, Roger Mortimer who squealed like a piglet, and dragged him back to the tunnel." Their eyes cast around the sandstone walls, as if expecting to hear the squealing earl or glimpse the young prince and his companions as they dragged their prisoner into the tunnel. "Follow me and I'll show you where an escape could have been made. Quietly now," she added, with a finger to her lips. They responded to the impromptu theatre and followed her down the steps on tip toe. Even I did.

Halfway they passed the wide openings in the side of the cave tunnel. "Are these windows?" asked a young girl who held onto her mum with one hand and pointed with the other.

"We don't know what they were for," answered Anna, "but you have a clear view to the south from here." She gazed out and paused for a moment. I wondered if she recalled the broad horizon after so many days in the pit, or so she would have me believe. "Maybe Edward and his men passed here and looked out. They wouldn't have seen roads or rooftops, but marshland and the river, lit by the moon."

She stepped back to let them crowd around the cave mouths and search their imaginations. Not far from the castle, I could see the dull sheen off the leaded roofs of Her Majesty's Revenue & Customs offices. The irony of putting the tax collectors in Nottingham, now famous for the tales of taking from the rich and giving back to the poor, put a wry grin on my lips.

I could see Anna had become distracted. She was looking back up the steps of the sandstone tunnel, peering around the corner as if she were watching something or someone. I didn't interrupt her. Eventually she turned back to her audience, now waiting to go on with the tour. She seemed to cuff away a tear with her baggy coat sleeve, then beamed a heart-warming smile and led us all down to the bottom. After many more questions, which she fielded like a pro, she waved them off home and they waved back like they had just found a new one.

"Have you got a moment?" I asked Anna. I wanted to ask her about the tears in the cave tunnel. Perhaps she was still traumatised by the attempted rape, or just missing her family?

She looked awkward. "Er, is it okay if we talk later? Only I must go into town now. It is my lunch break," she added a little defensively.

"Of course, you go ahead. There's no hurry and it's nothing to worry about." I assured her. I watched her walk off down the hill and hoped I hadn't made her fret.

Later, as the last visitors were leaving, I found her by the gatehouse, waving them off. "I hope you had a good lunch, Anna?"

"Sorry I couldn't stop earlier."

"Did you go to the library again?" I asked. "I was fascinated by those historical questions you asked recently. Any more progress on your family tree?"

"No, not today. I was helping... at a street kitchen. I'm a volunteer at Tina's Pantry. It *is* my free time," she added. She sounded defensive again, as if helping the homeless were something to be ashamed of. Or perhaps she thought I'd be angry at her having two jobs.

"That's wonderful Anna," I could see her relax a little. "I'm proud to see our staff help out in the city. You seem to have made yourself at home here."

"I'm doing okay now, but I'm not sure if I'm quite home yet."

I studied her face. I wondered if I detected a hint of determination. "I'm sure you'll get there. I only wanted to ask you about this morning."

Her frown returned. "I'm sorry I got distracted in the tunnel this morning, Doctor Briars."

"Angela. We've known each other long enough now, Anna. And I certainly wasn't going to tell you off, I was just concerned. You looked as if you'd seen a... well, you seemed a bit emotional."

I waited while she looked away. Anna's confidence seemed to have grown since working here, but she still puts up a barrier at times. "Were you having one of your... insights?" I ventured.

Anna smiled. The same warm uplifting smile I saw that morning. "Yes. But I know you're still sceptical."

"Humour me."

"I wonder... would you help me with something first?"

"Sure," I said. I had no idea then. None.

Brightmoor Street, Nottingham, May 2022

"This is where you're going to sit?" I asked Anna. We were standing in the corner of an under-croft at the edge of an empty car park off Brightmoor Street. The sun had sunk so the air was cooling, though I couldn't understand why she was wearing that awful overcoat.

"Yes, against this wall," said Anna. "It's out of sight from the street so hopefully no one should see us."

"What exactly am I looking for again?" I asked. Anna had been coy about asking me to come with her, but I was both fascinated and anxious for her. Part of me wanted to believe in the impossible: that Anna could really travel through time. Yet the rational part of me wanted to be there for her when I saw that it was just her extraordinary imagination. She would be embarrassed. Perhaps distraught. She would need someone to reassure her.

"Not sure," she said, "That's why I need you to watch."

Perhaps that made sense if she thought she couldn't see what happened to herself. "And you want me to record you on your phone," I waved Anna's new Samsung, hoping I wouldn't make a mess of the recording. Though I wondered whether I should make a mess of it to save her from seeing that nothing had happened.

"Please. Thank you, Doctor Briars."

"Angela. You must get used to calling me Angela. For heavens sake, I'm squatting in a backyard filming you on a journey to the past, we can't get more informal than that. Can we?"

Anna made a crooked smile from the corner of her mouth. "Thanks, you're a star."

"Look, I'm filming you." I waved my hand at her, "Perform!"

Anna closed her eyes, looking self-conscious. I suppose it was the first time she had been watched and recorded. She peeked through one eye.

"I'm still here," I assured her, getting impatient. "Get on with it!"

I'm not sure what I expected her to do, but what happened next was shocking. At first, her eyelids started fluttering, like in REM sleep. It was deeply unsettling, as if she might be about to have a seizure. Then I wondered if my glasses had fogged. Anna seemed to be growing a little indistinct, like a blurred photo. I gave them a wipe with my free hand, still filming. Then she became translucent. It was like the special effects department had doctored a film to make her fade out, only it was really happening right there in front of me, and it definitely wasn't my glasses.

I held my breath.

A few moments later I saw a shimmer in the air where she had been and then she started materialising again. And as she reappeared, I noticed she was holding a man's jacket and tie. I lost my balance and fell over.

"Hey, Angela, are you okay?" Anna rushed over and put her arm around me to help me up. "What happened?" she asked.

I stared at her, unsure whether to be horrified at her supernatural reappearance or relieved she was okay. "I was hoping you'd tell me," and I handed Anna her phone. It was still recording so she stopped and re-played.

Anna watched, fascinated. She obviously had no idea what happened to her when she went wherever or whenever the hell she went. I watched it too, to make sure I hadn't dreamed the whole episode. But there it was. It was real. She was real, and she really wasn't imagining what she could do. At least, she had the power to disappear and reappear at will. What happened to her in between was still a matter of trust, though my understanding of reality had just been rudely upended and I was prepared to take anything she said next on trust.

'Hey, Angela, are you okay?' the recording of Anna said, so she hit the pause button. "Wow! I guess you're a bit freaked out?" Even she seemed to be.

"Just a bit," I said, still in shock. "It's the first time you called me Angela."

For a moment she looked blankly at me, then burst out laughing. I couldn't help but laugh too. Nervous excited laughter which subsided as her face became serious, as if sliding into shadow. Anna was about to prove to me that she could indeed go... somewhen. She had brought proof.

"Where the hell did those come from?" I pointed at the jacket and tie beside Anna.

"From a man who didn't deserve them," she said, sourly. I waited for her to explain. What she said was equally upsetting and amazing. She told me she had travelled three years into the past to confront a man who had tried to rape her. She had waited for him, where she knew he would be, then tripped him up so that her younger self could get away. That bit totally boiled my noggin. In my own discipline of archaeology I'm used to timelines being sequential. She told me she had squirted pepper spray in his eyes to stop him, which petrified me. What if she'd missed? What if he'd grabbed her?

She told me how she had been travelling back in time over and over to find him, follow him, discover who he was and where he lived. That made me even more scared for her. What if she had been seen? What if he had caught her? She said she'd explained all this to the man and threatened to expose him to the police if he ever tried to rape someone again. That she would be watching him like a phantom following his every step. I expect that would have freaked him out. It did me.

I don't know whether she felt she needed to give me proof or whether she wanted another taste of revenge, but she made him give her his jacket and tie and left him there, like a ghost in her past.

"You could have been killed!" I said. "You knew he was dangerous. If I had any idea what you were doing, I'd never have..."

"No, you wouldn't," agreed Anna. "Which is why I didn't say." I was beginning to glimpse another side of Anna Partington. A tough and ruthless side. If I'm honest with myself I'd always guessed at it, yet here the real Anna was and I wouldn't want to mess with her. "But I got him," she continued. "I scared him. Perhaps I terrified him almost as much as he terrified me and maybe, just maybe, he might not try to rape anyone again."

"That was the most reckless, stupid, brave and downright bloody weird thing I've ever known anyone do. Don't ever do it again!"

Anna didn't answer that.

She didn't look shaken by the danger, she looked strangely calm. As if she had exorcised some terrible demon spirit that had been haunting her. "Bless you Anna Partington," I said, shaking my head, "there aren't many women who can go back and confront their attacker like that or live to tell the tale."

"S'pose so. I s'pose there aren't many who can go back in time."

"Of that I am sure," The full emotional enormity of what she had done was beginning to dawn on me. "I'm really sorry, Anna."

"For what?"

"For ever doubting you could time travel."

"I'd have doubted it if I were you."

"You were like... like a ghost. You just faded out and came back again. Holding that jacket and tie, out of nowhere." I paused as a thought came into my head and immediately felt awful.

"What?" she asked, reading my face.

"No, that was really wrong of me to even think of it."

"Go on, what were you thinking?"

"It was a terrible thought. I was thinking how much we would all discover if you were to go back to key moments in time to investigate the past. Real facts about the past, no educated guesses from fragments of pots and belt buckles. But... that'd be exploitation. No, worse, I'd be putting you at risk for my own professional gain."

"It's what I've spent my life doing in case you don't remember. Go on, name a time and place. I'll go take a peek for you. I'd even take you with me. You deserve it after helping me."

The offer tempted me sorely. Who wouldn't want to go back in time to find out what actually happened? Especially an archaeologist! "No, Anna. Every time you travel in time, you put yourself at risk. I won't have you doing that on my account."

"How 'bout I tell you all about it when I come back from a journey of my choosing?"

I hesitated. She must have read my expression.

"No one will ever stop me," she said.

I believed her. I just didn't want to make it more dangerous for her. But if she chose to go and found out something that would be of interest to me... "Deal," I said, "But no more stunts like that." I hesitated again. All the work that Anna had been doing in her spare time suddenly made sense to me. "That's what you've been up to! Researching that family tree of yours, and the questions you were asking me. You're going on a search for your family, aren't you?"

Anna nodded.

"Oh..." And now the true bravery of young Anna came to me at last. "You're going to start by seeing your mum again, before she died of cancer."

"Yes," Anna's voice sounded small.

"Come here," I hugged her tight. I found it hard to resolve her slight figure with the enormous courage she showed. It was almost as if her ridiculously large coat was worn to show people how big her heart was.

"Well, I've found out one thing today, with your help," said Anna, stepping back. "I take my body with me, whenever I go. It wasn't what I wanted to find," she paused. I wondered whether she was thinking of her friend, Rob. Robin Hood. "And I guess now I can tell you what I saw at the Castle the other day.".

I nodded for her to go on.

She told me she felt a familiar tingle at the edge of her conscious mind. A memory of the past: her own past, at The Castle. When she looked back up the stairs of the cave tunnel, she said she saw a young man in a dark green hooded cloak edging backwards down the steps, bow raised and shooting at foes above. A moment later a fair-haired woman, a red-haired man and a bald man edged down either side of him, all reaching for arrows in the quivers on their backs. The first man turned and saw Anna. He had looked shocked, but shock gave way to understanding, which in turn gave way to a sly grin.

"I recognised that grin," Anna said. "It reminded me I still have friends in the past. My family. It reminded me of a promise I made one Christmas night long ago. And it made me smile too."

EVERYDAY GHOSTS

THE END

Acknowledgements

I am thankful for many sources of knowledge about Nottingham's history including 'Sandstone Caves of Nottingham' by Tony Waltham, and 'Nottingham – The Buried Past of a Historic City Revealed' by Scott Lomax. I found the Mapperley & Sherwood History Group articles, and the material from the 'Picture Nottingham' site most helpful. All errors are mine.

The places mentioned in the story are all real, as are their historical background. Nottingham's caves offer us a wealth of stories about the past, including the sand mine, the entertaining hall under the house in The Park, the well and the castle tunnels.

Nottingham really was caught up in the wars fought by King Richard and his younger brother John, though I suspect we may never know if either of them met an awkward young lad with a strong sense of social justice, or a stubborn young time-hopping woman. Anna is of course fictitious.

I thank Pete Castle for his 'Nottinghamshire Folk Tales', which refreshed my memory of the best-known tale and drew my attention to some of the less well known, such as the wise people of Gotham.

Seeing the truth behind the tales of Robin Hood is fraught with challenges, though there is much to suggest that the name was assumed by a variety of people who sought to challenge power. The longbow was symbolic of the peasantry and was used to devastating effect to bring noble knights low during the Hundred Years War.

Because I am lucky enough to have never experienced poverty, I read Kerry Hudson's excellent autobiography, 'Lowborn' and began to understand a little of the challenges facing those who deal with daily inequality. Again, all misunderstandings are mine.

I am sincerely grateful for Rosie Fiore's enthusiasm, ideas, and excellent professional advice. The story has been transformed for the better. And most of all I thank Niamh for her patience, encouragement, and endless cups of tea.

Other books by Chris Gregory

Science Fiction by **Chris D Gregory**
Seconders
Second Generation
Distant Son

Rescue

Urban Fantasy by **Chris Gregory**
Everyday Ghosts
Everyday Spirits
Everyday Legends

Historical Fiction by **CD Gregory**
Crystal
Resister

Pendragons
Uthyr Pendragon

About Chris Gregory

I live in Hertfordshire where I'm lucky to see trees and a glimpse of water from my window. Sometimes I look away from the view and get some work done. Sometimes I receive orders to provide food and attention to my demanding cat (or creative director as she is often referred to). Sometimes I have the luxury of sitting with my laptop to write a story. All these moments are golden.

I have been writing stories for over fifteen years and if you enjoyed this one, I'm delighted. Please remember to leave a review of my book at your favourite retailer. If you wish to find out about the other stories I've written, then please peruse the list of other books below and my website:

http://www.chrisgregory.uk

www.ingramcontent.com/pod-product-compliance
Lightning Source LLC
Chambersburg PA
CBHW021423150726
47989CB00001B/89